Sticks

T GEPHART

Sticks

For Jenna and Liam -

my greatest achievements.

Oh. Fuck.

Fuck.

Fuck.

F. U. C. K.

That's exactly what should be displayed in the window of that plastic contraption shaking in my hand instead of that obnoxious plus sign. The bright blue horizontal and vertical line against a stark white background. Taunting me as I stood there hoping it was some cruel optical illusion.

But it wasn't.

Oh my God, I was going to be sick.

My head spun as I sunk to my ass on the cold tile floor. The stick that ten minutes ago had been so innocent and harmless was still in my hand as I struggled not to hyperventilate. This couldn't be happening.

I was pregnant.

As waves of nausea rolled through my body—something I'd been experiencing a lot lately—my brain tried to reconcile my new reality. My life as I knew it was well and truly over.

I am going to be someone's mother.

My hand had barely managed to lift the lid of the toilet as I lost my battle with my stomach. The full body heave expelled not only my breakfast but also my soul into the bowl as the evil EPT wand fell out of my hand and onto the floor. My future—as well as my blueberry bagel— now in the toilet.

I had done a lot of stupid stuff in my time. I'll be the first to admit that, but Joey Shaw was by far the dumbest.

Unlike most of the girls he seemed to entertain, I'd known Joey for years. Our bands had crossed paths from time to time on the bar circuit, even sharing the stage once or twice. The appreciation we had for each other was mutual, both professionally and otherwise. He was good looking, sexy and had a body built for sin. It was only a matter of time before we ended up doing the in-between-the-sheets tango; I was impressed at how long I'd resisted.

Driven by hormones instead of brains, our little game of flirting came to a very lustful, sexy conclusion last month. That mouth of his wasn't only talking up a good show, with every single egotistical boast coming out of it not even close to the mind-blowing orgasm he'd given me. His body absolutely delivered on the promise of crazy and unrestrained sex. It had been a night that wasn't going to be easy to forget. Now it seemed, he had gifted me a permanent reminder.

Fuck.

I was so screwed.

We had barely even spoken since our hook-up, happy for it to be a casual thing between friends. It's not like I was looking to date him. Ha. Not in this lifetime. I wasn't *that* delusional. The man was hot. Not denying that, but I'd had longer relationships with a pizza than Joey had with women. So, I was happy to collect on the toe-curling sex without the side order of is-he-ever-going-to-call-me-again. God damn it. How could I have been so freaking stupid?

Ugh. My stomach churned again as my brain rationalized spending most of the day locked in my bathroom. It seemed like a solid idea, one that would see me postpone the what-the-hell-did-I-do-now that was begging to be dealt with. Ha! As if.

This year had started out with so much promise. The band was doing great. While no record deals had come our way, our song had gotten thousands of hits on YouTube. And there wasn't a Saturday night where we didn't play. Not just dive bars but actually great gigs. We were even making decent money too. Life was pretty awesome. *Was.* Past tense. Now, of course, I was a few months away from hawking my six-string at PawnRUs and getting a day job at *Denny's*.

Poor Joey.

The sexy six-foot, dark-haired drummer had no idea that our baby was going to be the first and last child he would father, his balls soon to be hanging from my rearview mirror. I'd be sure to inform him and offer my condolences when I ripped them from his still-breathing body. His dick also at risk of ending up a hood ornament. It was only fair seeing as my body would be waving its red flag of rebellion in the coming months that his should suffer too. Might as well wear my skinny jeans while they still fit me, lord knows I was going to be rocking elastic waistbands and stretchy pants in the very near future. My wardrobe, the least of my worries.

Huh. I was going to have a baby. My hand uncon-sciously brushed against my flat-for-now belly, the life its dumbass parents created growing inside of me despite my lack of a clue. A missed period and some wicked fatigue the only hint that something was amiss. And in an instant, it had all changed. Knocked up, sitting on my bathroom floor with my head down a toilet, and I had absolutely no idea of how I was going to be someone's mom.

Inside of me there was a tiny life. A little helpless human who needed my love and protection, who hadn't asked to be born but had been put there nonetheless. Trusting that I would keep him or her safe until he or she was ready to enter into the world. My baby. Mine.

Great. Now my eyes were leaking. The fucking body

rebellion I had expected months from now had already started as tears streamed uncontrollably.

What the hell was happening to me? I wasn't one of those emotional girls who wept when they lost their favorite purse. I played in a rock band for God's sake; I didn't do crying. It was Joey's fault. Yes. Let's blame that asshole and his potent freaking sperm. He was the reason I had apparently lost my mind and would soon have a full uterus. And now I was back to being mad again.

Awesome.

This was so going to be fun.

Oh, please let me not kill him.

Joey

"**D**ude!" Max yelled from the door. "Your fucking phone has been ringing all morning. Either answer the piece of shit or switch it to silent." The phone that had apparently been an asshole came sailing through the air and landed with a thud beside my head.

Max was being a bastard. Jealous that, while my phone had been getting more action than a high school quarterback on prom night, his hadn't so much as buzzed since last night. Not my fault the ladies wanted me more. Sure, I was pushing the boundaries a little, but I was young, single and in a rock band.

This is what I had dreamed about since I strummed my first chord. I'd never cared about being good at sports or doing well in school; to me it just got in the way.

I'd gone from dead-end job to dead-end job completely okay with waiting it out until it happened. My folks might not have been pleased by my lack of commitment to the regular workforce, but they respected my determination. I wanted to be in a band for as long as I could remember. The only time I was happy was when I was playing in front of a crowd, and now that it was happening, they couldn't be prouder. My gamble had paid off. The major leagues were knocking at our door and I was more than ready.

We'd worked hard to get to where we were and I felt the party was past due. We had choices, and there was nothing wrong with what I was doing. Besides, the asshole could have totally smashed my screen with his doorway toss. And it was my third phone in as many months.

"Don't be hating on me because you went home alone." The screen lit up with the notification of my missed call. The name of my mystery caller revealed.

"Kenzie?" I wasn't sure if I'd said her name out loud or in my head. Any conversation with me before ten in the morning was questionable at best.

"Yes, it's Kenzie, and she's called three times already." He leaned against the doorjamb, his hand getting cozy with the back of his neck. "So either someone's died or she really needs to get a hold of you."

"Oh yeah, she can get a hold of me anytime she likes." The thought of her hand around my dick making me smile. Would have made me hard too, except I was already rocking the morning wood. "That girl has some wicked skills and I'm not talking her hands on the fret board."

"Right." Max's voice dripped with sarcasm. "Like Kenzie would fuck *you*. She has better taste than that." The bastard proved how much he didn't know, our little side action kept under wraps.

"Well, obviously she doesn't." I could barely contain my smug smile. "Because me and her—happened. It was beautiful too. She is a complete freak in the sack, dude, and didn't act all weird after we fucked. It was perfect casual sex. I'm getting emotional just thinking about it."

From the minute I'd seen Kenzie, I'd instantly wanted her. No shit. She was five different shades of hot with her Malibu Barbie dark-blonde hair and blue eyes. But unlike the *California Dreaming* fantasy, it had actually taken some effort on my part to get inside the tight dress—the reality exceeding even my wildest wet dreams.

With a set of double D's that were a complete gift from God and an ass that made you sit up and take notice, I was willing to do almost anything to get a taste of that. She didn't buy into my usual bullshit, which was sort of refreshing and I really enjoyed getting to know her. Hanging out, flirting—it was sort of fun, and as it turned out, she was totally into me too. The time we'd both invested paying off when we finally had sex.

"Yeah, sure you did." Max rolled his eyes, not buying that I had tapped that. "And if she hears you talking shit, she's going to hand you your balls."

"I'm not talking shit. It fucking happened," I snapped, a

little annoyed he would think I didn't get enough real pussy that I'd started to fictionalize it. "She was all over me at Josh's party last month. We barely made it back to her house before we'd fucked. She may want her hands on my balls, my friend, but not for the reason you're claiming."

The sex hadn't *just* been good. It had been out-freaking-standing. So awesome in fact we hadn't even waited for the bed. My dick getting inside of her the minute we'd walked into her apartment. Her tight pussy gripped me like a fucking fist, my need to come at fucking Defcon levels with the first time barely long enough for me to tease an orgasm out of her before I'd blown my load all over her stomach. First time I'd gone bare in a long time, neither of us able to wait until I got the rubber on. Of course that situation was rectified an hour or so later when I got suited up and fucked her again. It was even better the second time. The memory got my morning wood even harder, if that was possible—the visual would be put to good use in the shower when I jerked off later. Wouldn't be the first time I'd recalled that bad boy.

"Dude, whatever. You fucked her, you didn't fuck her—not my biz. But for fuck's sake, handle your shit so I can get some sleep." The big guy shot me a yawn. "We've got the album launch tonight. I'd rather not show up looking like shit."

"Truth, right?" The yawn contagious as my mouth

followed suit. "Whatever Kenzie wants can wait until tomorrow." With no messages being left, I could only assume she was keen to recapture the magic, something I'd be more than happy to recreate after I'd had an appropriate amount of shut eye. It had been something I'd been thinking about myself. "I'm going to kill the phone and get some more Z's. Set your alarm so we don't sleep through; Angie will kick our asses if we're late."

"Done. Later."

Max flipped me a half-hearted wave as he disappeared from my open doorway, our plans for the morning cemented. Possibly even some of the afternoon. It's not like we had anything better to do, and considering the time we crawled home this morning, it wasn't unreasonable. What *was* unreasonable was that I ever had to deal with mornings. Didn't I give that shit up when we signed a record deal? Sure as hell should have been in the fine print, and if it wasn't I was going to have words with our lawyer.

"Don't forget the alarm," I warned, not needing the heat we'd catch from our front woman if we turned up late. "Just gonna sleep a little more . . ."

...

"Fuck! Joey, you need to get up. We need to be in Midtown in a couple of hours." Max's usually chilled voice was hitting the panic as I cracked open an eye. That alarm we had spoken about, obviously not been set.

"Ah shit." I pulled my vibrating phone out from underneath my pillow. A barrage of missed calls dominating my screen, the one currently trying to get my attention was from Rusty, our guitarist and one of my closest friends.

"Yo, what's happening?" I answered without the need for the hello. The reason for his call wasn't really a mystery, the *you-better-not-be-late* more expected from Angie than our leading axe-man. Still, the bastard was co-piloting our rise to rock stardom, so who was I to complain.

"Good morning, sunshine. Oh, wait. Look at that, it's fucking evening. Huh. It's not morning after all." The sarcasm wasn't missed even though he didn't sound pissed.

"Yeah, yeah. We've had a busy few days. Just because you and Angie have given up the life doesn't mean I have to. I'm just picking up the slack, brother. Someone has to take care of the ladies now that you're off the market. Just trying to do my share."

Rusty was more than just the guitarist; he had been Black Addiction's biggest player—and I don't mean on the stage. There weren't many nights the dude hadn't had a girl or two hanging off his arm. Not that I'd been jealous. I got plenty of girls. Okay, so maybe not as many as he did but still, shit loads.

"Hmm. Sure you are." Rusty barked out a laugh. "I'm

eternally grateful for the service you're providing. Not sure the girls are though."

"They fucking love it, trust me. No one is leaving disappointed." I would happily provide a list of endorsements.

"Awesome. You think you can tear yourself away from your selfless act of community service and show up tonight for this launch? Call me crazy, but I'd like for my rhythm section to be there."

"We'll be there," I assured him, my body already shifted out of the covers. "Trust me, we've been waiting for this all week."

"Fantastic. The label is sending a car around soon. Get your shit together."

"Yep, all good. See ya soon." My hand did a midair wave for no reason in particular as Max rolled his eyes.

"See you soon." Rusty killed the call, and I tossed the phone back onto the bed.

"That was Rus." The grin on my face not hiding the fact I'd been thrilled it had been *me* he'd called.

Out of the two of us, it was usually Max who was trusted with information, but in this instance, it had been yours truly who was called to action.

"Need to jump in the shower and put on some clean clothes. The label is sending a car." The message relayed for Max's benefit because he hadn't been important enough to get it first hand like I had.

"Don't get too excited. I got Angie, she used more

swear words." His smug-ass grin clued me in that I hadn't been so special. "Let's get the show on the road, shall we?"

Our label, Metamorphous, happened to be captained by none other than Power Station. If we were a big deal, their success was astronomical and it helped we'd known them from before they'd made the big time. They made allowances for us because of history, but I wouldn't want to fuck them over either. Being late wouldn't only piss off Angie and Rus.

Thankfully neither of us were packing a set of tits, which meant the shower, change and out the door was achieved within the thirty minute window. So by the time the sweet high-end SUV had pulled up to our pad, we were ready to rock and get out the door, our big night hopefully more than just a bunch of handshaking and head-nodding. I mean really, what was the point of all of this adulation if it didn't translate into at least a blowjob?

Yeah, maybe I was conceited, and probably acting like a pig but it was sort of expected, and I was more than happy to play the part. I gave zero shit about the rock star title; but if the spoils were going to find themselves in my lap, who was I to say no.

Usually I liked to be the one behind the wheel, but the guy pulling the driving-Miss-Daisy was epic. Dude had us weaving in and out of traffic like a fucking champ, the stop-start-crawl left behind for tourists or amateurs. Whatever time we were chasing from leaving the apartment, we'd made up on the road, arriving at the club right on schedule.

"Much respect, my friend." I peeled off a twenty and handed it over to the guy who'd been captaining our ride. "Those were some of the coolest moves I've seen off a stage."

"No tip needed." He nodded with a smile. "Just doing my job." The door opened from the outside before I could argue.

Tonight was our homecoming. And while I would have preferred to play the songs live, some asshole DJ was gonna spin the album in the club instead. Let the people hear what we'd been holed up doing for the last few months and give them a chance to rub shoulders with us while we partied. The show-and-tell was the part I was pretty keen to get started.

A crowd had gathered out the front. Some of the faces I recognized from previous gigs, some obviously new, but everyone was wearing a smile. Made my chest puff out a little more as the security ushered us in, a girl or two grabbing at our arms as we bypassed the red rope and went straight inside.

A long way from the shady bars we used to play—the kind of service we were receiving now, something I would have no problem getting used to—the security tripped over themselves to make us feel welcomed. Fucking awesome. My grin got wider as we moved further into the club.

"You made it." Rus smirked, his hot girlfriend wielding a clipboard not far from his side. The hand on her ass made it plainly obvious they were together in case anyone missed the fucking loved-up vibe they were blasting when they looked at each other. They kissed a lot too, the PDAs not a problem for either of them.

Alison wasn't just playing tonsil hockey with our guitar player, but also worked for our record label as well. Oh, and she also shared blood ties with Max, so you needed a Venn diagram to keep up with all the freaky overlaps. Trust me, my brain hurt just thinking about it.

"Told you we would." I tipped my chin toward Rusty before turning my attention to his girl. "Hey, Ali." My eyebrow rose to check out her cute outfit. She might've been with Rusty, but I hadn't suddenly developed blindness. Those tits of hers—fucking magical—and they looked pretty damn awesome tonight.

"Hey, Joey. Hey, Max." She gave the douchebag beside me a hug. Figured it was fair he got some attention first being that he was her uncle, besides you always save the best till last. "You guys are over here." The love she'd shown my bass player finally extended to me as she gave me a quick squeeze. "Angie and Jase are already there." Her head tipped to the direction where the two dumbasses were standing given her hands were still wrapped around me.

Angie and Jase were pretty much a package deal these days. Our lead singer was also proud mama to a baby boy, the baby daddy not straying too far from his pack. The dude was intense too, so sure as hell no one was going to tell him he wasn't welcome. Not that we gave a shit—Jase was good people and also part owner of the label we were now signed to. Another fucking diagram needed for that complicated relationship. In any case, he and his Power Station buddies had seen to it that we not only got a good deal but also the best producer this side of the equator. That alone got him and his in my good graces; the fact Angie was deliriously happy was just another gold star for the dude.

"Look at you." Angie smiled as we rounded the corner. "You're even wearing a button-down shirt." Her observation one hundred percent correct that I had made an extra effort tonight.

"Had to make myself pretty for the fans." I nodded, my wordless hello to Jase reciprocated with a wave. "And you thought I didn't know how to dress." The threads I was wearing a result of the recent pay injection we'd received. Not that I'd ever cop to it, but I didn't mind getting in touch with my inner-GQ.

"We would have been here sooner, but the buttons confused him." Max weighed in, the asshole not adding anything helpful. "Where do you want us, ladies?" Bored with me, he turned his attention to Angie and Ali.

Jesus, he was a smooth bastard, both the ladies rewarding him with a grin. I mentally made a note I would have to up my game tonight if Max was going the gentleman route. For some reason girls found it irresistible.

"Press is going to want to take some photos, so if you can group around the bar to start with, it would be good." Alison shifted into all business as she gave us the run down. "The PR team is already on the floor. They'll give you any further direction."

The formal theme of the night wasn't what we were used to, our approach being more laid back. Jase and his Power Station buddies figured this was a good way to go, promo the songs without worrying about sounding tight just yet. It was probably smart given it had been awhile since we'd played live. We'd already earned some early praise for the new album and if the dog and pony was required then I'd do it with a smile on my face.

It wasn't hard, a drink or two were shoved in our hands while we smiled and laughed for the cameras. The ladies were kept away for the start of the evening—something I wasn't thrilled about—with *important* people getting our attention. I didn't really know these people or why they were so important, but the "good work" and "well done" they were throwing my way was really fucking nice.

Every set of eyes were on us as we stood together on an elevated podium. The lights around the periphery dimmed as did most of the noise out of the speaker. The hollering from the pit below didn't stand a chance in dying down though as the DJ announced our first track to the excited crowd, their chanting getting louder as the opening bars rang out.

It was weird standing there without a drum kit in front of me. The four of us in a place which two to three years ago we probably wouldn't have been allowed through the door, let alone invited as special guests. Not going to lie but part of me was really digging the ass kissing we were getting these days, the yes-sir, no-sir that came with this new gig was fucking sweet. Call me conceited, but we had more than earned it, our dues finally being paid in full.

"Joey!" I heard a chick below me calling out my name, her voice straining over our latest tune.

That was another thing I wouldn't get sick of—girls screaming for me. And fuck me if it didn't make me smile that someone was trying to get my attention even though Max and Rusty were standing right beside me.

"Joey." My head turned as I tried to find the origin of the voice and reward her with a smile. Least I could do for now, hopefully I'd get to give her a little more later. The grin got wider as I thought of her screaming my name with a little more intensity, the lips attached to the voice still not coming into focus.

"Joey, you asshole!"

Wait. What?

That wasn't what they were supposed to be screaming.

"Sounds like your fan club is here." Max smirked, the bastard obviously hearing it too. "How nice for you."

"Whatever, loser." I elbowed him in the ribs trying to

see who in the hell was calling me. Not sure why she sounded so dissatisfied. I made it my mission to make sure when girls left, everyone got what they needed. I prided myself on it. It was like a golden guarantee. *Maybe* once or twice I'd forgotten to call when I'd *promised* to, but that couldn't be helped. I was fucking busy. And I didn't have the best memory. Surely they understood.

"Joey, you dumbass. Answer your damn phone." My eyes caught on the flash of dark-blonde hair, Kenzie giving me a look so dirty I was surprised I was still standing. "I've been calling you for hours." The eye-glare of death continued.

"Hey, is that Kenzie?" Rusty shot her a wave, his lips spreading into an appreciative grin.

The dude had known her just as long as I had, and while the two of them had never swapped bodily fluids, they had that whole guitarist respect going for them. An unspoken appreciation of each other's talent. And while I was happy they were friends, I was glad they hadn't fucked.

"Sure is. Cool of her to stop by, huh?" Max slapped me on the back like a douche. He wasn't hiding the fact he was enjoying it—Kenzie being in a mood.

Looking at her down in that pit, her face full of fury, reminded me exactly why she had been worth the wait. Not only did she rate radioactive on the good-looking scale, but also she was feisty as hell. She wasn't the kind of girl who sat on her ass, and damn if that didn't make me even more interested. Her attitude was just as sexy as the rest of her, and she was so freaking talented. Smart too, but without the ivy-league chip on her shoulder. And as soon as we worked out whatever had gotten her panties in a wad, I was definitely going to be trying for more of *that*.

My eyes shifted for not more than a second but it had been enough to lose her in the crowd. The beautiful blonde disappeared as the sea of non-descript girls vied for my attention while the music played. None of them even scratching my interest now that I'd seen her.

Considering I hadn't heard from Kenzie in weeks, I was more than a little curious as to why she was seeking me out. Not that I hadn't wanted to see her, it was just the way things had worked out. There was some urgency in her voice that I hadn't expected, which made me sort of proud. Obviously our time together left an impression. Hell, the thought alone was juicing me up; we should definitely repeat that performance.

"Where did she go?" My head whipped around to Rusty hoping he'd have a better vantage point, Max's non-committal shrug already answered he had no idea.

"She's behind us." Angie laughed, turning around and stepping off the podium. The girl in question standing crossed armed right next to the DJ booth looking very much pissed off.

"I told you she was going to find out you had been running your mouth." Max was the next one to step down, Rusty following suit soon after.

The club continued their fevered appreciation despite us moving away from the attention. The noise just as loud as it had been even though we were now facing away from the crowd. The DJ didn't miss a beat, launching into the very next song as we took a "break," his explanation for why there was no Black Addiction still standing on the makeshift stage.

"Hey, Kenzie." Rusty schmoozed, the charming asshole still quick with a smile despite his dick being under lock and key. "You here alone?" he continued, his head doing a swivel to see if any of her band had ridden shotgun.

"You. Are. An. Asshole." Kenzie completely ignored Rus, Max and Angie as she unleashed a tirade of rage at me. "I have been trying to call you."

The explosion earned some heated stares from my band, but they kept their mouths shut. Obviously there had been some kind of misunderstanding and rather than give me shit about it, the guys stepped back a bit so she could move closer to me.

"Relax, baby. I was going to call you later." The smile crept up on my lips. The wide-eyed what-the-fuck I was getting from my band intensified as I put my arm around her. "You need a little Joey time? All you had to do was ask, babe."

"You've done enough." She pushed angrily against my chest. "And the only purpose I have for your dick right now is to shove it in your ear." Every single word seethed with fury. I wasn't sure if I should be scared or turned on, my dick going with the second option.

"Uh-oh." Rus laughed. "Joe, you want some privacy, brother?"

"No."

"Yes."

Kenzie's answer in the affirmative drowning out my no, the look on her face telling me she wasn't kidding.

"O-kay." Max sidestepped away from us, his feet giving him some distance. "You two love-birds have fun. Beer sounds good." His head nodded toward the direction of the bar. Not obvious at all.

"Yeah, drinks all round seems like the way to go." Rus rounded up both Alison and Angie, his take-care-of-your-business broadcasted loud and clear via the eyeball he was giving me. All of them did a quick evac of our general space, leaving with as much awkwardness as they did speed. Whatever was about to go down, I had a lot of explaining to do later.

"Babe, did I leave the toilet seat up or something? Because last time I saw you, you were a fan of my dick." My hand automatically found her hip as I closed the distance between us.

Despite the venom she tossed my way, she looked even more beautiful than the last time I'd seen her. And, not sure if she was going for understated, but that loose flowing dress she was wearing wasn't doing *jack* to hide those deadly fucking curves. She could be rocking a muumuu and still look hotter than most of the chicks in the club. Did I mention how nice her ass was?

"I'm pregnant, dumbass. So consider my fondness of your dick suspended," she said with zero segue.

An imaginary Mack truck rolled through and collected me in its grill as I struggled to understand the words she was saying.

"Say what?" The words spilled from my mouth as a sheen of sweat broke across my skin—the temperature around us suddenly rivaling that of Satan's ass.

"I have a baby inside me." She spoke slowly, pausing between each word.

"It's yours." She took a breath. "I'm pregnant."

"Sorry, I don't understand?" The words still not making any sense.

"Are you deliberately trying to piss me off, Joey? I'm already tempted to rip your balls off with my bare hands; you really want to push it?" Her face got even more infuriated, if that were even possible.

Honestly, I wasn't trying to be an asshole. Or piss her off. But I didn't understand how the two of us could have possibly made a human. I mean . . . how?

"How?" She barked back at me, obviously my question coming out of my mouth as well as rolling around in my head. "You seriously have no idea?" She glared at me, my open-mouthed silent routine doing the answering for me. "When a girl and guy get naked and have a special hug—"

"Kenzie, I know that." I may have barely finished high

school but the birds and the bees part I had down pat. "I mean . . . I didn't even come in you."

The sex wasn't something I was going to forget anytime soon. The memory of that night and coming *outside* of her was still very much burned into my brain. And last time I checked, the baby batter had to actually go to the place where the magic happened in order for it to do its thing. And when I *had* eventually come inside her, my cock had been well and truly wrapped.

"Well, obviously that doesn't matter." Her beautiful blue eyes shot me daggers. "Whatever time in there was enough to knock me up. You're the last guy I've had sex with. We had sex without a condom, and now I'm pregnant."

"Are you sure?" I wondered if the question was going to piss her off further. It seemed like she was on a hair trigger and had already said terrible things about my balls.

"I've taken about ten tests. I'd say I'm either extremely unlucky or pregnant."

Fuck.

The heat I'd felt before was nothing like what was breathing down my neck now. My lungs weren't doing great with the in-and-out they were supposed to do automatically, each breath seeming to take more effort than it should.

It was funny how the lights had dimmed too, not at all as bright as they'd been ten minutes ago, the edges darkening like we were in some kind of a tunnel. Actually, were we in a tunnel? Why did the noise sound so far away? Where had the crowd gone and why did it feel like my heartbeat was ringing in my ears?

"Joey?" Kenzie grabbed my arms, her eyes filled with an emotion I couldn't quite place. Concern? Or maybe it was just an extension of pissed off. I couldn't be sure either way as she dug her fingernails into my skin. "Are you going to pass out?" She moved her head closer, her eyes getting wider.

Me? Pass out? Not a fucking chance.

I wasn't a pussy who went lights out at the drop of a hat.

Why was it so hot in here?

And why the hell couldn't I fucking breathe?

"What the fuck?" The world suddenly snapped back into focus, the slap across my face helping it along. "Did you just hit me?" My palm moved to my cheek where the sting was still spreading across my skin.

Her hand hitting me had thawed some of the evil, a slight smile creeping up at the edges of her lips. "You looked like you were going to collapse, I had to do something."

"Thanks."

"Don't mention it. Do you want me to hit you again?" The offer giving her more pleasure than it ought to, her smile widened as she raised her hand.

"No, I think I've got it from here."

It was reassuring to see I wasn't the only one who had freaked the hell out. Joey's face had paled to the color of the DJ's new Adidas, gravity fighting him while he tried to remain upright.

I knew the feeling, the same terror had gripped me a few hours before—I'd just had a little more time to get used to it. And while I was mad as hell he hadn't returned my phone calls from earlier today, I wasn't a complete heartless bitch.

"I didn't want to do this here." My eyes floated around the room filled to capacity with Black Addiction fans, drinking and laughing oblivious to the occupation in my uterus. "But I tried calling you all day, and I didn't know if you would call back."

We didn't do the lets-chat on the phone. The conversations we'd had were pretty limited, either sexting or face-to-face. So given we didn't have the kind of relationship that involved burning my AT&T minutes, there was a very real chance I was going to be getting intimate with his voicemail. Which is why I needed to take matters into my own hands, and why I was here instead of curled up in a fetal position on my bed like I had been hours earlier.

"I thought you were calling to—" He stopped midsentence, a hand rising to rub the back of his neck. "Last time had been pretty hard to forget." There was no sarcasm in his voice.

"Considering the result, I'd say neither of us are going to forget in a hurry." *Yeah, I was incubating the lifelong reminder as we spoke.*

"Should we go somewhere? And talk?" The cool calm exterior he usually radiated was missing in action as he glanced around the room of bodies. "Outside?"

"Is that what you really want to do?" My eyes darted around the club with no sign of a reprieve. The wall-to-wall people didn't give us much opportunity for privacy. Outside wasn't going to be any better, not unless he was packing an invisibility cloak in his pocket. What was in his pants was kind of magical, unfortunately not of the Hogwarts variety, which is what we needed.

I hadn't given this whole exercise much thought past my grand announcement. It wasn't my brain that put me in the car and drove from Brooklyn to Midtown. Oh hell no. It was pure emotion. First panic when he wouldn't answer my calls, followed by anger that he was ignoring me.

Irrationality was the voice that shouted the loudest as I convinced myself that coming down to the club and announcing to him he was about to become a father was a good idea. Now I wasn't so sold it was the best course of action. A little late to be having second thoughts—the baby in my belly further proof that I needed better forward planning.

"Fuck, I'm not sure what we're supposed to do." He looked around helplessly; the crowd around us oblivious to what was going on. His confusion and uncertainty were unable to be hidden, even if the color had started to come back into his face.

"Well, I'm not exactly sure either," I admitted, my game plan completely being fly-by-the-seat-of-my-pants. "I freaked out earlier; the calm I've got going on at the moment is a complete ruse." I neglected to mention how many times I'd thrown up as well. No point being completely vulnerable.

"Are you going to keep it?" His face grimaced like he wasn't sure it was the right thing to say. My hand had not so long ago slapped his face, so it was a very real possibility my palm would find its way back there. I'll admit, I thought about it. My fingers twitching at things I really didn't want to hear.

"Yes. I'm going to keep *it*. I'm not having an abortion." The words came out a lot terser than I'd intended. "I'm having this baby."

Sure it would be easier if the problem just went away.

I'd even entertained the idea for about two seconds before I realized I could never actually follow through with it. No, even if it meant raising this baby alone, I was going to bring this baby into the world.

"You guys cool?" Max interrupted our intimate conversation. Neither of us having noticed his return, the beer in his hand the only proof he'd left in the first place.

"Yeah. All good. Everything's fine." Joey's head nodded as random assurances were rapidly fired out of his mouth.

"O-Kay." He looked skeptical as he turned his attention to me. "Kenzie, you sticking around? You want a beer?"

"No," Joey shot back before I'd managed to respond. "She can't drink beer. Are you crazy?" The crazy clearly coming from the man who was speaking rather than the dude offering me the beer.

"Thanks, Max." I didn't even bother to explain Joey's erratic behavior. "I'm driving tonight so no beer for me." The only excuse I could think of made its way out of my mouth. "Better to be safe than sorry," I lamely added, because I was one hundred percent sold no one would be convinced that operating a car would be a good reason to turn down *one* beer.

"You guys are both acting strange." Max's eyes ping-ponged between us. The beer bottle in his hand lifted to his lips as he took a swallow. "Someone want to clue me in on what's going on?"

"Nothing." We both answered in stereo, neither of us

ready to share our news just yet.

"Right." Max smirked not even trying to hide how much he didn't believe us. "Well, Joey, if you can tear yourself away from the *nothing* you have going on, we have some people you should meet." His head jerked to where the rest of the band was hanging out. Men in suits smiled as Rusty and Angie signed some promotional posters while smart phones documented every second.

"Ummm." Joey looked between me and the group Max had urged him to join. Genuine fear flashed through his eyes. "Can you stay?" His hand reached for mine, his fingers gently moving up my arm making my skin tingle. "Please. I'll get done as soon as I can and then we'll talk. Don't leave."

Well. Fuck.

While I still had fantasies of ripping body parts off his still-breathing body—namely the parts that got us into this mess in the first place—I couldn't deny how charming he was. It was that charm that had made him so unbelievably attractive in the first place. That, and his body looking like it was designed by God as my own personal playground. The button-down shirt he was wearing did little to hide the ripped torso that was housed underneath and his jeans were doing wonderful things for his ass.

Ugh.

This would have been easier on the phone when I didn't have to look at all of *that.*

"Maybe you can stop by my place after you're done. It will be easier to talk there." My mouth volunteered without proper consultation with my brain.

See? Clearly I can't be trusted when I'm around him because I make stupid decisions. The first being unprotected sex despite not being on the pill. Then asking him to come back to my place because it worked out so well for us the last time I invited him back. Did I even have an ounce of common sense left? Surely this had bad idea written all over it.

"Thanks." His hand made its way down my arm as the smile that always seemed to sucker me in spread across his lips. "I won't be long."

While Max didn't seem sold on the *we're-okay* we'd tried to convince him of, he didn't push it any further. A weary look was shot my way as he and Joey shuffled off in the direction where Angie and Rusty where standing. The crowd quickly engulfed them and they disappeared from sight, leaving me standing alone with a room full of people I had no interest in.

God this sucked.

Any other time this was exactly the kind of party I'd be into. It didn't even matter that it wasn't my band whose success we were celebrating, just that someone we knew made it.

Now, I stood in the crowded bar feeling like all of that had passed me by. A reminder that my life was going to take a detour.

Fuck these emotions.

I needed to go home before I either threw up or cried.

•••

"Hey." Joey stood on my front stoop, the knock at the door happening a few moments earlier. "Sorry I'm late, I tried to get away earlier." The wide-eyed surprise still being the most visible emotion he displayed.

"It's fine, I wasn't expecting you to drop everything." I motioned my head at him to come inside, sparing my neighbors from having to hear about my irresponsibility. It was the least I could do given I kept them up some-times with late night guitar practice. The door closed noisily behind him as he walked into my hallway.

"So . . ." Joey followed me into my living room. "I was thinking." His restless hands tapped an unheard rhythm against his thigh as I turned to face him.

Clearly the idea had had some time to marinate. My big announcement in the club had shaken his usual cocky demeanor, the guy in front of me not the same guy I'd slept with a month and a half ago. I fought the urge to smile; secretly glad he was just as rattled as I had been. Even if it showed me no indication of what it was that he was actually *thinking*.

"Awesome. You want to share these genius thoughts?" My hands found their way onto my hips as I waited to be wowed by whatever bright idea he'd concocted.

Joey had talent. What he could do in a bedroom was only surpassed by what he could make happen on a drum kit. And in those two areas, he really was the master of his domain. But that's where those talents ended. Bright ideas weren't really his thing.

"Okay . . ." His face paled again as he dropped to one knee.

"Oh God!" My eyes peeled back to maximum capacity as I tried to make sense of what was happening. "Please tell me you aren't about to propose?" My hands automatically slammed down onto his arms, my urgent tugging trying to get him to stand. My mind hoped like hell I was wrong, but unless he was trying to tie his shoe or go down on me, he had very little reason to be down there. Considering both his boots were well laced and I was still wearing panties, I'd say . . . FUCK. No. He could *not* be serious.

"Isn't that what I'm supposed to do?" Joey looked at me confused as he slowly rose to his feet. "I know I should have a ring, but I didn't have time to shop."

"You can't be serious right now. You're just going to ask me to marry you? What the hell kind of idea is that?"

Sure, he was freaking out. I was freaking out. But, holy mother of God. Marriage? Did he trip on the way over here? He must be concussed. That would be the only reason why he would think us getting hitched was a good plan.

"Kenzie, I have no idea what I'm supposed to do." His

hand raked through his hair in frustration. "Aren't we supposed to get married? I mean, I knocked you up. I'm not going to bail on you like an asshole."

So *maybe* I'd had thoughts about dismembering him when I first found out. But that was just the shock. Well, at least I thought it was. But the urge to rip any appendage from his body had passed for now, at least for the short term. I mean, I could still inflict grievous bodily harm if he mentioned my boobs were bigger than they usually were, but for the most part, I'd prefer if the father of my unborn child remained whole.

But as far as I was concerned there was only *one* reason to slip a ring on my finger, and having a baby wasn't it.

"Do you love me?" I asked as Joey nervously shifted on his feet, the bewilderment on his face sort of adorable. Ugh. These hormones really were going to be my undoing.

"Um. Is this a trick question?" He rubbed the back of his neck as his eyes met mine. "You know I confuse easily."

"No, it's not a trick question." I couldn't help but laugh. Like I said, Joey was sexy; smart . . . not so much. "Just answer me, do you love me?"

"Well, I like you a lot and the sex is ama—"

"Yes or no." I stopped his not-so-subtle dance around the question.

"No, no I don't love you." The words leapt of his

mouth; the oh-shit look on his face followed soon after. "I mean . . . not right now . . . maybe I could."

"Good." I smiled, deciding to put the poor guy out of his misery. "Because I don't love you either. And being in love is the *only* reason to get hitched. So given neither of us are in love with each other, getting married would be a really stupid idea."

"But you're pregnant." He leaned forward and whispered. Not sure why he'd lowered his voice; there were only two of us in the room. Both of us aware of my newfound status.

"Yes, I am," I said slightly louder than I needed, not feeling the same urgency to keep my voice down.

"Kenz, you really need to help me out here." He shook his head, his hands shoved into his pockets. "The last thing I want to do is piss you off, but I have no idea what you want me to do."

"Joey, I'm having this baby and I know it's taken us both by surprise but I'm not asking you for anything."

At no point did I think that carrying Baby Shaw was going to be an opportunity to further my financial development. There would be no shake down, no asking him to put me up in a nice apartment on the Upper West Side. Fuck that. No way. My uterus and I were not going to be holding this guy ransom despite his increased cash flow. And if his album got even half the anticipated sales the industry heavyweights were predicting, green would be his new favorite color.

But I also wasn't going to be one of those girls who ignored the fact it took two of us to get me in this situation. Freezing him out and then have him find out when his kid turned sixteen and asked questions was not the kind of mother I wanted to be.

"I couldn't *not* tell you. You deserved to know." My voice was quieter than I'd intended, those ugly emotions rearing their head.

"But . . . It's my baby too, right?" His head nodded as if to confirm the fact. "I don't want him or her growing up without me. I need to be there too. I need to be a part of my kid's life."

There were times in life that shocked the hell out of me.

The positive sign on the pregnancy stick was one, and now this, *this* was another.

I was half prepared for him to give me a pat on the back, tell me good luck and have a nice day. Thanks but no thanks, but I'm not geared to be a father. Perhaps even throw some money at me and ask me to sign some NDA in case it hurt his precious image. Of course the latter option would have induced a punch right in the kidney, so I'm glad he didn't go that route.

But him wanting to be involved? Like be an actual part of it?

Maybe I was the one who was concussed.

Does pregnancy induce psychosis? God, I hope not.

"I would never stop that," I said a little too quickly. "If

you want to, you should be involved." Before my mouth followed up with. "But we don't have to be together for that to happen."

"So we raise our kid and not be *together*?" Joey eyes narrowed as he tested the waters, not convinced he wasn't going to have to shack up with me, aka baby momma.

"Sure, who says we can't? Lots of people do it."

Where was the rule that said we couldn't? And if he was climbing on board the crazy train with me, then I sure as hell wasn't telling him no. The way I saw it was if this kid had two parents who loved and supported it then why did those two people have to be together? Fuck the establishment. We would do it our way. Conventions could kiss my ass.

"I don't know." Joey shot me a weary sideways glance. Obviously needing more convincing. Or perhaps wondering if this was an elaborate test, I'll admit even I was surprised at how calm I'd become.

"Okay, let me put it to you this way." I shifted on my feet, realizing I hadn't even asked him to sit down. Hell, no point now. Besides I wasn't convinced he wasn't going to get down on one knee again, so standing was definitely preferred.

"We like each other, and other than wanting to rip your balls off when I found out, I haven't had any other murderous thoughts toward you." Which was a plus. Some of Joey's ex girlfriends didn't share the same understanding I had; he wasn't a great boyfriend and add to the fact he seemed to attract psychos . . . yeah, you do the math.

"Some parents end up hating each other. Plotting each other's demise. And let's face it, you're too pretty for jail."

"You seriously wanted to rip off my balls? I thought you were kidding." His eyes got wide as he completely disregarded more than half of what I had said. Typical, mention of sexual organs and I'd lost him. It wasn't an accident I was wearing the least-sexual outfit I owned.

"Your dick too, but that's 'cause I was in shock." I couldn't help but throw in. Might as well come entirely clean. It would have made a nice conversation piece on my mantle.

"Jesus. How does that make it better?" Joey took the seat I hadn't offered him and sat down on my couch. His eyes not leaving mine as he ran his hands through his hair.

"It's better because we're being honest. We won't disappoint each other trying to be something we aren't. And it will be easier for us not to be forced together for the baby's sake, only to end up hating each other." I slid onto the seat beside him, my hand unconsciously moving to his thigh.

It was surprisingly effortless to be around him. I saw through his ego crap and appreciated him for the fun guy he was underneath. There was captivating charm about him, and despite being incredibly cocky, he was surprisingly honest. What you saw was what you got, unfiltered. And those eyes and smile made you feel like you were the only woman in the room. Probably the reason why we'd ended up naked the last time. That and he made my insides tingle. Joey with his shirt off was pretty damn amazing. *Mmmmm, sexy didn't even come close.*

I shook my head trying to forget all about Joey naked and how good it had been. "And there is no way in hell I'm having a shotgun wedding."

The whole white dress and walking down the aisle was a whole other argument, as in probably would never happen—ever. In fact, the institution itself was on shaky ground. Not sure I'd ever want to be with one guy my whole life. He'd have to be pretty damn spectacular and I'd yet to find one who wasn't intimidated by my lifestyle. Besides, I wasn't sure I'd ever been in love, so being forced into it wasn't happening.

"Well, that kinda makes sense." Joey agreed, hopefully shelving all talks of engagements and happily-ever-afters. "As long as ripping my balls off is no longer on the table." A slow smile crept across his lips, some of the panic evaporating as he eased back into the couch.

"Not at the moment," I smiled, the tension in my body slowly easing. "But I'm moody so I could go either way."

Joey

Finding out I was going to be a father was like a kick to the nuts. Like all the air had been sucked out of my lungs and the windbags had suddenly forgotten their purpose.

I'd been careful *most* of the time; able to count on one hand the number of times I'd gone bare with a girl. Not that it mattered now. All the being *careful* in the world wasn't going to un-knock up Kenzie.

There was a baby in her.

Mine.

"Do we need to get you to a doctor? I know when Angie was pregnant they made her take vitamins. We should get those." My mind kicked into gear as I tried to man-up. Or at least be fucking helpful. Right now I wasn't doing much other than taking up room on her couch. The whole shocked vibe was still my main mood. It was probably going to be awhile, so I wasn't going to be too hard on myself. After all, it's not every day you find out you made a person.

"I have an appointment with my OB/GYN on Monday morning. I guess I'll find everything out then." She crossed her legs as she leaned back into the couch, her blonde hair getting tossed off her shoulders.

"I should go with you." It came out of my mouth without thinking.

"You don't have to."

There weren't many women in the world who'd have thrown out that line. *You don't have to.* In fact, I'd beg to differ that almost any other chick would be holding a knife to my balls telling me exactly the kind of *have to* I needed to be doing. Heading to an appointment probably the least of it.

"I want to." I sucked in a breath and I repeated myself like a loser. "I want to go."

"We can ask about a paternity test while we're there." She did this weird thing to her hair and twisted it into a bun, the hand action almost distracting me as much as the words did.

Paternity test? As in there was a possibility the kid wasn't mine?

It had been a stressful few hours. The album launch, being told I was going to be a dad—shit, I was still marveling that my brain hadn't exploded. Patting myself on the back was not out of the question, and at the risk of getting another slap to the face—I needed to ask.

"Do you mean you're not sure I'm the father?"

I waited for the hand to come flying toward my cheek. My balls also retreated a few inches as well in case the aggression was redirected. You could never tell these days and she'd already threatened worse.

"Yes, *I'm* sure." She rolled her eyes but gave me nothing more than a backhand across my bicep. The half-hearted hit barely leaving a mark. "The last person I had sex with was with you, so unless I'm walking around with the second coming of Jesus, this baby is yours."

Kenzie wasn't the Virgin Mary or any virgin for that matter, but she wasn't a whore either. Like me, she enjoyed sex, and was really fucking good at it. The difference was she didn't have a different dude every night. Obviously I mean girls in my case, but you get the drift. And looking like she did, it was totally *not* because of lack of opportunity. Hell, I remember what *I* had to do to get her in the sack, screwing around wasn't her style.

"So why do we need the test?"

She leaned forward, her eyes going wide as her mouth dropped open like I'd asked her to blow me, or something. "Aren't you the slightest bit worried I could be taking you for a ride?"

"Well, no." I laughed, the thought not even crossing my mind. "It's you. You wouldn't do that."

"Joey, do you understand that you guys are sort of famous?" She spoke slowly, confused why the thought hadn't occurred to me. "And with the new album you're probably going to be even *more* famous. People are probably going to take advantage of that."

"What? Pretend they're having my kid? Seems like a lot of effort. I remember who I've had sex with."

The extra attention we got these days sure was nice. Most of the time I didn't even have to try and get girls, they just kind of found their way onto my lap. It's like my cock had become a pussy magnet, and I can't say I was disappointed. We had definitely made some waves in the industry and getting recognized was really kind of cool, but we weren't tossing Benjamins around or crusin' in Bentley's just yet. No point in anyone trying to shake me down. I didn't even own a house. So unless you wanted a share in my DW drum endorsement or to pink slip my new truck, there was little reason for anyone to come after me. Other than my dick of course, but that was the burden I was just going to have to bear.

"Please, do everyone a favor and not be so trusting, okay?" Kenzie rubbed my arm, her concern sort of touching. "We'll get the test and you can give the paperwork to your lawyers. It will make this whole process easier."

"Whoa. Lawyers? What for?"

First tests, then lawyers. This shit had gone from zero to a hundred in like a second. Shit needed to slow the hell down. The last thing I wanted was to turn this over to anyone else. This was between Kenzie and me.

"They are going to want proof. Trust me." She continued with her line of conversation, obviously dealing with shit a lot better than I was.

"Fuck the lawyers. If you say it's mine, it's mine. I know you." Not sure why we were still discussing this. We'd already established that Kenzie wasn't the kind of girl to fuck me over, and I'd already said I believed it was my kid. I didn't give a fuck whatever anyone had to say about it.

"God, I hope this child doesn't have your blind faith. That kind of talk is how people wake up in an ice bath with no recollection of why they are missing half their internal organs. News flash, Joey. Not everyone is a good guy." The look Kenzie gave me hovered between disbelief and confusion with a little frustration thrown in.

"Fine, we'll do whatever you want but no more talking of ice baths and missing organs." And especially not violence directed at me. "Just to be sure, I think we need to hide the knives for a while."

"You don't need to hide my knives, but you should probably leave." She tried unsuccessfully to kill a yawn, her tired eyes also clueing me in that it was way past her bedtime. "I get really tired these days."

While she wasn't wearing the sexy threads I was used to seeing her in— and my brain had been fried with information overload—there was no denying that the girl in front of me was still knockout beautiful. That and the fact she had *my*-bun-in-*her*-oven meant leaving didn't seem like such a good idea. Maybe it was some caveman throw back, but heading back to my place wasn't what I wanted to do. It wouldn't be the first time I'd stayed over, so it wouldn't be totally crazy to suggest it.

"You sure you don't want me to stick around?" Not really sure why I felt so compelled, yet leaving didn't feel right.

"Do you seriously think I'm going to have sex with you?" Kenzie's voice rose as her ass levitated off the couch so fast I wasn't sure if she'd gotten some wicked superpowers with the new mama status. No exaggeration, she was on her feet before I realized what the hell was going on.

"No. Of course not." I scoffed. I hadn't meant stick around so we could fuck. Well that hadn't been my first thought anyway. Although, now that she brought it up, I wouldn't say no. She was still freaking hot beyond words and those fucking tits were enough to get me on my knees. "I mean, unless you wanted to. Then I would totally be okay with it."

"Joey." Her head tipped to the side, the edge to her voice gone. Obviously she wasn't as mad as I thought she would be. Bonus. I hadn't even planned on sex tonight, so that was pretty fucking sweet.

"Yeah, baby?" The grin spread across my face as the front of my jeans started to get a little tighter. My dick needed very little encouragement and the woman in front of me was always able to give me a hard-on.

"I think you should hide those knives." A chill blasted through the air.

"So is that a no?" I had to be sure. It's not like she hadn't played hard-to-get initially. Maybe she just wanted me to chase her a little more. Make her feel wanted. My dick and I were certainly *up* for that.

"Get out." Surprisingly she didn't yell. Though the evil look she was throwing my way clued me in she wasn't kidding. Her finger pointing to the door was another hint in case I needed it.

"Fine, I'm leaving." I moved off her couch and got my feet heading toward the door. "Call me about the appointment on Monday. I'm coming to the Obi-Gee Kenobi." Whether I was sleeping with her or not, that shit was non-negotiable. I was going even if I didn't know what the hell I was walking into.

"OB/GYN," she corrected, fighting the slight grin that was working its way across her lips. "And I'll call you, so you can leave now."

"Leaving." I raised my hands in mock surrender as I crossed the floor to the door. My feet hesitantly took me the rest of the way out of her apartment.

Leaving Kenzie wasn't exactly what I wanted to be doing. Putting aside the sex part, which as I mentioned I totally would have been on board with, spending time with her was never hard. Unless by *hard* you were talking about my dick, which was most of the time when she was around. It wasn't his fault though. Not when she looked like that.

But it was more; she wasn't like the other girls. Maybe

it was because she'd never wanted anything from me, or perhaps it was because she was in a band so totally got the lifestyle. Who knew the reason, but she was more than just a fuck, she'd been a friend first and if I had any say in it, I was keeping her as one. This was one relationship I couldn't afford to screw up, especially not now.

The drive back to my pad in the Bronx was brutal, and not because of my ride. Since we'd signed the deal and gotten a little coin, I'd traded my old Chevy Blazer for a brand new, fully loaded Ford F350. But even the sweet new pair of wheels hadn't made the trip more enjoyable. The thoughts turned in my head on an endless loop, with my mood flipping between disbelief and holy shit as I put the miles between Kenz and me. I really shouldn't have left her.

"Bye, sexy." The chick Max had obviously spent some quality time with was standing in the doorway when I climbed the front steps. "Thanks for tonight." She giggled before turning to me. "Hey, Joey. Missed seeing you. You have fun?"

Clearly she knew who I was even though I was playing guess-who.

"Yeah, had an awesome time. Looks like I missed the party." Not that she'd offered or that I would have been into a threesome. Well, not tonight anyway.

"Maybe next time." She ignored me, her attention being on the dude who'd obviously made her come. "See ya, Max." She gave him a little finger wave that I never really understood. Was it supposed to be cute? Anyway, whatever.

"See ya, babe." The smooth bastard gave her a smile as we both watched her climb into her Hyundai. The ignition broke the silence as she started her piece of shit five-door and drove off.

"It's not like you to push them out the door." The raised eyebrow was unavoidable as I walked past Max and into our place. Not going to lie, the company leaving was a positive given the mood I was in tonight, but Max was usually classier than that. Him doing the bacon-and-eggs deal in the morning wasn't uncommon and he didn't do drive-by fucking.

"She has work in the morning, and you're one to talk. When was the last time you let a girl stay over?" Max laughed as he followed me inside, the door slamming behind him as we made our way into the living room.

"Yeah, well I can't sleep with people in my bed." My ass sunk into the couch, my mind too juiced up to sleep. "I run hot, all that cuddling shit just makes it difficult. They get annoyed when you tell them to lay off the hugs after sex."

Real talk. I could cuddle like a champ until it was time for lights out, then I wanted to be left the hell alone. I didn't need a human throw rug. Fuck. That. I wanted to spread out, chill and sleep. Girls unfortunately didn't really dig being told to stay on their side of the bed. It's not like there wasn't room, there was no need for them to be all up in my grill when we were catching Z's.

"Imagine that." Max laughed as he planted his ass in the opposite armchair. "Everyone is so sensitive these days."

"Right?" I nodded in agreement, the dude obviously on the same page.

"So, you going to tell me why you had to fly out the door like the club was on fire the minute we'd finished the formalities? If I had to guess, I'd say it had to do with a certain blonde guitar player who looked pretty pissed."

I'd assumed that I'd be getting twenty questions when I eventually got home. It's not like they hadn't seen A: Kenzie call me an asshole and B: Me bail on the band the minute the launch was over. If Rusty and Angie were here, I'd be catching heat from them too, so I should be thankful it was only my best friend who was doing the grilling.

"Yeah, well. You'd be right, my friend." My head fell back against the couch. "Kenzie and I had shit we needed to discuss. It couldn't wait."

"What kind of shit? Is she okay? Does she need help or something?" True to form, Max was concerned about Kenz and the situation. He had always been a smooth bastard, his nice guy routine getting him more than his fair share of pussy. He genuinely cared too, it wasn't just an act.

"*Okay* is not a word I can use tonight. And as for

helping, nothing you can really do." Or anyone for that matter. Hell, I could barely get my head around it and I'd had hours.

"What the fuck, Joe. What the hell is going on?" Max dug a little deeper, his need to know more from a place of concern than because he wanted to shoot the breeze. "And don't tell me *nothing*. Obviously there is *something* and it's serious because you haven't even made a crack about how good her tits looked tonight."

"You looked at her tits?" My head swiveled fast to face him. Max didn't like to double dip and him knowing Kenzie and I had history should have put her in the no-go zone. "Dude, don't fucking go there."

"No, I didn't *look*. But usually that would be the first thing out of your mouth, so I would say my point has been more than illustrated." He rolled his eyes, the needling used to get me to talk. "What gives?"

"So. Kenzie." I paused between each word wondering how the hell I was going to say it out loud. "Is pregnant." Yeah didn't sound any better hearing it from my mouth rather than letting it roll around in my brain. It still felt like a dream. Clearly the issue on whether or not we'd slept together had been put to rest. Ironically this was not the kind of proof I'd wanted, Max knowing there was no way on earth I'd ever joke about this.

"Holy shit. Are you serious?" Max's eyes peeled back in disbelief, the same what-the-fuck I'd been wearing for the last few hours.

"Yeah, that's what I said." The memory of my reaction in the not too distant past. "But it seems like I have super swimmers or something because even though I didn't finish inside her, we still made a baby." My fingers worked their way up to the bridge of my nose and gave it a squeeze. The headache that had taken up residence, the least of my problems.

"Please tell me you know you can still get a girl pregnant even if you don't finish inside her?" The bastard's voice rose in disbelief. Like the information should have been fucking obvious.

"C'mon, dude. What are the chances? I pulled out, there should have been like a zillion-to-one possibility of it happening."

And if the chances had been bigger they should be sign-posting that shit. Like instead of these dipshit infomercials trying to sell steam mops and Sham-Wows, a PSA should be circulating. Don't do drugs, stay in school and oh, even without the happy ending you can still be rocking a baby nine-months later.

"Well, it looks like your number came up, didn't it." Max stated the fucking obvious. No, seriously. Surely I had more chance of being struck by lightning.

"Yep." My head nodded, my eyes clocking him from across the room. "And before you ask, she's keeping it. We're going to do this together."

Or so was the plan. I had no clue of how this was going to work but I'll be damned if I was walking away. Fuck.

That. I was a man and I took care of my business, even if the business wasn't planned, and if I was honest, scared the fuck out of me.

"How is that going to work?" Max echoed my exact thoughts as he pushed a little further.

If it had been anyone other than him on the other side of this conversation, I'd have probably told them to go fuck themselves. A whole lot of none-of-your-business tossed in for extra measure. But with Max, I knew he had my back, his concern for me warranted in this instance, as I had no idea what the hell I was doing.

"Dude, don't even start." My head shook for as much my benefit as it did to illustrate the point. "She seems to have it figured out though so we should be fine. I asked her to marry me but she shot me down."

"Joey!" His voice echoed off the walls. "A chick is going to have your kid and you're going on tour in a couple months. Not to mention you threw in a proposal which she probably knew was offered under duress. No wonder she turned you down. Shit isn't *fine* my friend."

"Dude, my mind is already in fucking free fall. Please don't jump on my case as well. I thought I was doing the right thing. I seriously can't even think right now."

"Joe, you know I love you like a brother, but this is the big leagues my friend." There was no humor in his voice as he rose to his feet and got up in my personal space. His eyes so fucking serious I had to wonder whether or not he would take a swing. "You *cannot* fuck this up. That kid needs you to bring your A game, and if you can't do that then you are going to have to be honest with Kenzie. Need I remind you about the useless oxygen thief that is my brother?"

The reminder wasn't needed. Phil, the older brother of the guy in front of me, had sown his wild oats and then taken a hike. Didn't even know for sure whether or not his kid had been born. Just gave his ex-girlfriend a see-ya-later and good luck. Bastard not only turned his back on his responsibility but then twenty-five years after the fact decided he wanted to play daddy. Cue the-end-of-the-world-as-we-know-it when the daughter he abandoned ended up being Alison Williams, the girlfriend of our guitarist. There wasn't enough it's-a-small-world-after-all to get us over that shock.

"I'm not Phil, and I have no fucking plans on bailing." My ass lifted off the couch as I met him eye-to-eye. "I'll do whatever needs doing, and my kid is not going to be tossed aside because I wasn't ready. I'm *not* that guy."

Not exactly sure where all of that had come from, but I meant every single word. I wasn't ready. But that was my problem and I'll be damned if I let Kenzie do it alone. Or worse, let my kid grow up thinking his or her dad didn't give a shit. Oh hell no.

"Good." Max gave me a nod, the answer coming out of my mouth what he wanted to hear. "Go get some sleep, you're going to need it. Well talk more tomorrow if you want."

"Yeah, thanks, man." Not sure sleep was going to happen tonight but getting out of these clothes and horizontal sure seemed like a good idea.

"Night," Max called out as he followed his own advice and headed to his room.

"Goodnight."

My feet slowly ambled to my bedroom as my brain went through the scenario for the fifth billionth time. Yeah, sleep wasn't happening. Not tonight anyway.

Ugh.

I felt like shit.

Not sure if it was my momentous announcement to the father of my unborn child or the late night that subsequently followed that caused the feeling of utter crap I was dealing with today. Either or both could have been to blame as to why I was unable to close my eyes and get to sleep last night.

Oh trust me, I tried. Counting sheep, warm milk, masturbating—all of which did nothing but mildly entertain me during the hours while I lay awake in bed. Actually, that's a lie. The masturbating wasn't bad.

So it was official. Joey Shaw, my not-so-bright-friend-with-benefits, and I were going to raise this baby.

Together.

But not together.

Sure the particulars hadn't been ironed out—at least

we had a few months for that—but for the most part we seemed to agree. The baby deserved two loving parents, who for better or for worse, weren't going to be a couple.

It was for the best.

"Hey, Kenzie, you feeling okay? You don't look so hot." Sara sat down beside me, having arrived at my apartment five minutes before. Her green eyes looked me over with concern.

Sara Davis was not only the lead singer of our band but also my best friend. We had started Beauty Queens from Mars when we were both fifteen and bored with pretending to like the shit that was being flipped on the radio.

Neither of us were particularly athletic or popular so we banded together—literally—and celebrated our love for kick-ass female musicians who didn't give a shit. Our eclectic dress sense had the captain of the football team dub us "The Beauty Queens from Mars." He had meant it as an insult. I personally reveled in the title. Who wanted to be normal? Certainly not me. And so that's what we named the band.

We didn't get serious about the band until after high school though. With both Sara and I accepted into CUNY —yeah, one letter off from being a rather unfortunate acronym—we'd met Abbey and Becca at a MUSE appreciation night.

We graduated and tried to get regular jobs, but the band thing had always been a constant. Now it wasn't so much of a side project as it was the real deal. The rest was sort of history.

"Soooooooooooooo." I figured she would find out about it sooner than later, and truth be told could really use someone to talk to. "Remember how Joey and I hooked up?"

It's not like she could have forgotten in a hurry. I'd been high from the orgasms at the hands of that man for at least a week after. I didn't even kiss and tell; she had read it all over my face the next day.

"Please!" Sara smirked. "I'm still scarred from watching the two of you make out. It was like a porno. Except you were wearing clothes. How is Mr. Made-you-come-five-hundred-times?" The grin she'd been wearing getting wider.

"He's good. I guess." Well, at least he seemed *good*. I hadn't really asked, probably should have done that. Oh, well. A bit late now. "I saw him again last night."

"So that explains why you look tired. Nice." She gave me a knowing smile. Pity on this she was so waaaaaaayyy off. "I hope he didn't disappoint you. The sequels rarely live up to the original."

"I'm pregnant," I blurted out for the second time in as many days.

In my head I'd rehearsed it better, easing into the conversation. Apparently my mouth didn't get the memo as the smooth delivery was tossed aside for the stark reality. Meh, it was probably better that way. No one liked dragging out crap longer than it needed to be.

"It's Joey's. We're having a baby." My mouth spewed words that barely constituted a sentence. "Surprise!"

"Whoa. Hold the fucking phone. You're pregnant? To Joey? What?" Sara's kohl-rimmed eyes strained to maximum capacity. "Are you sure?"

I'm not sure how many times that question had been asked in the last twenty-four hours. By myself first, then Joey and now Sara. The answer always the same.

"Yes." My head nodded as I continued with my rundown of the facts. "Period MIA, fatigue, morning sickness—all pointing to the same conclusion. There were also the multiple pregnancy tests I took. Every brand CVS carried. Just to be *sure*."

"I'm assuming you're—"

"Yes, I'm following through with the pregnancy."

It was a valid question, considering I was a twenty-five-year old guitarist in a rock band, my only assets being my guitars and a used Chevy Malibu. I wasn't exactly the poster child for mommy material. Nor had I ever displayed any maternal tendencies, so the fact I was hardcore about this shocked the hell out of me just as much as everyone else.

"Even if I have to do it alone," I continued, no point stopping now. "But Joey says he's going to help." Unless he'd changed his mind since the last time we'd spoke. Either way, mine wouldn't be changing.

"So, are you two going to . . . date or something?" The

look on her face was skeptical like she wasn't going to be surprised by me saying no. She had known Joey as long as I had. His past history not the kind you look for when thinking long term.

"He asked me to marry him."

I'll admit I threw it out there more for shock value. More because it had almost knocked me right off my feet and I felt I should share the love. It was a lot funnier now; more so because I knew the proposal hadn't been legitimate.

Sort of like the child we were bringing into the world.

Okay. I needed to stop.

"The fuck?" Sara gave me the same holy-shit-he-can't-be-serious that I had experienced.

"He didn't mean it." My hand waved off her concern, putting it and the context into perspective. "And no we aren't dating. It's *Joey*. The man wouldn't know commitment if it bit him on the ass. And there is also the little fact that while we like each other just fine, I don't actually love him. So, no. No relationship."

"Sounds smart," Sara agreed, her mouth barely taking a breath before she continued. "So you're going to be a mom. Well, okay then. You are totally going to be kickass. Can you imagine how cool your kid is going to be? And I can help you with the baby. Kids love me. My nieces and nephews think I'm the best aunt ever." She folded her arms across her chest, a satisfied grin playing on her lips.

And that right there was why she was my best friend.

While another friend might have tried to tell me what a bad idea it was or how hard it was going to be, she did neither. She accepted my decision with a firm resolution to be by my side while I did it. Of course she'd had lots of practice. Most of the questionable situations we found ourselves in over the years had been my brainchildren. Still, her vote of confidence was reassuring even if I didn't believe everything she said.

"My folks are probably going to freak the fuck out. What do you think is an acceptable amount of time I can string this out?" My head flopped against the back of my sofa. The prospect of telling my parents didn't immediately fill me with joy. I'm sure they wouldn't have the same optimistic outlook as Sara, possibly some disappointment thrown in for good measure. Just because I lived my life with a mostly screw-you attitude, I still cared what *they* thought.

"When you can no longer wear regular pants," Sara said with all seriousness. "You can probably work the food-baby excuse for a bit and wear a baggy shirt, but the minute you need an elastic waistband, the jig is up."

"Yeah, you're right." While the timeline for my expanding waistline wasn't really certain, I expected it would get to the point that not even creative accessory placement would disguise it. That shit barely worked on television and they had a whole battalion of people to help them. "At least I don't have to do it this week, or the next. I have plenty of time."

"Kenz, they might be a little stunned, but they aren't going to disown you. You know that."

Sara was right. When it came to parents, I lucked out.

It might have been because I was the youngest of three—my older brother and sister paving the way, something they never let me forget—*or* it might have been that my parents realized I wasn't made for normalcy.

The band, the tattoos, the less than traditional job choice—they accepted it all. No under-breath comments about changing my lifestyle, no passive aggressive suggestions on how much prouder they'd be if I would just get a *real* job. Nothing. Just encouragement and love, even when my ideas weren't always the smartest. So they might not be thrilled about me being knocked up, but they would support my decision.

Just as they had always done.

Man, I had a lot to live up to if I was going to be half as good a parent as mine were.

"Yeah, I know. Still, let's leave the freak out for at least a week or two. By then I'll have been to the doctor and will have all the facts."

Not sure exactly what *facts* I needed to have. Considering I could pinpoint the date of conception, and had multiple confirmations via tests and other means, the medical degree giving me the *yes* seemed unnecessary. Perhaps having Joey's progeny inside me was making me lose brain cells; I could have sworn I was smarter than I had been sounding lately.

"Whatever, babes. It's your deal." Sara gave me a tight hug. "You want to get breakfast? I'd totally be cashing in on the eating-for-two card." Her wicked smile hinted she was more than happy to distract me with the promise of food. Total team player too because the distraction was exactly what I needed. Whether or not breakfast was a good idea was still yet to be decided.

"Yes. Breakfast. Let's go do that." I nodded between each word. My stomach hopefully on the same page as my brain and would not evacuate any food consumed a few hours later. Let's be honest, it could go either way.

●●●

"Joey." I answered the phone for the eleventh million time this weekend. All right, maybe I was exaggerating, but it had been a lot and we still had another twelve hours before we went to the doctor.

"Kenzie, so I was thinking." He blew out a long breath before continuing. "Are they going to need me to jack off there or am I cool to bring a sample from home? I'm good with either, but I'd just like to be prepared. Oh, and how am I supposed to store it? Tupperware container? I think I have an old *Miracle Whip* jar. Ha, actually that's kind of funny." His laugh bubbled from his throat.

"What the hell?" I pulled the phone away from my ear like it would suddenly spell out why I was having this conversation. "You want to help me work out why any-one would need you to jerk off, period?"

The phone calls I'd been fielding all weekend from him had been an involved game of twenty questions. At first they were sort of endearing, and I was glad he'd taken an interest, but as the hours wore on the questions got more and more bizarre. Joey would go online, read something and then call me to confirm. Like I was suddenly the oracle on all things pregnancy. WebMd had a lot to answer for.

"Well you said you want to do a paternity test." He answered like it should have been my first clue. "I already told you it wasn't necessary, but I'm on board with doing it if it makes everything easier. Do they have porn there or are we supposed to bring our own? Also, no pressure but if you want to help me out in the booth that is cool too. You can watch or you jerk me off, whatever level of participation you want is fine with me."

"Please tell me you're joking?" I shook my head wondering if this was an elaborate plan to push my buttons. Or some weird dare he had running with Max to see at what point I'd lose my shit. Surely, he had to know that paternity wasn't determined in *that* way.

"I never joke about jerking off. As I said, you tell me what you want and I am more than happy to comply. Do you need me to repeat the questions? Apparently preg-nant women forget shit a lot, it's nothing to be ashamed of or anything. I forget shit all the time."

At that moment I was glad for the distance. Glad it had been only his voice that was currently in my personal space and not his body, because if he had been here there was only so much restraint I could exert. And no jury in their right mind would punish me for killing him. I mean, seriously, he was obviously begging to die.

"Joey." His name barely escaped my clenched jaw. "I'm going to try and address one question at a time using small words so I'm sure you understand." My hand gripped the phone tighter. "You do not need to jerk off for a paternity test. They take a swab for your DNA from your *mouth*. The only time I can think of where you would actually *need* to jerk off is if you were donating sperm or for IVF, considering I'm already pregnant your donation has already been *banked*." I fought the urge to follow with no further withdrawals would be taken on my part.

"Also, I am not interested in touching or seeing your cock right now. In fact, I'd go out on a limb here and say my interest is permanently suspended on all things relating to you and sex." Unless sex was foot massages and bringing me Saltines and ginger ale, I wasn't interested in *any* man right now.

"And another thing." He wisely stayed silent while I continued my tirade a little longer. Had to say, at that point I probably would have kept talking regardless. "You can shove me *forgetting things* up your ass, there is nothing wrong with my memory. Baby brain is a fucking myth. I'm not going to suddenly turn stupid because I'm with child."

Silence.

And had I not heard the breathing on the other side of the line I might have thought he'd hung up.

"Joey?" I asked, wondering if he had zoned or passed out. Either was a possibility and I wasn't sure which one would make me less angry. Rewinding the conversation wasn't happening, so I could only hope anything else he said was less crazy than what he'd already treated me to.

"I'm here." I heard the long exhale like he'd been holding his breath. "Look, I'm not trying to piss you off but I honestly have no idea what I'm doing."

I wanted to stay angry.

To yell a lot more and maybe throw a few more curse words around. Not because I was upset with him, but because I too had no idea what I was doing. An instruction manual on how to do this didn't come with my vagina unfortunately, and I was just as clueless as he was. Okay—no one was that clueless—but you get the gist.

As always, there was something about him that threw off my game. Like I couldn't continue to be angry at him even though it seemed he had a tendency to say something either dumb or offensive when he opened his mouth.

"It's going to be fine." Who I was reassuring wasn't exactly clear, my own need to hear the words just as desperate as his.

"Yeah, it will be," he answered back, his voice thick with an emotion I couldn't quite place. "Talk to you later, Kenz."

"Bye, Joe." And with our see-ya-laters the call ended.

It wasn't late. The time on my phone display gave me a big middle finger as the numbers lit up. Only nine p.m. but it felt more like two a.m. and I was wiped out. It had been a big weekend, and I still had a few last dying moments left of it. At least none of the next few hours required me to get out of bed.

Beauty Queens from Mars had played their usual gig on Saturday night. I'd confessed my *condition* to Abbey and Becca when, just before we'd gone on stage, I'd had to spend some time praying to the porcelain gods. Their eyebrows rose further in suspicion when I'd passed on the beer after the show, so I figured I'd just come clean. Besides, they were as much family as my brother and sister were. Almost more so. And I wasn't sure if it was because they both were still buzzing from being on stage, or the few beers had taken them to their happy place, but both were supportive. Not one oh-shit-you-are-so-dumb had been uttered. It remained to be seen whether or not in the clear light of day and sober, if they'd still feel the same way.

Of course being on stage meant my phone had been left unattended for a while, something that wasn't usually a problem. That was *before* Joey had been informed I was incubating his seed. So when I eventually awoke the magical-rectangle-of-wonder from its silent seclusion it buzzed, vibrated and pinged like a firework on New Year's Eve.

Joey had texted, called, Facebook messaged, tweeted and then tried to text and call again. I wasn't sure if I should be calling him back or filing a restraining order. My silent debate on whether or not to call ended when my phone had once again lit up on my way home from the gig.

"Is something on fire because I have like eleven messages from you?" I shoved my guitar and amp in the back seat as I juggled opening the driver's door while keeping the phone at my ear. It was a complicated dance, my foot able to kick the back door shut before I climbed into the car.

"Hey, do you think we're having twins? It's just one baby, right?"

I sunk into the driver's seat as his speculation gave me another scenario I hadn't thought of. Awesome. Because having one child of his wasn't enough.

"I don't think so." The thought taunted me as I considered the possibility.

Oh, shit. Could I be having twins?

"Okay, just asking." The asshole added like it was no big deal, my non-committal answer obviously appeasing him.

"Bye, Joey."

I didn't bother explaining the mental minefield he'd just

opened up. Or the level of panic he'd thrown me in.

More for my own sake.

I was scared of what other possibility he'd throw into the ring. Triplets? Please God, let there only be one.

"See ya, Kenzie."

The calls had continued, each time another suggestion of shit that could either go wrong or some other internet half truths he needed to confirm. The finale of course had been the last one where we discussed masturbation and my memory. I was going to have to put my phone on silent. Or smother him. Either would work.

Literally any more *questions* and I was probably going to have a panic attack. Or put into action all the things I'd been thinking about doing to him. None he'd actually enjoy. Mood swings were common in pregnancy apparently.

Ugh.

I was tired.

And moody.

And emotional.

It was all a big ball of suck and I had zero answers. In fact, the only thing that looked remotely appealing was curling up in bed and trying to go to sleep. Because dealing with it hadn't worked out so well, except to make me panic. Oh, and to make me more tired and irritable.

So rather than fight the inevitable I trudged into my bedroom and collapsed onto my mattress. The weight of my body was accepted by the pillowy feather top as my eyes closed almost instantaneously. My body cocooned in my comforter seemed to know me better than I knew myself as I drifted off to sleep.

My breathing evened out as I allowed the exhaustion to wash over me.

Sleep was exactly what I needed.

Joey

It had been two days since I'd found out.

Or was it three?

Hours had mixed into each other, and to be honest a lot of it was a blur.

Let's just say it had been a *few* days since I'd found out. Yeah. Let's go with that.

So, it had been a *few* days and other than Max, I hadn't filled anyone in on Kenzie's status. And I wasn't good with secrets, so the fact I'd been able to keep my mouth shut this long was a miracle. Some sort of prize wasn't out of the question. Maybe even a medal. I had really impressed myself.

But while I had managed to keep my mouth from moving, my mind had been jacked up to eleven. Every scenario imaginable was downloaded into my memory banks, the thoughts churning constantly. My head felt like it was a crowded room full of E-swallowing ravers. With glow sticks. And the music sucked.

Angie had just done the mom thing, and that shit had been far from easy. Those fucking hormones were vicious; how Jase survived it is still a mystery. I'm not going to lie, she had scared the fuck out of me. Our once-reasonable friend turned into a *Sarah Connor* from Terminator, but without the kickass body. Not that I was bringing that shit up.

So to try and get myself up to speed—and to Google pic some images of Sarah Connor to try and calm me down—I did some searching on the 'Net. I wanted to be prepared and find out as much as I could, but instead of coming away with a crash course on being a dad, my search just suggested a whole heap of shit that could go wrong.

And who else was I going to talk to this shit about?

So I called her.

Just a few calls. More to see if we could work this shit out together. Strength in numbers or something like that.

Possibly *not* my smartest move.

She didn't sound thrilled.

In fact, I was able to feel the glare of death all the way through the phone, which took some wicked talent. My silent thanks that I decided it was better not to go over and have the conversation face-to-face. Who said there wasn't a God? That right there was proof he existed.

My internet searches and subsequent calls to Kenzie were not appreciated. See, the fucking Godzilla shit had already started and we were only in the first trimester. We had months before the irritability was supposed to hit—or so said the internet.

And that place was a fucking trap if ever I saw one. Those websites just added more questions rather than give fucking answers. And don't even get me started on the fucking pictures. Trust me, that shit cannot be unseen. Do not Google *cervical dilation*. Hand-on-heart, you do not want to know.

And another thing. Apparently they didn't need my baby-making juice to see if the baby was mine. Seemed like the logical way to see if I was the dad was to check my jizz. I was more than happy to give it—because I'm that kind of guy—and what better way than to go straight to the source. Right?

This shit and more was what kept me tossing and turning through the night. Not even watching porn helped; the orgasm empty as I jerked off into my hand. When my lids finally agreed to stay shut it was time to roll out of bed. Absolute bullshit.

●●●

Thankfully I'd convinced Kenzie to take my car to see her doc. No point in us taking two, seeing as we were going to the same place, and the car she was driving was a piece of shit. Legit. POS. Not that I'd ever tell her that. I liked my balls where they were, thank you very much.

So when I rolled up at her place at some god-awful time of the morning when no person should be awake, I was surprised to find her sitting on her front stoop. Awake and alert and fucking beautiful. Her hair was loose, just the way I liked it and she looked every bit the sex bomb I knew she was. She'd lost the dress she'd been wearing Friday night and instead was wearing the stuff I was used to seeing her in. Tight blue jeans, a pair of chucks and a T-shirt that showed off the curve of her tits. My dick immediately took an interest in what was going on.

"Hey." She looked up as I pulled up to the curb. "You're on time." The look of genuine surprise flooded her eyes as she walked toward the passenger side door.

"Here, let me get that for you." I hit the door and jumped from the cab before she'd reached for the handle. My hand did the honors as her foot stepped on the side running board. "I told you, I'd be on time." I waited for her to climb into my truck.

Honestly, her concerns I'd be late were valid; I was not a morning person. I'd had to set ten alarms on my phone and left the bastard in a chair on the opposite side of the room so I wouldn't be able to silence the thing and go back to sleep. I'll admit, there were at least two I'd shut off that gave me an extra five minutes. Every little bit counted. The main thing was that my system worked, I was on time and ready to rock despite the fact I was running on vapors. I was going to have to be mainlining caffeine if I even had a hope of getting through the day. The two cups I'd had on the way over, weren't cutting it.

"You ready?" she asked once I'd climbed back into the truck, her hands knotted in her lap. The on-edge vibe echoed through the interior.

"Yep, I'm ready." I fucking lied, thinking it was better than telling the truth. I was so *not* ready.

The drive was short with the only noise being the tunes coming out of my stereo speakers. She hadn't said anything, and every time I'd opened my mouth over the last few days I'd seemed to put my foot in it so I let shit be. So we sat in a weird kind of silence.

Thank fuck we arrived at the doctor's office before shit got too awkward. My truck pulled up to the address she'd given me as I cracked open my window to get a better view. It didn't look like much, just a plain building with a tiny door in front. The sign on the lawn the only thing wising me up that it wasn't someone's house.

I managed to find a spot on the street to park—which was a miracle in itself—and ejected from the car. Kenzie didn't give me a chance to get around to her door, her feet hitting the asphalt before I'd made my way to her.

"You good?" I asked, wondering what the hell I was supposed to be doing. Holding her hand? Giving her a hug? Fist bump? The options made my head hurt. I'd never lost my game when it came to a girl, but currently —with her—I was more nervous than when I'd lost my virginity.

"I was a little sick this morning but I'll be okay." She yawned as we walked on the sidewalk the short distance to the doctor's office. It hadn't been just me who thought the early hour of this appointment was bullshit.

"Sick as in . . ." I waited for her to elaborate.

I'd seen Angie, our singer, blow chunks on more than one occasion. Not on fucking purpose either, but it was hard to miss that shit when you are stuck in a booth recording an album. So as far as the morning sickness thing, I got. It happens, you puke, it's over.

What I didn't know was whether *that* was what we were dealing with, or if it was something else. Trust me, I had a list as long as my arm of fucking worst-case scenarios. Most of which made my blood run cold, so I knew enough that "a little sick" could mean major bad news.

"As in I throw up pretty much as soon as my feet hit the floor." She walked beside me as we made our way to the door. "It's gross, but considering my last few mornings have been much of the same, I'm expecting it's nothing to be worried about," she said with little conviction.

She gave no clue as to whether she was avoiding or she genuinely wasn't concerned, her tone dialed down and tight. So rather than push the issue, I swallowed any other questions and opened the door, Kenzie giving me a weak smile as she stepped through the doorway.

"This gentleman stuff is really throwing me off." She

played nervously with her bottom lip.

"You and me both," I admitted, the laugh making its way up my throat even though nothing was really funny. Unless by funny you mean scary as fuck and then it was hilarious. Fuck, I hoped this was over quick.

Either the ridiculous time of day didn't affect the baby doctor place or Oprah was in there giving away cars because the room was filled to capacity. Patients in various stages of mom-dom were parked, waiting their turn—most of them not looking too happy.

Kenz either completely ignored the fact that BabysRUs had exploded in the room, or she had Jedi-mind tricked herself into a state of Zen, heading straight toward reception. She didn't even blink, flexing her nerves of fucking steel as she stood there. I'd always known she was one hell of a badass, but this took it to a new level of respect.

That wasn't the only thing that got my attention as my head did a swivel, my feet still glued to the floor at the entrance. The fact I had a dick put me *well* into the minority.

Seriously, I was out-numbered by like twenty to one— and not in a good way. I had to wonder if the excessive estrogen wasn't going to mess with my balls, it couldn't be a good thing and I wasn't excited at the prospect of finding out. *Hang in there, buddies*, I tried to give my nuts a pep talk. Hoping they could withstand the sonic boom of chick hormones they were experiencing. I was showering straight after this, just to be sure.

There was one other dude in here, and if the look on his face was anything to go by, his stones were already sitting in his Mrs.' purse. I couldn't tell if he was freaking scared shitless or broken. He just sat beside his chick—her belly close to popping—with a dead, blank stare.

Jesus Christ.

This was not good.

We'd barely been here five minutes and it felt like Armageddon.

Beads of sweat prickled my neck as I let my hands drop casually in front of my crotch—I figured I'd give the boys a fighting chance and offer them some protection. Next time we came here I was definitely wearing a cup.

Even though my brain really didn't have its shit together, my feet thankfully did their thing and got walking. The one-foot-in-front-of-the-other took me away from the doorway looking like a douche to where Kenzie was standing at reception.

Her blonde hair covered her face as she leaned over the counter, filling out some kind of forms—completely oblivious to the lack-of-happy happening in the room.

No shit. I didn't see one person crack a smile, except for the chick sitting behind the desk. And her hair had been pulled so tight she'd have no choice but to give you a cheesy grin. Oh, and she was way too cheery for this time of the morning, so I immediately didn't trust her.

"We'll just take a sample after you're done with the

forms." I caught the tail end of the conversation as freaky-smile-reception-chick put a specimen jar on the desk. "The bathroom is just on the left."

See!

I freaking knew it.

I had tried to tell Kenzie there was going to be jerking off involved, but noooooo, she laid on the that's-not-how-they-do-it BS. Vindicated. She might be smarter than I am—but on this, clearly I was right.

Of course, I'd already cleaned the pipes this morning—I'd needed some way to make myself less hostile from the early wake-up—but I didn't anticipate a problem. Probably just as well too, because the jar they'd provided was tiny. I'd need at least five of them. Maybe even ten. Even now it would be touch-and-go. My load was pretty legendary. Case in point, the baby it had made purely on pre-cum. Fuck, I wonder how strong my swimmers were when I actually came? Medal winning probably. My mouth automatically curled into a proud grin at the thought.

Anyway, I figured I'd save her the *I-told-you-so* I was entitled too. I was a team player and was more than willing to step up to prove it. Besides, I had a job to do, and jerking off was one thing I excelled at.

So, while Kenzie was busy filling out a bunch of paperwork, I figured I'd grab the jar and get started. I mean, there was no time like the present and if we could move this process along a little, it would be better for everyone. She didn't even look up as I snagged the jar and headed to where the desk chick had motioned where the bathrooms were. You think they could have provided something a little more welcoming. A booth maybe? With some porn. Surely that wasn't too much to ask.

With the jar tucked up tight in my mitt, I pushed open the door to the bathroom to find there was only one stall. Thankfully, given there weren't many people in the room sporting the Y chromosome, I had the place to myself. Even better. While I would have been happy to just take care of business out in the open—like I said, I was a complete team player—I figured I should probably head into the stall anyway, and do it with less chance of an audience.

The dude out in the waiting room looked scared enough as it was, I didn't want the poor guy to feel inferior if he happened to wander in and see what I was packing. Not to brag, but my dick was pretty fucking awesome. The thought alone made me smile as I got to where I needed to be and unzipped my pants, shoving the jar into my pocket for safe keeping.

My hand went to my dick and pulled it free from my boxers, and while the beast wasn't hard, it didn't take more than a few tugs before he suddenly took an interest in what was going on. The effort helped along by how happy I knew it would make Kenzie, my initiative hopefully earning me some brownie points. Maybe even a blowjob later. One could only hope.

Hmm. My fingers curled around my shaft as I pictured her beautiful red lips around my cock. Her mouth bobbing up and down as she took more of me, her tongue flicking the head on the way out. Fuck yeah. My hand moved faster, as I fixated on every detail of Kenzie's face, the way she had looked at me when the blowjob had been less daydream and more reality, the curl of her smile when she had me almost begging to let me blow my load.

Yeah.

So close.

Just a little more.

The beast hardened even more, giving me his seal of approval on the mental imagery my gray matter was tossing around, with my hand on autopilot as the fantasy kicked up an extra notch.

"Fuck me, Joey," she'd demanded, pulling her lips from my dick. Her need to have me in her matching my own as she tore her clothes off and showed me that what was underneath was waaaaaaaaayyyy better than I'd conjured in my head. Her perfect tits heaved up and down as my eyes steamrolled her entire body, a crime not to take a minute and appreciate how fucking unbelievably beautiful she was.

"Anything you want, babe," I'd said, one hundred percent on board with her plan to get inside of her ASAP. The anticipation alone made me want to come, but I wouldn't give myself that pleasure until I'd heard her moan my name. I wanted to feel her clamp around me so tight

and shake, knowing those cries had been at my hand—or dick as the case was.

"Yes." The word rushed out as I bent her over the back of the couch and pushed in half way, her wet pussy more than ready for me. My balls cursed the hell out of me as I held there for a minute letting the sensation travel up the length of my dick, wanting it to last as long as possible.

"You want that, baby?" I'd pushed in a little more, holding back on giving her all that I had. The cry that came out of her giving me all the thanks I needed as I teased her a little more.

Fuck. I bit down on my lip as the recall got me closer, faster than I'd anticipated. The fucking daydream faded as reality put me right back in the bathroom where I'd been handling my business. Usually I could stave off the urge, but I wasn't sure if it was the subject matter or something else that had my need to come at desperation levels.

Oh shit. The special jar I needed was still tucked into my pocket, my pants pushed down around my hips as I looked down at the beast literally seconds from blowing its load. I probably could have planned it better, had it open or something but I had zero contingency plan as my skin tingled and any self control I had went out the window. My free hand managed to grab some toilet paper just in time before I sprayed my jizz all along the toilet door. The fucking feeling so outstanding that my legs buckled under me and my ass hit the toilet seat as my body gave one last shiver.

Wow.

"Joey?" A tentative voice called from the door, the same voice that a few seconds ago had been rattling around in my head begging me to fuck her.

"Hey, Kenzie." My fingers still curled around my dick gave it one last tug. "I'm going to need another few minutes, babe."

At least I *should* be able to get hard again. Another ten or fifteen minutes tops, maybe even less. I'd never needed to be on the clock before, but I wasn't going to punk out on the challenge. No, sir. Not this guy.

"O-kay." Her voice wavered, not sounding any closer. Obviously she was still chilling at the door. "Um, you haven't seen that jar that was on the counter have you? I really need it."

Well *there* went the element of surprise. My plan to produce the thing filled without her asking, foiled. Still, intentions had to count for something, right? It's not like I hadn't performed. And had I thought slightly ahead, I would have totally achieved my objective. It was poor planning not lack of trying which had the jar empty and my jizz everywhere else.

"Yeah, I screwed up on the first try but I'll be more prepared the second time around. Just give me a few minutes." No point trying to hide the fact, hopefully my good intentions would be recognized.

"Oh God. Please tell me you aren't doing what I *think*

you're doing." Her voice sounded closer, like she'd stepped into the room but given there was a door between us I wasn't actually sure where she was and what look she was wearing. Her voice certainly didn't have the praise and adulation I'd expected. She could have been a little happier; I was doing this for her benefit after all.

Using more toilet paper to finish the clean up, I shoved my dick into my pants and cracked open the door. Sure enough, Kenz was now standing inside the men's room, the look on her face matching the horror I'd heard in her voice just moments earlier. And not that I could read minds, but if I had to hedge a guess, I'd say she wasn't pleased. Probably because she knew for once I'd been right on the money about this.

"Look, I wasn't going to tell you *I told you so* but, I told you so." I stepped out of the stall and watched her eyes widen. "And I didn't want to make you feel bad about being wrong, so I thought I'd just come in here and quickly get it over with." Really, when you thought about it, I was actually being a gentleman. The least she could is act a little grateful.

"Joey." My name was blown out like a curse. "That jar was for *me*. They needed *my* sample. Not yours." She waved her hands around for extra effect, in case the look on her face wasn't deadly enough.

"What the hell kind of sample do they need from you?" I shrugged mentally trying to work out what the hell she was supposed to do with the jar.

Nope.

Nothing.

"*Pee,* you moron." Her voice rose higher as her tightly wrapped fists dropped to her side. "They need me to *pee* in that jar."

She sounded mad, she was probably mad.

"Ooooohhhhh." My head nodded as the last piece of the puzzle finally clicked. Yeah, I'd read about that. Screening for shit in a pregnant chick's pee. Completely mind dumped on that info.

"Well, I guess then there's no need for round two then." I reached into my pocket and pulled out the jar. The size made a lot of sense now that I knew its purpose. "Here you go. Ready for action, babe." My hand tilted offering it to her.

"Ewwww. You didn't wash your hands. I'm not touching that." She screwed up her face like I'd asked her to lick the bathroom floor, her body repelling in disgust.

"Babe, you've sucked my dick." I couldn't help but laugh. "And you are currently carrying my kid, so I think it's a little late to be worried about my cooties."

"It's not the same thing and you know it." Her hands planted on her hips, a smile trying not to spread on her lips. She might have been pissed I'd pointed out the obvious but she wasn't denying it either. The memory made me grin.

"I'll ask for another one. One that hasn't been tainted."

Her eyes narrowed as they moved from me to the jar still chilling in my hand.

"Fine, babe. Whatever makes you happy." I shrugged not understanding what the big deal was, but I wasn't about to argue.

"What would make me *happy* is to go home." She blew out a breath of defeat. "Instead I'm here and about to have someone I don't know poking me and possibly taking a look at my vagina. Excuse me if I'm not in the best of moods."

So it hadn't been *me* that had pissed her off, the situation being responsible for the shitty mood. The revelation relieved me slightly as I gave her my best grin.

"Well, if it makes you feel any better, your pussy is pretty damn spectacular, so the doctor is in for one hell of a treat."

This wasn't some instance where I told a girl her ass didn't-look-big-in-those-jeans trying to make her feel better. Not that I'd ever had a problem with a big ass, which is why I had no problem with the lie. But in this case, I was telling the absolutely truth. Her pussy *was* fucking spectacular and I personally hadn't seen enough of it.

"Can you please dial down the freaking crazy and just come sit down?" Her lips twitched into a slight grin, hinting that she'd lost some of the edge.

"I'm crazy?" My smile got wider. "*You're* the one in the men's room, Kenz." My hand motioned to the very obvious urinal signposting exactly where this conversation was happening.

"Well, lucky I got here when I did or you would have defiled the jar." She bit back her grin.

"Why don't you head back into the waiting room and I'll make sure I take care of the defiled jar *and* wash my hands." My feet unconsciously moved closer, inching their way to where she was standing.

"Wow, such a gentleman." The sarcasm defused by the way she was grinning at me.

"It's kind of what I've been trying to tell you." I barked out a laugh.

"This kid is so screwed." She rolled her eyes, not convinced by my declaration.

"Nah, our kid is going to be brilliant."

It was the first time we'd spoken about the baby without one of us having a panic attack. And while the location wasn't great, I was glad we'd both broken down that wall. Our kid *was* going to be brilliant because it had us as parents.

"I'm going to go." Her voice turned serious and I'd guessed her mind had gone to the same place mine had.

"Yeah, I'll see you out there." My head nodded as I watched her walk out of the men's room, her hips catching my attention as she left. God she was beautiful and if we had a daughter and she was half as good looking as her mother, I was going to be in for a world of fucking trouble.

The small plastic container that had caused so much drama was tossed in the trash, the faucets my next stop, letting the water run over my hands.

By the time I'd made my way back into the waiting room, some of the crowd had thinned out. Kenz joined me a few moments later, her *sample* handed to a nurse on her way to the chairs.

"All good?" My brow rose, unable to hide my smirk. I'm almost positive I'd had more fun in that bathroom than she had.

She didn't respond, just shaking her head and mumbled something I couldn't quite make out under her breath. It possibly contained the word *crazy* in there somewhere.

It seemed that having an appointment didn't count for much in this place. Our scheduled time came and went with the wait making each minute feel longer than it I needed to be. They should have a coffee place or something in here. Seriously, if we were going to have to lose hours, the least they can do is provide me with an over priced latte and some free Wi-Fi.

"Kenzie Clark." The sound of her name broke the monotonous hum of *The Bold and the Beautiful* that I'd been forced to watch. And not a moment too soon, I was getting a headache trying to work out who was sleeping with who. And I thought we got a lot of action.

"That's me." Kenzie rose to her feet, giving the nurse chick holding a file a smile.

"You can come back now." Nurse chick signaled with a wave.

"You ready?" Instinct took over as I grabbed her hand.

I didn't ask if she wanted me to go in with her. Probably because there was a better than average chance she probably would have said no. And for whatever reason, it felt like I should go. After all, that's why I was here wasn't it? I wasn't about to punk out. Not when my kid and Kenzie were counting on me.

"Yeah, let's go."

"**O**kay, Kenzie you can put your legs down now. Feel free to put your underwear back on." Are not the words you want to hear from anyone you've just met. Even less when there is a guy whose only connection to you is hot drive-by sex sitting by your side.

Joey might have thought I'd missed the utter delight on his face when Dr. Brown asked me to get up on the examination table and drop my panties, but I wasn't blind. The muted groan was also hard to miss.

Thankfully some rather strategically placed sheets meant his peep show was short lived, with the good bits taking part under the covers. The internal exam also hadn't lived up to his fantasy. The wand-of-death—or as Dr. Brown called it, the internal ultrasound—had made him sit up a little straighter, but only until the grainy picture appeared on the screen. Then by some miracle he lost interest in the over-sized dildo contraption and fixated on the screen in front of us.

And there he or she was. No more than a blip, surrounded by a bunch of what looked to be white noise. So small it took me a few seconds to make it out, and marvel how something that tiny was making me feel so sick and tired.

"Well your blood results look good." Dr. Brown tapped notes into her computer as I moved back to the chair beside Joey, the lower half of my body no longer naked. Panties and jeans back where they should be. "And based on the dates you've given me and the size of the gestational sack, you are approximately six weeks pregnant."

Both Joey and I nodded wordlessly. Dr. Brown gathered a stack of information pamphlets and handed them to us with a list of appointments I was going to need to keep. The one on top with the words "Breast is best" getting Joey's attention. Great, he distracted easily enough when we weren't dealing with boobs, pulling him back from that would be tough. His eyes immediately dipped down to my barely-exposed cleavage before giving me a grin. See? The man was predicable.

The issue of establishing paternity would have to wait a couple of weeks; the doc explaining it was usually performed around the eight-week mark. Not that Joey seemed to mind, although he did ask about the process. No doubt interested to see exactly how they were going to collect his DNA. I stopped short of suggesting they swab the men's bathroom, the thought of what he did in there halfway between hilarious and mortifying. This was the father of my child, ladies and gentleman. Yep. I mentally flipped off my subconscious for stating the obvious.

"So, November twenty-seventh." Joey recited my due date as we walked back to his truck. "Poor kid is going to have a birthday and then Christmas straight after."

"Yeah, I guess so." Less than a month between the two occasions to be exact. Though I wasn't really sure how that timing was relevant. Honestly, didn't we have bigger things to worry about?

"And then like nothing for another eleven months. That sort of sucks," he continued; the conversation still stuck on the date. His brow scrunched in confusion as he held open the passenger side door.

"Sucks?" I dared to open the can of worms that was Joey's thought process.

"Because all the presents come at once and then you have to wait forever." He threw up his hands like it should have been obvious. "And there will be none of that combining presents shit. Trust me, as a person born in January I'm here to tell you, that's just lazy."

At first I thought he was joking, his way of adjusting that come November the small and grainy blimp was going to be a real, tangible baby. But judging from the look on his face, he was deadly serious. Wow. I didn't know whether to laugh or shudder in disbelief. *Presents* were what he was thinking about?

"That is the biggest worry on your mind right now?" I asked as I hopped into the truck. "That our baby might get combined presents?"

"Well, you're healthy and the baby is healthy." He closed the door and moved around to the driver's side before continuing his argument. "I need to focus on important stuff. See, you wouldn't know. Your birthday is in June so you get a six-month rotation. I'm here to tell you it blows." He slid into his seat and shut the door.

"Joey, my birthday is in *September*. Not June." I wasn't even going to speculate as to why he assumed I was born in June. Considering he'd been at my birthday party last year and the year before that, I would have thought at least the month would have stuck. The edible panties he'd gifted me from my most recent celebration were still sitting in my dresser drawer untouched.

"Oh. Well. Same difference." He'd shrugged like it was no big deal. The few months in between would beg to differ, I'm sure. So would I.

"I'm not even going to try and work out how that is the same, but whatever." There just wasn't enough time in the day to work on Joey logic, besides I had bigger issues to worry about. But if that would keep him awake at night, then I had no problem agreeing to his no-doubling-up clause. "There will be no combined presents okay, not from me at least."

"Good." He seemed appeased by my commitment, turning on the ignition as he clipped in his seatbelt.

Unlike Joey, my mind was not preoccupied with the close proximity of our child's birthday with Christmas. There were a million more pressing issues that were swirling around in my head.

The first thing that gained my attention was the astronomical amount of money one doctor's visit had cost. Joey had pulled out his wallet and covered it before I'd gotten a chance to swipe my Visa, but there was no way I was expecting him to foot the entire bill. Nope. No way. There might be other girls who would be happy with that arrangement but I certainly wasn't one of them, paying my own way since college. I'd have to find a way to at least pay half. It's not like I had medical insurance, something my parents had badgered me about since I left college and was no longer covered under their policy.

Now, I wished I had listened. Coulda, woulda, shoulda —too late.

Much like the condom I didn't use.

I swear I'm not stupid.

The hospital costs also made my heart skip a beat. What I first thought was a typo with a few too many zeros was quickly confirmed as the actual figure. Yep, that's how much it costs to bring a human into the world. More than what I'd spent on my first car. Then there were diapers, bottles, clothes, stroller . . . the list extended for miles, all while the money kept adding up.

So as you can imagine, the last thing on my mind was whether or not when junior blows out his or her candles, the present they open that might count for Christmas as well. As this rate, no one was getting presents.

"What are you thinking about?" Joey speared me with a sideways glance, my silence longer than I'd thought.

"Just stuff," I answered, not willing to share my load. It's not like I wanted to admit that I was mentally calculating how long I could live off my savings. Assuming I could play until I went into labor, I could probably get by for six months? Maybe longer if I really, really saved.

"What kind of stuff?" He probed further, his eyes on the road as we got closer to my apartment.

"Just about how long I can probably gig until I have to stop." I gave him the amended truth. "Angie played the night before she had her baby; I can probably go right to the end too."

Which was my *only* plan. Because other than the money I earned through playing, what else was I going to do? There was no way I was taking up knitting. And I didn't do sitting around and waiting well, so to keep playing sounded like the best idea.

"Hmm. Yeah. I gu-ess." The broken words tumbled out of his mouth awkwardly. His hands gripped the steering wheel a little tighter.

"What now?"

Joey was a bad liar. Extremely bad. The kind of bad that you almost feel sorry for, except then you realize that he's a successful drummer making bucket loads of cash doing what he loves. Then the fact he can't bend the truth convincingly doesn't really seem to be so bad. It was just nature's way of evening the score.

"I'm going on tour in a couple of months. Which means I won't be around. And I figured maybe you might come visit me on the road." He stopped and took a breath between each new idea, almost like starting a new conversation after each new point.

"Well, I didn't think you were going to be hanging around for the next eight months or so." I settled back into my seat. I had assumed he would leave soon, even if the idea didn't thrill me. "But I'm not going to be able to come visit you on tour. I've got my own band who is going to need me." Sure, that's what it was about. The fact the band couldn't live without me, not the fact that I needed every last cent I could make or that I felt I didn't have much purpose outside of that. God damn these fucking hormones. Now I was feeling fucking insecure. Great. Just great.

And not to mention that the last thing I wanted to do when I'm the size of a *Sea World* performing whale and barely able to walk was hop onto a tour bus. Sure, that sounded like fun, being close to giving birth and watching the father of my child make out with groupies. Not that he wasn't entitled to sleep with and kiss whomever he wanted to, but I didn't want to have to see it.

"I guess we'll work it out later." Joey shifted uncomfortably in his seat, obviously not thrilled I hadn't jumped at the chance to follow him around the country.

I'm sure turndowns were new to him, the oh-yes-whatever-you-want more to his liking.

"Yeah, absolutely. We'll work it out later." My head nodded even though my brain wasn't so sure. "Look, we should probably talk."

God, I hated conversations that started like that and yet here I was, my mouth saying words that made me cringe. Why the hell did I have to be the responsible one? Though between two of us, there wasn't much of a choice.

"Sure." Joey's eyes glanced over at me, guiding the truck to a stop in front of my apartment. His hands twitched at the ignition a beat before he made the decision and shut it off. "You want to go inside?" His head tilted to my front door.

Yeah, right.

That was not happening.

"I think we should talk out here." My body turned to face him.

Every single reason why I had been attracted to him in the first place still made sense—his dark brown mussed up hair, his sexy bedroom eyes, the smile you knew meant trouble. While all those things still made my girlie parts tingle, I was smart enough to know we shouldn't go down that road now. And let's face it, there was nothing to say I wouldn't potentially have another moment of weakness, and wouldn't that just be freaking awesome.

Nothing like complicating an already complicated situation.

So *couldn't* go there.

"Joey, I don't want it to be weird between us." Which is exactly what would happen if I let him come inside. "We're in this for the long haul, right?" Not sure whom exactly I was reassuring, I mentally stopped myself from grabbing his face and telepathically trying to extract the answer.

"Kenz, I'm a lot of things, but my word is my word. I said I'm going to be there." His hand brushed up against mine and I had to remind myself the touch didn't mean what I thought it meant.

Which was . . .

Yeah, so I had no idea what the touch actually meant but I was *sure* it wasn't romantic. Which is just as well, because we weren't doing that. Even if I wasn't pregnant, it had never been that way with us, so he wasn't about to start now. Right?

Why was my head so scrambled? I was beginning to think I was going to need a refund on my college degree, the piece of paper hanging on my wall not living up to its side of the bargain.

"Good, maybe we should give it a few days. Just so we can process this all. And I'll give you a call next week or something."

It's not that I didn't want to talk to him—sure, maybe not five million times a day like the past weekend—but I thought the break would be good for us. Give us some time to adjust to it all. Get my head around the truckload of feelings that had been FedEx'd to my door.

"You want me to *not* call you?" Joey tilted his head genuinely surprised like he'd never had a girl ask that of him. Granted, the girls he knew usually demanded it so my request was probably a foreign concept.

Actually, on paper it sounded ridiculous. Hey, you knocked me up but keep your distance for a while. Yep, we're just going to have this kid but don't even think about sending me a text.

I was officially a dumbass.

And yet, I needed the break.

"Yeah, just for a bit. I mean if there is something important, then of course call, but I just need some space." And to gain some of my sanity back. Shit had been skating close to crazy for more days than I cared to remember and after the last few hours, I was even more confused. It was for the best.

"Is this about me in the bathroom?" Joey's lips edged into a smile. "Because I already told you I was sorry about that."

"No, it's nothing to do with that."

Although seriously, who jerks off in a public bathroom? He could barely handle *himself*, how in the hell was he going to deal with our child? "But I really wish you would listen to me next time." And possibly keep the self-pleasuring to the confines of your own house. Just the bedroom would be better, but maybe that would be asking too much.

"Fine, next time I try and be helpful, I'll ask." He threw his hands up in defeat, hopefully meaning what he said.

"That's great, but I'm still going to need a few days." At the very least, even that was a stretch. The hope of a few days to give me the clarity I needed seemed like a tough task. Still, I didn't have a lot of options.

"Okay, so I can't call you for few days. I can handle that." He offered with little rebuttal, agreeing to give me my space. Not that he had much choice, it was either that or he was going to be spending some quality time with my voicemail.

"Thank you."

"Hey, whatever. It's cool." He shrugged, unable to hide his confusion about why I needed the distance. "You want me to walk you in?"

"No, I've got it from here. Thanks for the ride." My hand popped open the passenger side door as my ass slid off the seat. "Talk soon." The off-handed goodbye automatically leaving my mouth before I'd had a chance to stop it.

"Yep." He nodded watching me jump out of the truck, my feet hitting the sidewalk.

"Bye." The wave I offered was lame, much like the reasoning I had offered for the radio silence. Yeah, I seriously needed to get my shit together.

"Bye."

He waited until I'd pulled open the security door before starting his Ford and driving away, the noise of his truck heading up the road making my body sag in relief.

It was good to be alone.

It was what I needed.

My feet trudged inside through the now-opened doorway, my plans for the day including nothing more than yoga pants and possibly a couch. Hopefully no vomiting—but I wasn't about to be too crazy, it was still early and lunch could still throw me a curve ball.

Lunch.

Just the thought made me want to throw up.

Well, at least I wasn't thinking about Joey. Well I hadn't been . . .

I fumbled with my keys, barely pulling them out of the lock in my door when I heard my cell buzzing from my purse. The ringer still silenced from earlier.

"Ugh." I groaned both internally and verbally, wondering why I couldn't at least get into my apartment and out of my pants before I had to deal with the world. My free hand pulled the vibrating culprit from the depths of my bag, the illuminating screen displaying the name of the caller.

Joey.

It had been five minutes tops.

He really sucked with directions.

"Yes?" I answered, my mind hadn't decided if it was happy or agitated.

"Does the no calling thing start from now or from tomorrow?" I was almost positive I heard the smile in his voice.

"You called me to ask me when not to call me?" Surely he could see how ridiculous it sounded.

"Sure, how else was I going to know?" He answered like I was the one who was being stupid.

"To clarify, it's from now." My fingertips squeezed the bridge of my nose, having a conversation with Joey was like herding cats, and I didn't have the brainpower or the energy right now. Although, if I was honest with myself, I wasn't entirely pissed off.

"Cool. Just so I know." I imagined him grinning, pleased with himself.

"Great, glad we got that sorted out." I stepped into my living room and tossed the keys onto the side table by the door. My feet toed off my Cons as I worked toward my goal of getting into yoga pants and comfortable regardless of the interruption.

"Hey, Kenz." Joey hesitated, his breath drawing in sharply as he waited for me to answer.

"Yeah?" My mouth responded before my brain could signal that it might not be the wisest choice.

"I'm glad it's you."

I waited for the rest of the sentence, maybe the part where it made sense, but it didn't come.

The line hummed with silence.

Nope, he was leaving it at that.

"What do you mean?" It was obvious the only way I was going to get an elaboration was to ask for one.

"Like if I was going to accidentally get someone pregnant, I'm glad it was you."

A lump formed in my throat.

God, I was the worst person in the world.

Unlike Joey, I had wished the paternity of my unborn child had fallen at someone else's feet. Well, at least I had when I first found out. Someone more stable, more responsible and possibly someone who knew pizza wasn't the most efficient way to cover all five food groups in one hit.

But those doubts hadn't entered into his mind, and he really had been incredibly sweet. Even though deep down he was probably just as worried as I was. Maybe he was right about this. Maybe I should have been glad it was him.

"Anything else, Joey?" I couldn't help but smile. No matter how much he pushed my buttons, I could never be mad at him for long. He was just too adorable, even if he could sometimes act like a dumbass.

"Nah, I'm good. Take care of yourself, and if you need anything you can call me. I promise I'll answer."

My head nodded silently even though he couldn't see it. "I'll promise I'll call if I need anything."

And with that we said our second goodbye, my emotions all over the place as I hung up the phone.

Yoga pants.

My mind reminded me as I pushed away the urge to call him back and talk to him a little longer. My jeans shimmied down my hips as I undressed on my way to the bedroom, the denim falling to the floor as I shoved them down past my knees. So much better.

The yoga pants could wait, my plan derailed as soon as my butt sat on my mattress. Maybe I could crawl under the covers and just not deal with pants at all for a few hours. The internal battle lasted mere seconds as I crawled under my comforter and snuggled onto my side.

I *was* glad it was him.

The question I had tried to push aside got answered anyway. The smile crept on my lips as I imagined if he or she would have his amazing dark-brown eyes. Yeah, I'd like that, for our baby to look like him. His sense of humor too maybe, just toned down a little. And his laugh. Oh, and definitely his smile. But most of all, his kindness —he was way kinder than I could ever be.

Yeah, I was glad.

Glad it was him.

Seven

Joey

When I eventually made it back to my house, my only plans were to get reacquainted with my mattress. It's not like there was any good reason for me to continue to be awake. And my brain was already pushed to the limit with information overload. So my head on my pillow was exactly the kind of reset I was going to need. Sleep, the main objective. Getting rid of the current headache an added bonus.

"Hey, how was it?" my roommate and best friend asked as soon as my boots hit the kitchen. Seemed early mornings didn't serve up the same kind of misery for him, the dude looking pretty freaking refreshed sipping a cup of coffee.

"Yeah, let's just say shit got jacked up to eleven." My ass sunk on the barstool parked against the breakfast bar. "You got any more of that coffee? I'm going to either tap a vein with that shit or head to bed for the next five-to-six hours."

More likely ten, and even then I didn't think the shuteye was going to be enough. Hell, I could sleep for a week and it wouldn't make a difference.

"And why the hell are you up so early?" I asked as a cup of steaming hot Joe was placed on the counter in front of me like magic. Max was awesome like that. One day he was going to make someone an awesome wife.

"It's eleven-thirty." He shot me a look like the statement in itself should mean something significant. "Besides, Rus and Ange had some stuff they wanted to go over. I assumed you got the message?"

Firstly, just because those two had decided to ball-and-chain it, didn't mean we needed to start acting like different people i.e. get up early to work. I didn't bitch when we were recording—okay so maybe I bitched a little—but for the most part I played nice because my eye was on the prize. Now? There was no need for it. The album was done so there wasn't any reason we couldn't dial down the let's-get-shit-done till at least three. It just seemed like cruel and unusual punishment to have a *meeting* any earlier. Surely there was a Geneva Convention against this shit, and if there wasn't there damn well should be.

"Everyone knows I'm no good to anyone before noon, and even that's a stretch. So why we are all of a sudden starting with fucking early mornings is beyond me." I fished out my phone to see that I had in fact missed the all-important summons from Angie. The unread message spelling out we had business today.

"Do I need to remind you that you are already awake?" Max smirked from behind his coffee cup, the bastard giving me zero sympathy. "Or am I sitting here talking to myself?"

Wise-ass.

I needed new friends. And I was just about to tell him about my disappointment in my current circle when Rusty and Angie—both without their significant others—arrived before I'd had the chance. The door I'd forgotten to lock making their entrance happen without the need for a knock.

"Holy shit. It must be an apparition." Rusty clutched at his chest as he mock stumbled into the living room. "It looks like Joey, but it's before noon so I know it can't be. Can someone go check his pulse and make sure he didn't die in his sleep?"

"Very funny, Rus. I had shit to do this morning. Besides, I've already heard it from Max." My chin tipped toward the direction of the big guy grabbing a few extra cups of java. Total wife material.

"Did you even go to bed? You're dressed and every-thing. And—" Angie moved closer, her nose sniffing the air around me. "You showered. Wow. I think Rus might be right. We should definitely check his pulse." Our feisty lead singer smiled.

"I went to bed." I rolled my eyes, the heat I was

catching not unusual. We liked to talk shit to each other; it was like terms of endearment. "So, what's so important?"

"Okay, well it's good you're up." Rus took the lead, Angie shooting him an appreciative nod. "Angie and I were fully prepared for having to hang around until you woke from your usual coma but this saves us a lot of time."

"Sounds serious." Max echoed my exact thoughts, the words shooting out of his mouth before they'd gotten a chance to leave mine.

"We convinced the label to do another launch." Angie smiled, the *we* in the conversation obviously meaning her and Rus; the label, Metamorphous AKA Power Station also happened to include her husband. "One where we *play*." The smile got a little wider. "Last weekend was sort of lame. When Jase and the guys first suggested the party it seemed like the right way to go, but I felt like a moron sitting around while they piped our stuff through speakers. That's *not* us."

It was good to know that it hadn't been just me. Sure, it had been nice to get the attention. Have people scream your name and want a piece of you, but I'd rather be sitting behind a kit than standing on stage with my dick in my hand. Not that I'd had much time to enjoy the last launch, the whole loving the attention being shelved pretty quickly after Kenzie's arrival. So I was definitely up for a redo.

"Sweet." My head nodded, the excitement freaking real as I waited for the details. I'd been itching to play, and with what had been going down in my personal life, hitting the crap out of a drum or two sure sounded like a good idea. In truth, I could use the distraction.

"You just give me the time and place." Max grinned, the bastard beside me also having a tough time with the hiatus. It had been months since we'd played live, and we were more than ready.

"Oh, you're going to love this." Rus grinned; the smug douchebag paused for effect before continuing. "I got us a gig at CJ's."

Fuck me.

Maybe I did die?

Or this was a way for the big guy upstairs to repay me for man-ing up when it came to Kenzie. Not that I'd expected a reward, but I sure as hell wasn't turning it down. It almost seemed too good to be true.

CJ's was a hybrid bar/club that went beyond being just an establishment. It was an institution. It had been the breeding ground for the punk rock movement and then had followed the progression into rock, with every band worth its salt vying for the chance to play there. There were urban legends of bands begging the owner to play. Blowjobs, money, trips to Bermuda—whatever it took. The Ramones had graced the stage too many times to count, where they likened the experience to spiritual.

While the building itself looking like a complete

shithole, it wasn't the dive bar it was disguised as. Those diehard twenty-one-year-olds from the 70's, 80's and 90's had all grown up and we're packing money clips bigger than my bank account. And while those kids were now drinking overpriced boutique beer and Dom Pérignon, they still had rock deep in their roots—those rich bastards knew how to have a good time.

"Holy shit." Max once again stole my line, the shock making my words get stuck in my throat. "Dude, bands kill to play there. The crowd is intense."

"Uh-huh." Angie nodded, she couldn't have wiped the smile off her face if she tried. "And any band who plays there usually either has a spike in album sales or is decimated, never to be heard from again."

We'd played big arenas on the support docket with Power Station, but this was different. This was getting the nod all on our own. Kneeling down, kissing the ring and being accepted into the famiglia.

"It's time to sink or swim, boys." Max weighed in, the grin slipping from his face. "Not for the press, not for the suits—I'm talking old school. We play and get them on our side—"

"Platinum, baby." My pulse started to hammer just at the thought.

Yeah, I was over simplifying it, but getting a nod from the crowd at CJ's was one hell of an endorsement. Not to mention half of them were in the industry, which meant exposure to radio, interviews, and stadium tours—this time our own.

"Let's not get too excited," Angie played devil's advocate. "Even if they love us, the album still has to sell. There are no guarantees."

"Fuck guarantees." My fist pumped in the air, unable to keep the excitement that had been bubbling, locked down. "This is exactly how we do this."

"All right." Rusty gave me a nod. Even though he was trying to play it cool, I could see he was just as excited as I was. "So, let's meet later at Angie's; we'll go through the set. We're not getting up there and playing half cocked. We get one shot at this, we're going to make it count."

"Considering we haven't played for the public since the night before I had Zack, we're going to need the practice to work out the kinks." Angie was being practical but deep down we knew we could play those songs in our sleep.

"Yeah, that's the gig I'd sooner forget." Rusty's recall slightly different from that of our front woman. While it had been the night before she brought her little dude into the world, it had also been the gig that Max's brother had chosen to do his hey-you're-my-kid to Alison.

"Let's hope no one else shows up claiming to be someone's dad." Angie laughed, her joke earning me a sharp look from Max. Neither of us laughing.

"Uh-hum. Yep." The sidestep wasn't as smooth as I hoped; I really hadn't counted on the topic coming up so soon. What were the chances? It's not as if topic of kids and dads came up often.

"And what was *that?*" Rusty's eyebrow rose in question, the dude not missing a beat. I hated that he was so smart. And observant. He needed to keep that Mentalist bullshit for the ladies, not direct it at me.

"What?" I scoffed, trying to think of something convincing to say. Yep, completely blank. "It was nothing."

"Like hell, *nothing.*" Rusty not satisfied pushed a little further. "If Phil is back in town and we're going to have problems then you need to disclose that shit now. No more surprises."

Thankfully Max's piece of shit brother wasn't the problem. Like we'd all predicted, his need to have a Hallmark-moment with his kid had lasted about twenty seconds before he'd decided he didn't want to wait around. Because giving his kid a few months to adjust to the shock of having a father was *obviously* unreasonable. No, the *surprise* was something totally different this time around.

"Phil is a ghost. He took off a few months ago, and last I heard of him he was in California. Besides, you know there is no way I'd let him ever come to one of our gigs. If I could cut all ties with him I would." Max cleared his throat, the love for his dumbass sibling dwindling to non-existent.

"Then who else is missing a dad, because last time I checked, all our family trees were decked out." Rus looked around the room, demanding answers.

"I guess that would be me." The words not coming out exactly how I'd meant them. I wasn't great with improv, so it was the best I could manage without preparation.

"Dude, seriously." Rus shot me a raised eyebrow, the added head shake thrown in for good measure. "You look *exactly* like your dad. Don't even try and tell me you're adopted."

"No, not *my* dad," I clarified. "As in, I'm going to be one."

"Shut. The. Fuck. Up." Angie's hands shoved me in the chest, her mouth dropping open to match the wide-eyed expression she had going on. Yeah, not what she was expecting I'm sure.

"Kenzie. November." The two words serving as the explanation. There was more to it, but my brain couldn't connect the sentences to make them come out right. My mouth and my mind on two different wave lengths. Not that it mattered; they were smart guys, they could fill in the blanks.

"You had sex with Kenzie? *And* you got her pregnant?" Angie continued with the third degree, apparently needing clarification on the situation.

"Obviously it wasn't planned, but yes." The attention I was getting making me edgy. I had every intention of telling them but would have preferred to have this conversation under different circumstances, ones where I actually knew what to say.

"So what, the condom broke?" Angie was like a dog with a fucking bone, and seriously who gave a shit? Did we really need to CSI the particulars? Kenzie was pregnant, enough said.

Silence.

A bunch of eyeballs flew in my direction; my mouth stayed clamped shut in response. The lack of answer enough for everyone to connect the dots; it's not like I had ever been shy about talking about a girl.

"You didn't *use* a condom. Yet you're surprised there's a baby." Angie rolled her eyes, but saved me from the are-you-serious I was expecting. I'd seen her do much worse; I could only assume she was cutting me a break.

"Yes, yes. I know. I'm an idiot." Not that it changed anything. Fuck, the *how* didn't even matter at this point so I saw no need to continue talking about it. Besides, this wasn't going to be something I fucked up, even if the shit had been unplanned.

"Well congratulations." Angie pulled me in for a hug, her tight smile clueing me in that she wasn't going to ride me about it any further. It was hard for her not to I'm sure. Her gift to me I guess.

"Ooooooooh." Rusty's voice broke the silence, our heads swiveling to his direction. "So *that's* why she was so pissed the other night. Makes sense now."

Uh-huh.

The nod of my head was all that was needed, the events of the night in the club snapping into focus. I mean, it's not every day a hot chick calls me an asshole in public. Well, not anymore.

"Yeah, we just found out."

While I could tell Angie and Rusty probably had more questions, thankfully they kept their mouths shut and didn't make me go over the story. The guys were awesome like that. When it counted, they'd shelve the name-calling and sarcasm and get behind whichever one of us needed it. Blind faith and absolute unwavering support is what I got back. They didn't heap on the expectations, just let it be and let me pick the pace and because they did, it made me want to open up. My mouth got busy and gave them the low down about Kenz and I being on the same page with raising the kid together. And other than earning me a few concerned looks, I was saved the twenty questions. Everyone had their manners in place, not pushing me to talk more than I wanted. All of them telling me they were there for whatever was needed.

What I'd said before about needing new friends was bullshit.

They didn't get better than the three standing around me now.

Honestly, I was relieved. At least it was out in the open, and other than telling my folks they were going to be grandparents—which would happen eventually—I didn't have to worry about slipping up and saying something I shouldn't have.

Well, at least not to do with the pregnancy. My mouth could still get me into trouble; it's not like that shit stopped just because I was suddenly going to be someone's dad. Fuck, I was probably going to have to stop swearing too. Shit. I mean, shoot. Yeah, that was going to be hard. Thank God I had some time to sort it out. I might have to try and swear out my fucks before November.

"That didn't go so bad." Max wandered back into the living room, Angie and Rus heading out soon after my big reveal.

"Yep. That went a lot better than I'd imagined."

Neither of them giving me the irresponsibility lecture or throwing the lawyer talk at me like Kenz assumed they would. Like I said, when it counted those guys had my back. And with one less thing taking up my mental space I could concentrate on other things. Like not calling Kenzie.

"So you want to talk about the appointment?" Max, took a seat on the couch. "Or anything else? If you don't, that's cool too. Whatever you need."

The dude had a built-in sense of what I needed; he pretty much knew me better than I knew myself, so it came as no surprise he was leaving the ball in my court.

"We're going to cool it for a few days. Kenzie needed some space." I started the debrief, not that I entirely understood it myself. Not that it mattered, I'd told her I'd respect her wishes and that's what I was going to do.

"Dude, it's a lot. I think if she needs space then give it to her. She's not packing up and moving anywhere, so a few days to let the dust settle isn't such a bad thing."

Of course what he was saying was absolutely true, probably slicker than what I could have managed. Things had moved pretty damn fast in the past few days. Slowing shit a little would probably do us both some good. And it's not like she was far, I could still hightail it across the Brooklyn Bridge anytime I needed.

"Yeah, you're right." I agreed.

"What the hell is that?" I pointed accusingly at the plant that had been dumped on my counter top, a bright red ribbon tied around the pot.

"I figured you can practice on it—you know—for the baby." Sara spruced up the leaves; her bright pink fingertips fluffing it like a King Charles Caviler ready for *Best in Show*. "What do you think?" She turned it to face me.

"I think I'm going to kill it. And it's hideous."

The weekend had been tough, Monday even tougher. So after I'd slept most of the day, fantasized about the double chocolate fudge cake from the Food Network, had a good cry—because that seemed to be my usual speed—and then thrown up a couple of times, I called Sara.

This time when I spilled my guts it was more metaphorically rather than literally, which made a nice change.

So on Tuesday morning when Sara landed on my doorstep with what looked to be a small tree in hand, I knew it was bad news. For me and the tree. FYI, I had no green fingers or thumbs, and the thought of gardening gave me hives.

"Oh, come on Kenzie." She shoved the plant closer, presenting it to me like some strange sacrificial offering. "Think of it as a science experiment. Just make sure you water it, talk to it and don't kill it. Simple. I think we should call him Hendrix. That's a good name." She was way too excited about this fucking science experiment. Proof that she needed a project, one that didn't include me.

I surveyed my newly acquired botanical child, knowing my friend was just trying to help. That phone call Sara had been on the receiving end of had been one of a rambling, scared and insecure little girl, something I'd never been. Like the life that had been implanted in me sucked out my previous courage. And that's what scared me most of all, that in only a few days I'd been reduced to a mess. It wasn't me, and I didn't like the feeling.

"Fine, I'll play nice with the plant."

"Hendrix," she whispered, covering its leaves with her palms like my words would mortally wound its ego. Honestly, if anyone were capable of sending flora to therapy, it would probably be me.

"*Hendrix*, I'll play nice with Hendrix." I lifted the pot,

bringing it closer, my sweetened tone for Sara's benefit, not the plant.

"That's the spirit." She gave me a quick side hug. "So what do you want to do now?

"Take Hendrix to get his first lap dance and buy him a forty ounce malt liquor." I laughed, glad for some semi normal conversation. It had been about the baby and me almost every time we spoke, and I was glad for the distraction.

"Ha, see I know you don't mean that because you can't stand malt liquor." Sara grinned, not skipping a beat.

"Oh, but the lap dance is completely okay?" I laughed, loving the lighter tone of the conversation. How long had it been since I genuinely laughed? Too long, if I had to ask.

"Actually, if you wanted to do mother-of-the-year right, you would be *performing* the lap dance." She popped her hip to the side and danced suggestively, her hands roaming over her body despite me being her only audience. "Right up until you delivered. I hear that's a kink."

"Ewwww. Sara. Too fucking far." I both mentally and physically shivered. The visual not one I would be able to get rid of in hurry.

"Hey." I stopped giggling and looked at my beautiful friend, the act of kindness going beyond the gift she'd brought me. "Thanks, I really needed the laugh and I know I can be myself around you without you thinking

I'm being an asshole."

"Kenz, I brought you a fucking *plant*. I willingly walked into a nursery, picked it out, paid money for it and hauled it here. I'd say no one in this room has any grounds to pass judgment."

"I just want you to know how much this all means to me." I stopped talking before the lump in my throat got any bigger. There really wasn't any need for words, none of which would do the feelings I had justice anyway.

"Awww, Kenz." She pulled me into a hug. "You know I love you."

"I love you too." I hugged her back, fighting back the tears that seemed to be on constant rotation these days.

"All right, enough of this shit." Sara straightened, her shoulders squaring off in a move I knew meant business. "We're getting out of this apartment and doing something normal for a change."

Other than the gigs on the weekend and the doctor's visit, I'd been pretty much in lockdown. Granted it had been self imposed, born out of a whole lot of what-the-hell-is-going-to-happen-next, but my exile had been long enough.

"Please don't say day spa," I pleaded. I'd happily go almost anywhere with Sara, anywhere but there. "You know I don't like strange people touching me."

"You say that with a womb that is bearing Joey Shaw's fruit." She raised an eyebrow, the added smirk to soften the blow. "Strange people have already touched you."

"Ha. Ha." I mock laughed. "Seriously, what do women see in those places? Let's all get naked together and have overpriced mud smeared into our skin."

"Firstly, I am completely bummed you don't want to get naked with me after I just showed you my moves." She shook her head feigning offense. "Secondly, day spa? When have I ever suggested that? I said normal, not crazy talk."

"Do I need to point out the obvious?" My head tipped toward the bright green-leafed visitor she had brought to my house. "You and crazy—cannot be ruled out."

"Fair call."

"Actually, I have an idea of something we could do." The mental stretch felt good after the emotion of the last few days.

"I'm already liking this idea." Sara grinned, holding up her arms in victory "Kenzie Clark is back ladies and gentlemen."

"Dom has been dying to collaborate, you know they just got signed to a minor label."

"Ah, Dom. He's so fucking hot. Just looking at him makes me want to touch myself inappropriately."

"Well, hopefully you can keep your hands on the mic stand so we can get something down. They've got paid studio time and everything. If the label likes what we do, who knows? We might get on the album."

Two things.

I loved music passionately. It wasn't just what I did,

but also an expression of who I was. Writing music that people got to hear was a high you couldn't describe. And there was no better way for me to process emotions other than putting them into notes and playing them.

Bad boyfriends, heartache, happy times, disappointments—all of it manifested into the music and provided me with a kind of therapy that kept me sane. Which brought me to my next point.

I hadn't written a song in months. Stuck in a weird purgatory of contentment, I just couldn't get inspired. As tragic as it was, bad stuff always breeds the better tune, and I had been baselining happy for a while. Trust me—I know how dumb it sounded, but you can't rationalize art. And Dom and his band had been itching to do something together, looking to spice up their darker, metal sound with something that had a bit more light. Which is why they had asked to team up. That, and I think for as much as Sara wanted to touch herself when it came to Dom, he had similar feelings as well.

Plus—in case everything else hadn't added up to enough good reason—if by chance the song did make it onto their album, there would be publishing royalties. Not that I was expecting six-figure checks, but even a few grand would go a long way to fattening my soon-to-be-anorexic bank account.

Time in the studio on their dime was the cherry on top.

"You want to put pen to paper and work on

something?" And hopefully break the dry spell I'd been battling.

"I was just wondering if the added cargo was going to kick start the creative process." Sara's smile enough of an endorsement.

"I'm going to make the call and see if they are still interested." Hopefully the offer hadn't expired in the time I'd been considering it. It was always a possibility, it's not like there weren't a thousand other bands in the city.

"They'll be interested. You're an amazing songwriter and I write kick ass lyrics, they are going to want us."

"We'll see."

•••

"Ladies." Dom greeted us at the door, his long dark hair pulled into a man bun, his dimples popping out proudly when he caught sight of Sara. She may have gone to some extra effort, her push-up bra/fitted shirt combo impossible to miss.

He had jumped out of his skin with excitement when I'd called him yesterday, asking if the offer was still on the table. What was supposed to be a quick conversation, ended up lasting longer than I had intended. Dom and I both tossing around ideas about what kind of song would work best with both our styles. It was hard enough to contain Sara on my side of the phone line, my BFF insisting that the call be put on speaker, which thankfully saved me from relaying the conversation back to her later.

Dom had wanted to get started as soon as possible on something new. If it even had a shot of being on their album then it would need to be written and recorded in the next few weeks. Not impossible, but certainly more pressure than what I was used to. Which is why when he suggested we catch up the next day and start nutting it out, I readily agreed. Anxious to get back to work and start writing again.

"Hey, Dom." I gave him a hug, my hands barely stretching around his torso, the effort made more difficult by a guitar in my hand. He wasn't just tall—topping out at six-foot-six—but he spent an obscene amount of time in the gym. While I preferred Joey's muscular, athletic build, Sara went gaga over the body-builder types, like the man in front of me whose body had so many ripples he could quite possibly be having an allergic reaction.

"Dom," Sara purred, not offering a hug like I had. Stepping through the doorway and commencing the thinly veiled dance she always did, pretending like she *didn't* want to jump his bones.

"Sara." His eyes traveled up the length of her body which left no doubt he was mentally undressing her. Seriously, these two needed a room already.

"So," I cleared my throat, not so subtly reminding them I was still in the room with them. "I've got some ideas for the song."

"Great, I can't wait to hear them." He closed the door behind us and walked into his living room. "I figure we can camp out on the couch and see where we end up." And unless he was deaf, he—like me, couldn't have missed Sara's erotic moan at his suggestion.

It was going to be a long day.

Lucky for all of us, after the initial flirting, they both dialed it back as we slipped into business mode. Dom really liked the melody I had been playing with in between vomiting this morning.

It had been a tough balance. Puke. Guitar strum. Puke. The cord progression churned in my head even while I had my head down the toilet, the ultimate in multi-tasking.

"You want to play it?" Dom's head nodded to my guitar laying idly against the floor, dragging over an acoustic one for himself. His smile, hopeful.

"It's rough, Dom." I watched as he visibly deflated like I'd just kicked his puppy. "But sure, we can wade through it."

"Awesome." His face lit up, giving a little fist pump. Oh, if only we were all so easily pleased.

While Dom and I tinkered with the notes, Sara scribbled furiously in her notepad, tapping out the beat on the page with her ballpoint. A few words here or there but no real lyrics yet, she sat bobbing her head and giving us a thumbs up whenever we got to a part she liked. It was song writing in its crudest form, but I was loving it.

The minutes had slipped into hours, the time passing quickly as we played. The foundation of the song slowly emerged from the melting pot of notes; what we'd written, sounding really, really good.

"You wanna grab something to eat and keep working?" Dom's search of his cupboards revealed nothing more than a few packs of Pringles, some Ramen noodles and Mac n Cheese. All of those options were going to get a pass from me.

"Sure." Sara agreed without even consulting with me, her flirty game back in play now we were off the clock.

"Hey, so you guys know Black Addiction, right?" Dom grabbed a stack of takeaway menus, perusing our dinner options. Sara sidling up right beside him in case he needed help.

"Um. We don't know them *that* well." My heartbeat went into express mode as I wondered why the hell Joey and his band were getting a mention. Was nowhere safe? Sara's eyes widened, completely negating the playing-it-cool I was going for.

"But you've played with them, hung out a few times." Dom very correctly pointed out that despite my oh-no-we-don't-really-know-them, the gigs we'd played were a matter of public record. Pretty sure he'd even been at one or two of those gigs himself. I had no idea where the hell this was going to go.

"Yeah, more so in the past." I tried to maneuver out of my lie. "They're not really in our circle anymore. You know how it is when a band gets a major deal."

I was so full of shit.

"Oh, really?" Dom asked like he couldn't believe the nice guys he'd met had turned into assholes. Probably because it wasn't true and despite their deal, Joey, Max, Rusty and Angie had all remained pretty humble.

"I just heard some shit today about them." Dom lost interest in the menus, tossing them aside for a minute so he could give the subject its proper attention. "You know, word on the street sort of stuff."

I was seriously contemplating asking Sara to pop a button or two to help derail the conversation. It would get us both what we wanted, and let's face it, she'd be more than happy to take one for the team.

"What kind of stuff?" Sara obviously didn't share the same sentiment as I did, that the less we spoke about it, the better.

"Come on, guys." I laughed, ready to go to the alternate play where *I* popped a button. Hey, whatever it took. "We really want to talk about Black Addiction? Who cares what they've got going on? It's probably bullshit anyway. Stupid industry talk."

Yep, let's go with that. Not like it wasn't partly true, especially at a local level. Some of the bullshit backstage feuds between rival acts were worse than shit that went on in high school. Rumors could easily be downplayed especially if you didn't buy into them.

"I want to know." Sara leaned in, giving Dom her full

attention and some extra encouragement. "What's the gossip?"

I was literally going to kill her.

Black Addiction had gone through a label change—their latest deal being offered by rock heavyweights, Power Station. So it wasn't likely the *gossip* could be about a deal. They had also just put out an album, which ruled out an upcoming release. The tour was imminent—but once again—not a secret, so that couldn't be their big news either. And given I had slightly exaggerated how little I knew of the band to Dom, I'd assumed that any major developments would have been confirmed by Joey. Which left only one piece of major news. The collaboration between Joey and I. This one, not for public release.

"Sara, really?"

Could she not see how badly this could end? I was happy for it to stay a rumor, the lack of confirmation by either of us hopefully knocking any wind out of its sails. After all, it was the music industry; unplanned pregnancies weren't exactly scandal material. What I couldn't deal with was the news being out there before I'd even had a chance to tell my parents. The Chinese whispers guaranteed to reach their ears despite them not moving in the same circles. How the hell did it get out? Maybe I'd postpone killing Sara, and go back to my original vendetta.

Joey. Fucking. Shaw.

"Well the source I heard is reliable, I don't think she'd lead me astray." Dom smiled, the mention that the source was a *girl* not getting the same reaction from Sara. "And from what she said they are probably going to announce it soon anyway. It's not like you can hide something like that for long. I mean, everyone is going to see it anyway."

God damn it. It was definitely about me.

"Maybe this girl is just full of shit," Sara snapped, picking up the forgotten menus.

Finally, she got on the same page, the one where we stopped talking about Black Addiction and whatever it was that people were talking about. It didn't even matter to me that jealousy had been her motivator, whatever it took. And I was totally fine with going right to Hell.

"Nah, she's in tight with Max." Dom shook off Sara's rebuttal, which wasn't going to earn him any favors with either of us. "Said she got it right from him. It's pretty big news, why would Max lie?"

Another name to add to my list of kills.

Joey.

Sara.

Max.

My murderous rampage was going to be keeping me busy. It's a good thing we got a jump on this song; I wasn't going to have a lot of downtime in the foreseeable future.

"How is it anyone's business?" I snapped, extremely pissed off, at what or whom was still yet to be decided.

"Just because they have more visibility these days, doesn't mean people are entitled to access their private life. And talking about it is only perpetuating the bullshit as well." I couldn't stop my mouth, the flood gates had opened as I continued to spew words. "I feel sorry for them, that parts of their lives are now open for public consumption. I'm pretty sure they didn't sign up for having every single detail of their existence being thrown under a microscope. People should shut their fucking mouths and go on with their lives. Assholes."

Silence.

Both Sara and Dom sat dumbfounded with their eyes glued to me, my anger running out of steam, as did my argument.

"Ummm." Dom looked at me awkwardly, no doubt putting two-and-two together. "I heard that they got a gig at CJ's."

"What?" My mouth dropped open making the only word out of it sound distorted. My brain misfired on the information he'd volunteered.

"Black Addiction is playing CJ's? How the fuck did they score that gig?" Sara completely missed that I looked like I was having an aneurism and continued to dig for details. The jealousy over the source shelved in favor of information.

"Well, that's what I heard." Dom confirmed, his eyes carefully examining me like he was trying to visually extract why I acted like a mental case.

While Sara was ignoring it, I didn't get so lucky when it came to him. He added another piece of information, his eyes on me as he added, "I think it will be announced later this week."

"Oh. Well . . . I guess that's good." I had no idea what I was saying. Not that I really cared, it wasn't valid at this point anyway. What mattered was I drew as little attention to myself as possible. Something I should have thought about before I opened my big, fat mouth.

"Wait. What did you think I was going to say?" Dom refused to let me off the hook.

"No, nothing. Congratulations to them I guess, it's a tough gig."

"Seriously, what do we have to do? Someone needs to tell me the fucking criteria."

It was as if Sara was in a conversation all by herself and that's where I'd left her. I had my own hole to dig out of; I wasn't looking to borrow extra trouble. Besides, it's not like she could arouse any more suspicion that I somehow had a secret. Nope, I had taken care of that all by myself.

"Obviously you had something in mind, you had a pretty strong reaction. After all, you don't really know them *that* well."

Dom wasn't stupid. He was fairly observant consider-ing. I guess when you stood a head above most of the population you gained a certain perspective. *I'm a giant and I can see through your bullshit.* Sadly, I was going to have to add him to my kill list. He knew too much.

"No, really. Nothing. I just hate social injustice. We need to stick together."

I was so full of shit.

And what's worse is that everyone in the room knew it.

"If you say so." Translation: I'm going to be a gentleman and let this go, but we both know you are hiding something. Oh, and you're a lying asshole. Okay, maybe the last bit had been just me, but that's exactly what he should be thinking.

"I panicked," I admitted, unable to continue with the spiral of lies anymore. "Yes, we know them. I'm sorry, I thought you were going to say something else."

If Dom had been anyone other than the nice guy that he was, I wouldn't have cared what he believed. Hell, I didn't live my life by anyone else's standards, but I hated seeing that look on his face. He would eventually find out and remember that at this moment I chose to flat out lie rather to respect him and trust he'd keep my secret.

"Please don't tell anyone." The weight of my body sagged against my chair, wondering if I shouldn't have tried to bluff my way out of it.

"Kenzie, we're tight." Dom gave me a slow nod. "If you need me to lock something down, you can take it to the bank I won't breathe a word to anyone else. Now, what's going on?"

"It's fine, Kenz. He won't tell anyone." Sara smiled,

reaching out and squeezing my hand. "Because if he does, I'm going to Bengay his underwear. Every single pair."

"Fuck, Sara." Dom coughed, the smile creeping on his face. "At the risk of the inferno that will be my ball sack, I'm not going to tell anyone."

"Not even the band," I warned, not needing there to be a loophole somewhere. *Oh, sorry. I thought you meant other people, not these people.*

"They are included in the collective of *everyone*, Kenz. Spill."

"I'm pregnant. Joey's the father."

On the upside, I was getting a lot more efficient with my announcements. By the time I got around to telling my parents, it was going to be a cakewalk. All right. Maybe that was being slightly optimistic.

"Wow. I didn't even know you guys were dating." He sat up a little straighter, the news obviously not what he was expecting.

"We weren't." Unless by *date* he meant having hot sex, and then yeah, that's exactly what we did. "Not in the traditional sense anyway."

"Does he know?" he asked slowly, my initial explanation lacking.

"Yeah, he knows. I just don't want everyone else to know right now."

"He being good to you, Kenz? The boys and I can have a word with him if he isn't." The caution in his voice wasn't manufactured, and I had no doubt that if I gave him the nod, Joey would find himself black and blue in a gutter.

"Dom, that's sweet, but he's been really wonderful about it. Honestly, I couldn't have hoped for better."

"Good." He seemed satisfied, happy he wasn't going to have to bust some heads. "So that's what you thought their big news was? That news of you and him had somehow gotten out."

And the penny dropped. My over sensitive tirade suddenly made sense. My motives less noble, being it had been my own ass that I was trying to protect.

"Well, there wasn't much else it could be." I didn't bother giving him and Sara the rundown on how I'd deduced *my* news had been the only possibility. Now, when I think about it, it was a little conceited. "He didn't mention the gig, but I haven't really spoken to him in the last few days."

"I thought you said he was being good about it?" Dom's eyebrow rose, wondering why if Joey had shared bodily fluids he wouldn't share his good news as well. Valid.

"He is. The not talking part was my doing." I still wasn't sure it had been the right thing to do. "I just need a break to take a breath. Just for a minute, you know?"

"Yeah, I get it." Dom shifted in his seat, his big frame looking slightly awkward. "Look, honestly, you don't have to worry about me. It's like you never told me, but I'm glad you did."

"Thanks, Dom. You're one of the good guys." I reached

out and gave his knee a squeeze.

"Don't let that shit get out, I have a reputation to uphold as a mean ass motherfucker. No one goes to listen to a rock band if they are *bunch of nice* guys." He gave me a grin.

"I guess we both have a secret to keep then."

"And Sara, you keep your hands off my underwear." He leveled her with a stare.

"Said like a man who hasn't had the pleasure yet." She blinked slowly, her hand moving suggestively down her chest.

"Jesus, girl. You're going to kill me." He coughed, the smirk a hint he was enjoying it as much as she was.

"You want me to leave so you can screw already?" I offered, feeling suddenly like the third wheel.

"Yes," they both echoed before erupting into laughter.

"And you call yourselves my friends." I scoffed, pretending to be offended. "Just for that I'm going to stick around and make you suffer."

Nine
Joey

Radio Silence.

Not a fucking word.

I'm sure she totally expected me to cave, but I had kept my word and hadn't dialed her at all in the last couple of days. Not to say I wasn't tempted—sure, I'd scrolled my contacts a few times—but I stayed rock solid and focused on everything else. Unfortunately for me, other than the gig we had lined up, there wasn't much going on. Which meant I had to distract myself in other ways. Probably was always going to end badly.

"You want to go get a burger or something?" Max toweled his hair as he walked into the living room.

His semi-dressed state clued me in that he hadn't decided exactly where he wanted to be heading just yet. The night was still young and we had no fucking plans, and sitting at home wasn't our usual speed.

"Okay, honest opinion." I swung around from my seat

in front of my laptop. "Do you think my hair looks like the dude's from Gossip Girl?"

"Excuse me?" The toweling off stopped as he looked at me like I'd asked him to lick my balls. The stunned confusion not exactly what I'd expected.

"My hair." I pointed to the stuff covering my head, like the words were obvious enough. "Do you think it looks like that douchebag's on the show?"

I'm not sure if Max just wanted to yank my chain, or maybe just string me along a little bit more, because other than goldfishing like an idiot, he didn't answer.

"Of course, I'm taking their word that this dickwad is even a real person," I added indignantly, pretty convinced that it was really some elaborate prank. "What kind of name is Chace Crawford? I bet he wouldn't even know what a pussy is, let alone be allowed inside one."

"Okay buddy, stay with me. I'm going to call 9-1-1." Max's feet got moving pretty quickly, closing the gap between him and me. His eyes locked on me the whole time. "Do you remember your name?" The words were slower than they needed to be, like there was something wrong with my hearing.

"Max, I'm serious." I waved him off, wondering why the dude couldn't just give me an answer. It was pretty simple, either yes or no. And if anyone was going to give it to me straight it was the guy in front of me.

"Joe, are you stroking out?" Max's eyes darted left and right like the walls might give him some extra info. "I don't even know what to do with that information."

"Look, I don't know who this fucktard is but I'm not liking that people are comparing him to me. Even if it is just hair—straight up, that show sucks balls and I want no part of it." Seriously, who was this piece of shit and why were people playing contrast-and-compare with us? The more I thought about it, the more it pissed me off.

"Dude, I think you are having some kind of psychotic episode." Max's ass sunk into a chair beside me, and if he was faking concern, he was doing a pretty good job of it. "Let's retrace your steps and see if I can't get my friend back. Now, help me, help you, Joe."

I'll admit that possibly without context it may have seemed like a bogus question. Even more so because I generally didn't give a rat's ass what anyone thought. But having to keep busy and having no real purpose today was the reason we were even having this discussion.

"I can't call Kenzie," I confessed. The whys of the situation not needed, considering he'd agreed I should give the phone tag a break. "Which shouldn't be hard, except that now she told me I can't, all I want to do is call her." It even made less sense saying it out loud. "And that is complete BS because you know if anyone isn't going to call back a girl, it's me."

For most guys getting the hey-don't-call-me was like winning a golden ticket. Not to be an asshole, but the pressure of remembering to call was a lot of wasted anxiety. And why were these calls even important in the first place unless it was to hook up again, in which case texting was just as efficient. And in the past I'd shrugged the responsibility on more than one occasion, Max or Rusty riding my ass about being disrespectful.

"I'm not sure *that's* a redeeming feature, but for the purpose of the exercise, sure I'll agree." Max rolled his eyes, knowing I was right.

"So, I needed to do something else to distract myself." I started to fill in the blanks, giving him the added info as to how I found myself where we were. "And Rusty was flapping his gums the other day about how shit I was doing was turning up online. Even though we both know that shit wasn't my fault, it's not like I can stop it from happening."

"And . . ." Max waved his hand urging me to continue.

"Which reminded me I hadn't Googled us in a while." Something I had no shame in admitting. After all, it was important to stay connected with our fans, and see what they thought.

"So I did a search and found some fan groups on Facebook. Did you know there's a group called *I want to ride Max's cock*? It has five thousand members, dude. Your dick actually has a fan page." I pointed to the laptop, happy to pull up the page if he needed further proof. "I may have *suggested* that mine was bigger, because you know I like to tell the truth, but these girls were convinced you're packing like an eighteen-inch shlong." It really was the charitable thing to do, not to be malicious but because if anyone's dick needed the love it was definitely mine.

"How the hell does the size of my dick have anything to do with your fucking hair?" Max's voice rose in frustration, his eyebrows bunching together as he spat out the rest. "You're making less sense as we go along. And I really hope that you logged in with an alias, and didn't announce to the word that Joey Fucking Shaw was discussing my cock in a chat room. I don't think the PR department has enough spin to come back from that."

"Please, what do you think this is, amateur hour?" The big guy really needed to give me more credit. It wasn't my first rodeo pretending to be someone I wasn't. I sure as shit didn't want to signpost I was so bored I was jerking off online. "I'm BigTits69; they think I'm a chick from Rhode Island." I nodded proudly, thinking I'd been pretty convincing as a girl. I even had a profile pic, that's how committed I was to the cause.

"I'm ninety-nine percent certain I'm going to regret asking you to continue, but go on, BigTits69." Max shook his head, not appreciating the genius of my profile. Seriously, it was two of my favorite things. The name was freaking perfect.

"Well, I got bored with your dick—"

"Okay, that is a sentence you can never say ever again." Max jabbed a finger in my chest, cutting me off before I could continue. "Like for real, Joey. I don't care about the context. Never. Not unless you want to die."

"You're such a fucking pussy." I blew out a breath wondering why he was being such a sensitive asshole. It's not like I was asking to see his dick to blue tick it for verification. "Anyway, whatever."

I tried again; hoping this time the bastard would let me speak.

"I got bored with—"

"Joe." He warned.

"*Someone's* dick, who isn't you," I amended, hoping he'd be happy.

"Dear God, please just give me a sign I should let him live." He shook his head, squeezing the bridge of his nose as I cracked a grin.

"And I found another fan page," I continued, ignoring him. "This time about *me*, and not to brag or anything but I had a thousand, two hundred and fifty-three more than yours."

"Please, if you won't take him, take me. It's been good up till now, I'm not sure I want to go any further." He lifted his arms up to the heavens in mock surrender; his voice bouncing off the ceiling like JC had the actual time to listen to his drama instead of doing important stuff.

"Which is where those girls were taking a fucking poll about my hair." I scoffed in disbelief, like there couldn't have been anything else noteworthy that people wanted to talk about. It had to be the lamest, fucking thing. "My *hair*, dude. On my fucking head." I truly did not understand it, even explaining it to Max I was still freaking bewildered. "And it's some asshole I don't even know." I hoped for his sake Chace Crawford and I never met up, but seriously there was nothing else?

"You get dick—"

"Jesus." Max barked out a laugh, his head sinking into his hands.

"—and I get fucking hair. How is that even possible?" And if I hadn't been masquerading as some chick, I would have totally demanded restitution. Seriously, my cock was fucking amazing.

"I'm going to go out on a limb here and say we need to retire *BigTits69*." The grin crept onto his mouth. "Nothing good can come of it, in fact everything that does come from it is bad, bad news." He gave me a tap on the shoulder, clearing his throat before he continued.

"Secondly, I get your life just got dumped on its ass, but I think there are more constructive ways to keep you from burning up the phone lines. Joe, who the fuck gives a shit what they think about your hair? Did you leave Black Addiction and join One Direction?" The last bit making him laugh.

"Fuck. You're right." I leaned back into my chair. Even though everyone was dead wrong—and I hated to be compared to whoever this douche monkey was—it shouldn't matter. I was a drummer for fuck's sake. What did I care what they thought of my hair?

"Look, why don't you get changed, I'll throw on a shirt and we'll get out of here. Let your friends distract you."

Max's hand clapped the back of my neck, his voice sincere in that he wanted to help.

"Well, I guess as dumb as it was to get bent over it at least I didn't call her." I shrugged, finding a silver lining. Because the whole time I was key tapping, I hadn't even thought about calling, which had been exactly the plan.

"True." Max grinned. "See. It wasn't a total waste." His hand gave me a little shake before he removed it and popped me in the arm. "We just need to work on a strategy for your downtime. Get you a hobby or something and keep you out of trouble. We can't have you going all keyboard warrior whenever you need to be distracted."

"Hey, but all that aside." I'll admit I was more than just a little curious. "Did you know about your dick page?"

"Hell, no." He laughed, "And I'd prefer to forget most of this conversation and never hear about it again."

"If I were you, I would totally embrace it." The title and appreciation obviously wasted on my friend, but I'd be proud of it. Possibly even get a billboard just to promote it. Also, I'd have more followers.

"Anytime you want to stop talking about my cock would be good, Joe." Max rolled his eyes, not seeing the wasted opportunity.

"Fine, fine. It's done. Let's get out of here and find something else for me to do." Hopefully keep my finger off the dial a little longer. Maybe even get my head straight, the whole last few days creating a shitstorm of thoughts I had no hope of deciphering.

"And delete the profile." Max pointed the laptop as he stood up. "Better to take temptation completely out of the equation."

"Yeah, whatever. I'll get rid of it." I was so not deleting it. "It's already gone." My fingers tapped on the keys pretending to deactivate the account as he walked away, heading to his bedroom.

Like I'd do something that stupid. You never know when you might need to go incognito. Hell, I was keeping that baby in my back pocket for a rainy day.

"Joey." He poked his head out from his bedroom doorway. "This is going to be fine. Trust me." The subtext of what he was talking about not needed. The guy had my back—those words right there—proof enough.

I swallowed, a lump forming in my throat.

"Thanks, dude." All I could manage.

•••

True to his word, Max not only got us out the door but recruited Rusty to join us, the guy not spending much time with us now that he was happily part of a pair. Not that it bothered me; I wouldn't be going out if I had that at home either.

While Alison was a sweetheart—as well as good looking— and we didn't usually care if she tagged along, it was good to have a night out with just the three of us. It had been too long.

The bar, as we affectionately called it—had been a mainstay for us for a few years. It was where we used to hang out, writing song lyrics on napkins before any of the other stuff started happening. It was also the place we'd come while we were recording the album, unwinding with a few beers after grueling days in the studio. It was almost like a second home, the staff knew us all by name, and by drink order.

"Hey, Joe." Rusty entered the bar, heads turning as he strode past. It didn't matter that he wasn't interested; girls still flocked to the good-looking SOB. "Interesting evening, I hear." The smirk giving me all the intel I needed to indicate that Max had already debriefed him.

"Yep, and aren't you pissed it's his dick and not yours which is getting all the attention?" I pulled out a chair, my chin giving him a hello as he sat down.

"Can we just leave my dick out of this?" Max shook his head, his bottle of beer lifting to his lips.

"Hey, I'm not the one who brought it up." I shrugged. If anyone should be catching heat for the mention it should be Rus. "I was just explaining."

"Whatever hard-on floats your boat, Joey. I'm not here to judge." Rusty laughed, amused at his own joke. His hand signaled a waitress to bring over his usual.

"Whatever, assholes. I'm secure in my sexuality." I lifted the longneck to my lips and took a swig. It was actually kind of nice to have the back and forth. Shit felt so normal and I'd forgotten how cool it was to just chill with these two, having a beer and some conversation.

"Hey, Rusty." Rochelle, an old friend of ours sidled up close to Rus, her hand sliding up his thigh in a way that was far from innocent. "It's been a while since I've seen you in here. I've missed you." Her tongue darted out to lick her cherry lips.

"Hi, Rochelle. You know I'm a one-lady-man these days." Rus peeled her hand off his thigh and gave her a smile. "And I'd rather not disrespect Ali or you by pretending otherwise." He gave her a front row seat to the trademark Rusty brush off. It was actually cool to watch, the dude was one hell of a smooth operator.

"Of course." She laughed, throwing her head back for effect. "Just teasing." She scrunched her nose in what I could only guess was flirting.

"Joey." Her hand slid down my back. "How have you been, baby?" She eased herself down onto my lap. "You been hiding too?" She asked the second question without giving me a chance to answer the first.

Rochelle Roberts was hot. And as far as distractions went, she was a pretty fucking attractive one.

Tits that were worth every single cent she'd paid, and a body that could bend in ways that would make a pretzel jealous. She could also give head like it was an Olympic sport and I knew this all from first-hand experience.

It didn't bother me that she flirted with Rus, a twisted part of me enjoyed the fact he kept turning her down.

And I still fucked her because, well . . . why wouldn't I? It was a tough gig and someone had to do it.

"Hey, babe." I leaned back, letting her ass shift in my lap. "I've been busy."

It wasn't difficult to know what she wanted. After all, we'd fucked a couple of times already, neither of us interested in more than the casual hook up. It didn't even bother me that she did the same to other guys. She was a nice girl who just happened to like sex. Nothing wrong with that.

"You want to go do something, baby?" She pushed her tits together, giving an even better view of her spectacular cleavage.

"Yeah, maybe later. I just want to hang with the guys for a bit." I gave her a grin, still undecided if I wanted company.

It had been a few days since I'd been with anyone other than my hand—the night before Kenzie's announcement to be precise. Part of it was the baby, but more importantly, I genuinely didn't want to. Be with someone that was, the sex I still very much wanted. The raging hard-on I woke up with every morning proving the point. But every time I thought about actually moving to the fucking part, I couldn't make myself go there. Lord knows I had a contact list full of willing participants. Maybe I should just get back on the horse. I didn't have any reason to be lock-and-keying my dick, and the thought of relieving some of that stress sounded mighty appealing.

"Sure, whatever you want. I'm going to go sit at the bar with Gina. Call me if you get lonely." She rocked against my cock a couple of times before climbing to her feet, a promise of what she was willing to do later. Sadly, I wasn't even hard. God, I hoped my dick wasn't broken.

"Will do." I watched as she walked away, my eyes sticking to her ass as she headed to the bar. Even with the hip sway, it still didn't even give me a semi.

"Asshole." Max snapped his finger in front of my face. "You really going to go there? Seriously?" He eyed me from the other side of the table, the dude looking less than pleased.

"Probably. Since when have you known me to turn down sex?" After all, the idea of tonight was to get my mind off things, couldn't think of a better way than being with a girl who knew exactly what she was getting. Not to mention I was slightly concerned by my lack of interest. And if Rochelle couldn't resuscitate my cock then there really wasn't much hope.

"Besides, she's knows the score, it's just casual. No harm, no foul." And no freaking hoping for a relationship either, which was just another positive.

"Have to agree with Max, Joe. Walk away." Rusty weighed in, the eyeball-of-death also getting shot my way from his side of the table.

"Why?" Neither of them had taken an interest in my love life before, I wasn't sure why they felt the sudden need to get involved. It's not like either of them were interested in her.

"Oh, I don't know, Joe." Max kept his voice tight, the noise of the bar not allowing anyone other than the three of us to hear the conversation. "You knocked up Kenz and now you're just going to go off and fuck someone else? Please tell me you're not that stupid."

The reason why the two of them tried to cock block me was finally laid on the table. They were worried I was cheating on Kenzie.

Which would have been a fair call except we weren't a couple. Far from it, and I was free to screw whoever I wanted. And while I hadn't taken the opportunity up until this point, there had been zero reason for it. None. I could have had sex a hundred times by now, why I hadn't I still didn't fully understand.

And another thing, as much as I liked to fuck around, I'd never cheated on a girl. The few times I'd been in a relationship, I'd kept my dick in my pants with no problems at all. I was a lot of things; scumbag wasn't one of them.

"It's not like that with us. We're not together. Trust me, Kenzie doesn't care who I fuck." Well at least that's what she'd led me to believe.

"So she can just fuck other dudes?" Rus asked, a smug grin creeping across his face. "Sorry, man. I didn't know. All right then, as you were."

"Don't be ridiculous. Kenzie is pregnant, she's not

fucking anyone." I scoffed, the idea of her getting down-and-dirty hilarious. I may not be the sharpest dude but my recollection was pretty clear—she had no interest in it.

"Pregnant woman have sex all the time, dumbass," Max added like he was the oracle, and knew all about pregnant chicks and their sexual urges.

"That's not what she said. From the vibe I got from her, if she never saw a dick again it would be too soon."

I replayed the conversation in my head. Yep, her own words were *her interest in my dick was suspended*. She'd also threatened to rip off my balls more than once. And that wasn't dirty talk or foreplay. She actually meant it.

"Yeah, that passes. Sometimes pretty quickly. And some get even hornier, wanting sex all the time." Rusty volunteered information, the conviction in his voice sounding like he knew what he was talking about.

"What the fuck? She is going to want sex?" A wave of panic washed through me, my body all of sudden having trouble running its internal thermostat.

"Yep. Probably a lot of it too." Rusty threw in, adding more fuel to the fire.

"No. No. No." I shook my head, not believing what I was hearing. "You mean to tell me that she will be having sex with some other dude?"

The idea that she would be with someone else was something I hadn't considered. Obviously we weren't together, but I just assumed . . . Fuck. I don't know what I assumed, but her screwing someone else wasn't it.

"Yep. It's good that you've got the agreement though." Max anchored his hands behind his head, his eyes not moving from me despite him relaxing into his chair. "Have to say, it's pretty admirable. Not sure I'd be so cool with it."

"No. I don't want her fucking other guys. This can't happen." More like, I'd do whatever the hell I needed to do so it wouldn't happen. It didn't even make sense as to why I didn't, but there was no rationalizing the fucking emotion.

"Didn't you just tell us how you guys aren't a couple?" Max's eyebrow rose, his voice steady as he made his point. "You can't expect her to not see anyone else if you're fucking anything that moves. Double standards much?"

"But my kid is in there."

"It's still her body. And a girl's got needs just like a guy." This time it was Rusty making the argument. The two of them tag-teaming me like a bad episode of WWE.

"I feel like I'm going to throw up." I didn't even care how much that made me sound like a pussy. The thought of Kenzie fucking some other guy while my kid was inside of her literally made me feel sick. Whatever agreement we had was fucking bullshit and I can't believe I'd been dumb enough to give it the nod.

"Breathe through it, buddy." Rusty, slapped me on the back. "You want me to call Rochelle back? Maybe she can give you a hand job and calm you down." The asshole throwing in the cheap shot for good measure. It wasn't needed—the point was well and truly made.

"What the hell am I going to do?" My eyes volleyed between them, hoping that one of them would have a freaking clue that would help get me out of this mess.

"I think instead of talking to us about it, maybe it's a conversation you need to have with her." Max's head nodded to the cell that was sitting in front of me. And wasn't that fucking ironic since the whole reason we were out here was so I didn't call her.

Oh well. This was important.

I'd never intentionally broken my word to anyone, but there was no way I could let this lie. We would have to sort it out and then if she wanted to go back to doing the phone avoid, then I'd play nice. Just as soon as we agreed on where we stood on the issue of fucking other people. Or more to the point, we would *not* be fucking other people.

"Hey, you guys cool if I bail? I'm not chancing this to a phone call." Besides, she might not answer, so the only way I saw this conversation happening was face to face. Which technically meant I didn't go back on my word, and this shit could still get straightened out. See? Who said I wasn't smart?

"Yep. Go do what you need to do. Max and I will hang here." Rus answered with a complete lack of surprise, taking another swig of his beer.

Max grabbed my arm as I went to get to my feet, the chair scraping the floor noisily as I scrambled to get up and get gone.

"Hey, I'm sure I don't need to remind you not to be an asshole, right?"

"Trust me, that's one thing you don't have to worry about. Not with me and not with her."

I wasn't entirely sure what those words meant but I knew that while I didn't love her, and she wasn't my girlfriend, it would be a cold day in hell before I'd hurt her. Add into the mix she was carrying my kid and I could guarantee I'd crawl through fire for her if she asked.

And what a fucking wake up call that was.

I was so incredibly fucked.

Pathetic.

I was tucked up in bed at nine p.m. and had been wearing PJ's since seven. And so was the glamorous life I was leading, my ass getting handed to me daily with every single ounce of energy disappearing into thin air.

Pity I couldn't make myself care. The idea of being snuggled down under my covers more appealing than heading out with the girls. Who knew the idea of sleep could make me excited, the ten-hour stretch I had planned literally making me giddy.

Just me, this bed and no interruptions. There wasn't a thing I wanted more.

What the hell?

The buzzer from my front door smashed through my zen-like contentment. The continuous, obnoxious noise refused to stop despite my mental urging.

It is just someone wanting the wrong apartment, I

rationalized, holding a pillow over my head to drown out the drone.

But despite my expectation that whoever it was would either stop, move on or spontaneously combust—yeah, slim chance, I know—the incessant buzz continued.

"God damn it." I kicked off my covers, ready to get medieval on the dumbass who dared derail my plans.

That poor bastard.

I hoped they'd had a nice life.

"Hang on," I huffed, not caring the demon spawn fixated on my buzzer couldn't hear me. "I'm fucking coming." Again, air was my only audience as my feet stomped loudly to my front door.

"What?" I breathed through the door not willing to open it. All pretenses of hello or manners went out the window, my mouth unable to lie. It could have very easily been *fuck off,* so the way I saw it, they were getting off lightly.

"Kenzie, it's me. Let me in." The muffled voice answered through the wood, my hostile greeting left unacknowledged.

"Joey?" The edge fell from my voice as I waited to confirm the origin of the disturbance, not willing to open the door until he'd given me the green light.

What was he doing here? It's late. Okay, so maybe not late but still we hadn't spoken in three days, the time out I'd called still in effect. And he had been so respectful about giving me space, he was the last person I expected on my doorstep.

"Is everything all right?" I asked as I searched for the keys to my deadlock, the stupid things not in the bowl where I usually left them.

"I need to see you. Please."

Crap. He sounded strange and he'd said please. Something was definitely wrong. Why hadn't he picked up the phone? My curiosity superseded my agitation as I finally found my keys and twisted the lock. My mumbled pleas that it not be anything serious continued as I swung open the door.

"Hey." I watched as he stood on my front step, the look of his face stone cold serious. God, please don't let him be dying.

"Okay, so here's the deal." He grabbed my arms and moved me through the doorway, back into my apartment. His resolution unwavering as he closed the door behind us. "We're not fucking anyone."

"I'm sorry? What?"

My face twitched like I'd had some kind of seizure as my brain tried to rehear the words he said. Even trying to rearrange them didn't help, feeling like I'd stepped into the twilight zone.

Was I dreaming?

Did I already fall asleep and this is some fucked up dream? It was surely too bizarre to be real.

"We aren't fucking other people," he reaffirmed, like the words made any more sense the second time around.

"I'm not going to sleep with anyone and I want you to do the same." His hand reached out and touched my arm completely discounting this as a dream.

Well, then.

I was out of ideas.

Unless he was drunk, but other than the weird talk his breath was noticeably absent of booze. His eyes were also clear and his stance completely devoid of the too-much-to-drink sway.

"Can you slow down and find the part of the conversation that I've obviously missed?" I'd say at least thirty minutes of it if I had to take a guess. The start of it probably happening when he'd left The Bronx, forgetting I actually had to be *there* to hear what he was saying.

"I know we aren't dating, and you don't owe me anything but I think we should do this," he continued, the elaboration not helping much more than the original explanation. Perhaps he could draw me a diagram, whatever he needed to say couldn't get any more lost in the translation than it already was.

"Do what exactly?" I blew out a breath, too exhausted to keep playing the guessing game. So far I'd gotten bits of puzzle words that didn't fit, their significance as much of a mystery as to why he was here in the first place.

"Not. Have. Sex." He said each word slowly and deliberate, like that somehow helped. "With other people and I'm serious. It's going to rely on an honor system but I swear, I'm not going to fuck another girl while you're pregnant."

The penny finally dropped.

What his whirlwind of confusion had failed to explain was spelled out plainly. He wanted fidelity. Something he'd never asked me for when we actually *were* sleeping together, now that we weren't—maybe he was dying?

"Why would you do that?" My voice was small, unable to pretend that I wasn't floored.

Hearing him say he wasn't going to sleep with other people was something I thought I'd never hear. Along with him voluntarily giving up sex because effectively that's what he was signing up for. We weren't fucking, so if there was no one else, he and his hand were going to get very close over the coming months.

"I'll be honest, first it was about me not wanting you to be with anyone while our kid was in there." His hands moved up my arms, his touch not having left me since he'd walked in. "The thought of some other dude being inside you while my . . . while *our* baby is in there too makes me want throw a chair through a wall." He took a breath continuing. "But on the drive over here I realized how much of an asshole I was."

He was definitely dying.

Or it was the end of the world.

But this was not the guy I'd slept with. This was not the man I knew.

"You got the rough end of the deal, Kenz." He steered me to the couch, my feet following without resistance.

"You're the one who's been sick, it's you who has to carry our baby."

I blinked, the back of my knees hitting the edge of the sofa and my brain not able to compute what to do next.

"You're the one who's going to have to go through god knows what when it's finally time for him or her to be born." He didn't blink an eye, easing me down onto the couch before joining me by my side.

"And as much as I can tell you I'm going to be there, nothing I say or do will change that it will have to be *you* who does the heavy lifting. Fucking around while you are doing that just isn't the right thing to do. It doesn't have anything to do with whether or not we're together, it's got to do with the fact I need to put someone else first. And you're giving up a hell of a lot more than I am during those eight months so the least I can do is keep my dick to myself."

My throat was tight, the lump that formed made it difficult for me to swallow as my eyes started to water. I couldn't help it, the tears I was so desperately trying to hold at bay crept at the edges and broke free. My body sagged against the cushions at my back but it didn't register, I could have been sitting on a bed of nails and my attention would have still be on nothing other than Joey. My heart thumped erratically as I tried to say something, but stunned silence was the only thing I was able to offer.

"Fuck, I'm sorry." His eyes darted across my face, my

tears being misinterpreted. "It sounded better in the car. I said it wrong."

"No, you didn't." I finally found my voice, another tear rolling down my cheek. "You said it all exactly right." My fingers reached out for his and interlocked. "I'm just really emotional because it's one of the nicest things you've ever said to me." Or any man for that matter.

The single most selfless act of putting *me* first, even when he didn't have to, knocked the wind out of me. If I hadn't already been sitting down I definitely would have needed to. Something else I was thankful to him for. My hospitality had been missing in action when he'd first walked in, so we might still be standing. Still, shock will do that to a girl.

"Wow, I'm really going to have to work on stuff I say to you because if that's the best, it's pretty bad." Joey smiled, not understanding how amazing those words had actually been.

"You're doing great." I smiled, my leaking eyes finally slowed as I tried to get a handle of my emotions. "Really, this is more than I expected."

"Well, we have to get through this together, right? So what do you say we try this?"

God he was sweet. And so incredibly tender I hated myself for every bad word I'd ever said about him. Conceited. Arrogant—sure. But the good bits far out-weighed the bad ones.

"You really think you can do this?" It's not that I

doubted his intentions, his eyes and words being crystal clear of his commitment. But theory and practice were two different things, and he was surrounded by beautiful women who *wanted* to sleep with him. It was like putting a drug addict into a crack house and then expecting them not to sample the product.

"It's a few months, no biggie." He shrugged like he expected it to be a walk in the park. "What about you? This here is a two-sided deal." He grinned. "You think you can hold out?"

He had definitely drawn the short straw. Sex, on my list of priorities was on par on with getting a root canal. I couldn't even imagine wanting it, let alone fighting the urge not to. In fact, I might never have sex again. It would probably be safer and any orgasms I'd be missing I could happily provide myself, if and when I felt like them.

"Joey, the no sex part isn't going to be a problem for me. Honestly, I can't even think about it right now without wanting to stab myself in the eye with a fork." Or stab a penis if it even looked like it was coming near me.

"Yeah, Max and Rusty said that's going to change and you're going to be super horny." He looked at me sideways, the smile curving at his lips.

"You spoke to Max and Rusty about *me* having sex?" I was trying to not fly off the handle given how sweet he was being, but the last thing I wanted was my bedroom habits being discussed with most of Black Addiction. I didn't even want to know the circumstances as to how it was brought up, let alone their opinions on it.

"It was more them talking to me about it." He tried to reason, like the alternative would be more palatable.

"Not any better." I shook my head. "As much as I love Rusty and Max, they are going to be wrong."

"So you *aren't* going to be super horny?" Joey's voice rose in disappointment. It was obvious he'd been secretly hoping.

"I can't see it happening."

"But if it does." He turned his head to the side, either contemplating or choosing his words before he continued. "And don't take this the wrong way—but I'll be happy to help you out."

"What? Like you'd service me? Jesus, Joey." The back of my hand flew across his chest only slightly offended. It sounded terrible even though I was sure he hadn't meant it that way.

"You know what I mean." He tried to dig himself out of the hole he'd put himself in. "And sex for us isn't all tangled up in all that other stuff, so I'm just saying if you *needed* me, I could do it." The smile he'd been wearing teased into a smirk, the direction his mind was currently heading plainly obvious.

"You really are trying for sainthood, aren't you?"

"I assure you, Kenz, it wouldn't be a sacrifice."

"It won't happen." My resolve so sure I'd probably reclaim my virginity.

"Well either way, I'm good." He leaned back, stretching

out his arms across the back of the couch.

"I bet." I laughed, the idea of Joey being my own personal sex toy would have been so appealing a month or two ago. Such a waste he was offering it now. Sometimes life was just unfair like that.

"Do you want to stay? I was just going to go to bed, but if you wanted to hang around, we could watch movies or something." Pushing him out the door and being alone didn't fill me with the same joy it had an hour or so ago.

"Sure, as long as I get to pick." His hand swooped down onto the coffee table and picked up the remote. "I'm giving up sex; there is no way I'm going get stuck watching bad TV as well. Oh and no *Gossip Girl*, that's like a rule."

"Fine, you can choose." It was a small concession given I'd probably fall asleep after an hour or so anyway. "And how do you even know about *Gossip Girl*, let alone have such strong feelings against it?"

Not that he'd have to worry about me wanting to watch it, but the mention of the teen hit drama had me curious. I should probably learn anything goes when we're talking about Joey's mind and his mouth. It was a crapshoot as to whether or not it would be relevant.

"Long story." He dismissed it with a wave of his hand, his finger hitting the remote to bring my television to life. "But just so you know, it's personally offensive to me. So as my friend, you should avoid it too."

I didn't bother pursuing it further, not sure I wanted to

know and too tired to care. "No sex and no *Gossip Girl.* All good." I stifled a yawn, the fatigue I'd been feeling earlier coming back to rear its ugly head.

"You want to do it here or the bedroom?" He shot me a sideways glance of concern. "The movie, I mean," he clarified, in case I'd misunderstood his intention. "We can go wherever you're most comfortable, and I won't even touch you even though your rack looks amazing in that top." His eyes dipped down to my fitted cotton sleep shirt, my lack of bra catching his attention.

"I wasn't expecting company."

"Hey, no hardship here." He let his eyes linger a little bit longer, the grin on his face indicating he was enjoying the view. "I noticed earlier but we were talking about serious stuff so I didn't bring it up."

"You definitely deserve a medal, I'm sure it was very hard for you." The words slipped out of my mouth before I'd had a chance to really process what I'd said, the double entendre no doubt wouldn't be missed.

"I mean difficult." I tried in vain to offer a more appropriate word substitution. "Do *not* make some wiseass comment about your penis, you know that's not what I meant."

"We can talk about him if you want, babe." The chuckle found its way out his throat. "You know that shit doesn't offend me. Actually, it's pretty awesome."

It was with an effortless calm that we fell into a more normal conversation, my body snuggling against his as I got comfortable on the couch. Any weirdness I had been worried about was AWOL as he put his arm around me and accepted my weight against him.

"You've been without sex for around five minutes and you're already begging to talk about your cock. You want to rethink that vow of celibacy, Joe?" I laughed, loving how easy it was to be around him. It was as it had always been with him. Uncomplicated.

"Babe, you brought up my *cock* not me, and don't pretend you aren't just as bad as I am. Ten to one says you cave before I do. Just remember our agreement when you do." He lost interest in channel surfing as he pulled me closer, his eyes fixed on mine.

"We aren't betting on which one of us is going to be begging for sex, Joey. And if anyone will cave, it's you my friend. I'm rock solid," I answered with no hesitation. It would be uncharitable to take that bet, I wasn't heartless.

"Well then, put your money where your mouth is. A little healthy competition should make it interesting." His eyebrow rose, daring me.

"Money is boring, what's the ante?"

If he was so hell bent on proving me wrong, who was I to deny him the opportunity? And he was right about one thing, it would make it more interesting.

"Ooooooooh. I've got something. The loser can't jerk off for a week." He smiled proudly, like he just offered the Kanye of all suggestions.

"What?" I laughed, the idea possibly the most

ridiculous I'd ever heard. "How can you even police that?"

"Honor system. I'll trust you, if you trust me." He smiled, the ease of his answer made it sound like it was me who was being ridiculous. "But I can tell you, I'm not losing this bet. Jerking off is all I'm going to have. I might as well giving up breathing, it would be easier."

"Well, you better start learning to hold your breath, because I'm not losing either."

Ha! If I wasn't in a generous mood I would have suggested two weeks but I was willing to keep playing nice. Besides, any more than a week would be a crime against humanity, he'd be climbing the walls by day two. For his band's sake I hoped they weren't on tour when he cracked.

Actually, that could be interesting.

I was so going right to Hell.

"I'm *not* losing." He held out his hand, expectantly. Big smile on his face.

"We'll see." I accepted his hand, and shook on it, my smile doing its best to match his.

"Just to clarify." I thought it best to probably go over the fine print, "We should probably define losing." Wondering if it meant him having sex with someone else.

Funny how I hadn't really thought about it until he'd offered it and now, I really didn't want him being with someone else. I'd even go a step further, and say the idea of him with some other girl made my blood run cold. The joy of winning not as appealing anymore.

Fuck, these mood swings were a bitch.

"I thought we already agreed. Losing is an admission." He'd seemed to read my subtext. "The first person to admit they can't go on any longer without is deemed the loser."

"Okay." I eased back into him, pushing aside the tug-of-war I had going on in my head. Did I want to keep talking or just enjoy being with him? I was really glad he had decided to stay.

"Fuck, yeah." Joey's attention turned back to the television we'd all but forgotten. "Scarface is on, I love this movie." He grinned at the screen. "*You wanna fuck with me?*" He echoed Pacino, reciting the move line for line as it played out. Usually that would have been grounds to punch someone right in the face, but strangely, I didn't mind.

The commentary continued as I struggled to keep my eyes open. The battle to stay awake slipping from my grasp as my lids finally closed. The gentle rock of his body when he laughed, lulling me to sleep.

"Kenz," Joey whispered in my ear in my dying moments of awareness, the dark tunnel of REM chasing me down like an unrelenting wave.

"Hmmm." I murmured, unable to get my lips to move and give him something more tangible. A word was going to be too much to ask.

"I'm gonna stay tonight, okay? Just try and remember not to freak out in the morning. I haven't had a chance to hide the knives." I felt his hand brush against my hair, my eyes refusing to open.

"Yeah, I'll remember." I felt my lips curl into a smile. "Don't touch my boobs while I sleep," by some miracle I managed to say before I finally drifted.

If any further conversation took place, I didn't remember. My breathing evened out as a calm washed through me. And despite my body not being tucked up in the perfectly good bed not very far away, I was more comfortable than I'd been all week.

Sleep.

I felt like I could sleep for a hundred years.

And right now, that's what I intended to do.

Joey

Kenzie had been a lightweight. She'd punk'd out on the Pacino marathon within the first half hour. Completely missed my amazing impersonations—and my stellar recollection of the script—but from what I could make out, she really needed to sleep.

Instead of leaving like I probably should, I decided to stick around. I may or may not have completely taken advantage of the fact she wasn't exactly coherent when I asked. But there had been an exchange and she had agreed so it counted.

The couch got old by the time the credits rolled around and as much as I wanted to hang around and watch the Godfather Trilogy, I figured we'd move our snuggle-party-of-two to the bed. She didn't even wake up when I'd carried her into her room. It felt nice to have her body tucked up tight against me until I'd laid her on the mattress. First time I took a girl there *without* the intention of fucking. Wonders would never cease.

Not going to lie, but seeing her splayed out in front of me wearing a top that did little to hide those gorgeous fucking tits didn't help the situation. My dick stirred in my jeans even though both of us knew nothing was going to happen. And unlike the chick I'd felt at the bar, Kenzie's body hadn't come with a price tag. Every inch of her the same God-given perfection she'd been born with. But true to my word, I didn't touch. Looking couldn't be helped unfortunately; a man can only be strong to a point.

She rolled over onto her side as I got undressed, tossing my clothes on the floor as I pulled them off— my boxers the only thing I left on.

Her sheets felt nice as I slipped in between them, obviously not the same Target special I had lying on my bed. Clearly that bullshit about thread count wasn't a scam after all. Who knew?

Realistically, I didn't give a rat's ass about the sheets. It was the fact I was in them that was important. And while usually I would have made sure I had a comfortable perimeter separating me from my fellow sleepee, I didn't even flinch at sidling up close to her. Not quite spooning. More like a ghosting, my body in a similar pose along side her with a couple of inches between us. Close enough that if my dick suddenly decided to take an interest, I'd be tapping her on the back. And I don't mean with my hands.

Rather than risk waking the Beast and having to deal

with the inconvenience of having to jerk off—sacrilegious to even think such things, I know—I shut my eyes and fell asleep.

The morning unfortunately was a completely different story.

"Joey." Two hands reached around my shoulders and shook me and I had no interest in anything that didn't get me ten more minutes of sleep. Where was the fucking fire? There was nowhere I needed to be.

"Joey."

Again with my name and the shaking. I don't know why assholes feel the need to wake up people who are obviously more interested in being asleep. You want to be all up-and-at-them like a fucking Pop Tart that's your deal, don't be discriminating against those who'd prefer to slumber.

"Hey, asshole."

Okay, so that got my attention.

"Huh?" I cracked open a lid and saw a fucking angel staring at me.

Of course I wasn't a moron, remembering I'd spent the night with Kenzie and the heavenly creature was actually the hot guitarist I'd slept beside last night. But as she looked down on me with her clear blue eyes, her dark-blonde hair framing her face, she looked too fucking beautiful to be human. Except she had a lot of tattoos, and probably cussed way too much to have a pair of wings.

"Hey, baby." My head lifted off the pillow and enjoyed

my morning view. That T-shirt I'd been such a fan of last night was still doing a stand-up job this morning. Must be a little chilly in here as well because her cute little peaks were standing to attention. Just the way I liked them.

"You need to take care of something." Her eyes floated down my body and landed on my cock. The bastard obviously had already received his wake up call, and was alert and ready for action.

"Was that a question or a statement?" I smiled knowing full well unless someone took care of it, I was going to be rocking the biggest set of blue balls for the rest of the day.

"Oh, no. I had it digging into my back for the past hour. It's all about you. Have fun with it. I'm going back to sleep." She flicked her hair over her shoulder and rolled back onto her side.

"Wait, so you woke *me* up because my hard-on was bugging *you*, and now you're just going to go back to sleep." My hand pulled on her shoulder, flipping her back against the mattress. "You could have just ignored it, you know. Let me deal with it when I got up."

It's not like my dick was going to jailbreak from my boxers and demand a blowjob or something. He and I were perfectly content to catch some more Z's until the natural course of progression woke us up. Then I could do what I usually did in the mornings, and jerk off in the shower.

"I was as polite as I'm gonna be." She waved it off like

it was *me* being unreasonable. "Every time I moved or turned around it poked me like I was a piñata." Her finger jabbed me in the chest in illustration. "My bed, my rules—and I don't need your hard-on trying to play *Marco Polo* while I sleep."

"Fine, it's too early in the morning to argue." I kicked off the covers, the culprit in question sticking out proudly from my hips. "You need anything else while I'm *up?*"

And yeah, I meant to say it exactly like that. We still had our wager on the table and if I got her to fold, I would happily kill two birds with one stone. Efficient and enjoyable, a much better way to wake up than the shake-n-bake she'd given me.

"Sure, if you're offering. Crackers would be nice, thanks." She smiled sweetly and then rolled away from me for the second time this morning. Her muffled laughter hinting she knew how much she was getting under my skin.

"Just so you know." This time it was my turn to grin. "I'm going to think of you." My feet hit the floor, as my ass lifted off the mattress.

"I'm not sure if I should be horrified or honored." She laughed, her body shaking gently under the sheets.

"You could be helpful if you really wanted," I offered, only half joking.

"Thanks but I'm sitting this one out. Besides, no point in both of us being awake." She yawned, keeping her back to me.

It would have been a minute, two at most before her slow, steady breathing returned. She was out like a light, and I couldn't help but stare.

I'd never really seen her like that; completely oblivious to how beautiful she looked right now. She seemed sort of vulnerable, her body tucked up tight in a ball as she lay on her side. A complete contradiction to what she was usually like.

Her face was another story. As I moved to the other side of the bed, I got an eyeful of her stunning features. From this side, she didn't look so vulnerable. She looked fierce, her forehead slightly crinkled in concentration even though she wasn't awake. Her eyelashes bouncing gently off the top of her cheeks as her sleep deepened. Yeah, it had definitely been my bad missing this.

As much as I would have enjoyed channeling my inner creeper and pulling up a chair, sitting here and watching all morning wasn't the plan. I didn't even want to be up in the first place, my renegade dick getting us both kicked out of bed. The sooner I got that taken care of, the sooner I could climb back in. Hopefully I'd be rewarded; a hand on her ass would cover it. I should have asked before I left.

Naturally I was a master at clearing the pipes, especially in the morning which meant a few minutes under the spray of the shower was all it took to get the big guy to go nocturnal. No promises he'd stay that way, especially if she let me touch her ass.

After a quick shower—I was there anyway might as well get clean after I'd gotten dirty—I made a quick pit stop in her kitchen. The tour of the house rounded out when I ended back in her bedroom with my ass on the mattress beside Sleeping Beauty.

"You smell nice." She rolled over to me, her eyes closed despite her smile. "Did you use my shampoo?"

"Yeah. I figured if I smelled like you it would help with the fantasy." I laughed, my reasoning about fifty percent true. "I got your crackers too. You want me to feed you? I think I have my palm leaf somewhere and I'm already wearing the towel."

"Is that a joke this early in the morning, Joe?" Her eyes cracked open and gave me a grin. "Wow, you're in rare form."

"It's these sheets I'm telling you." My hands stroked the whatever-thread count-insert country-here-cotton suggestively. "Best sleep I've had in awhile. Whatever they are, I'm getting like a hundred pair. In fact, fuck it. I'm going to wear them like togas. I could easily bring back that trend."

I put the crackers on the nightstand, more interested in the lady between the kick ass sheets.

"It's been working for Frat boys for years." She nodded, giving me her seal of approval. "I think if anyone has a shot. It's you."

"The only reason I'm sad I missed college." I held my hand over my heart. "You feeling okay?" She didn't *look* like she was going to puke, but I hadn't seen her toss her cookies, so I couldn't be sure this wasn't the face right before it happened.

"Yeah, usually it's when I get vertical things go south. I try to work my way up to it." She shuffled up slightly on the bed, her back resting against the headboard as she stayed under the covers. The sheet slipped down enough to give a spectacular money shot of her tits. Sadly, they were still in the top she'd worn to bed but it still was a nice good morning.

"Is there anything I can do?" Not that I had any nursing qualifications or knew what she needed, but I could improvise like a champ and my bedside manner was second to none.

"You can tell me about CJs." She smiled, spilling she had knowledge on something that currently was supposed be on need-to-know.

"How did you find out about that? We haven't been announced yet."

I hadn't told her. At least I didn't think I had. I did have a tendency to talk in my sleep, and could spill virtually anything after shooting my load but neither of these things had happened, so I was confident the weakest link hadn't been me. Write that on your calendar, peeps.

"I know everything, Joey. How many times do I have to tell you?" She held her hands in front on her like she was consulting her crystal ball.

"You know exactly what this means, Kenz. The

opportunity, it sort of feels like a fucking rite of passage. It's up there with playing the Garden, but it means a little bit more because this is all us."

It was good she knew because other than the band there really wasn't anyone to talk with about this. We weren't supposed to tell anyone yet—although obviously someone had failed on that part—and my family had no idea what it meant. Someone like Kenz knew exactly what I was feeling without the long story.

"Yeah, I get that. It's a big deal." She grabbed a cracker from her nightstand and bit a corner off, chewing thoughtful. I guess she hadn't made her mind up if she was going to puke either.

"You're going to be there, right?" The need to have her there suddenly important. "You'll come see us play? It's not for a couple of weeks but I want you there."

It was going to be a big night, possibly one of the biggest, so yeah I wanted her there. Plus, if she was there my kid would be there too and that was cool in itself; that I got to share that moment with them. Wow. Fuck. My kid. Yeah, I wanted them both there.

"Of course, I'll be there. It's been a while since I've seen you guys play." Her hand reached out and touched mine.

"Uh-hmm." I tried to move the lump in my throat and changed the subject. There were a few acceptable times to have a Kleenex moment, but having a chat in a bedroom wasn't it. "So, what's the thing on your kitchen table?"

I'd noticed the greenery on my way through and while I couldn't be sure it hadn't been here the last time I visited—we'd fucked in the kitchen but I hadn't looked—the big red bow was the tip off it was new. Its presence in itself was surprising, Kenzie more known for her fancy finger work than her green thumb.

"Ah, you met Hendrix." She nodded taking another nibble of the cracker, the first few bites staying put. "He's a gift from Sara, you know to practice looking after stuff."

"You named your plant, Hendrix? That is badass. Well done."

I was impressed she hadn't gone with something lame like Leafy or Walter, let's face it there wasn't a lot you could call a plant and it sound cool but she had most definitely achieved that.

"Sar named him, but I concurred. So I'll take badass by default." She grinned, another few nibbles on the cracker. "Have you thought about names for us?"

"You mean for the baby?" I asked like a dumbass.

"No, for us because twenty some-odd years with the same name is boring." She tossed me a look that told me she had made the same assessment. "*Of course* for the baby."

Well.

Fuck.

My eyes blinked rapidly as my brain short-circuited. And not in the kind of way where I pictured her naked. This was completely different.

"Ummm."

Nope, still nothing. On second thought, what the hell was my own name? Because at this point that wasn't flashing front and center either.

"We're not calling our kid *Ummm*, Joey." She eyeballed me with a smirk, the slight dig somehow making me feel better I'd had a complete mind dump.

"No, I just mean I hadn't thought about it. I just figured it was a long time away."

More like it seemed like an eternity away and the thought of being responsible for naming another human scared the fucking crap out of me.

"It is." She nodded with what seemed like a huge case of I'm-not-worried; how she had it all together was still a source of wonder. "I was just curious if you had any ideas, that's all."

Rather than prove I had no fucking idea, I decided to throw the ball in her court. Considering she was the only one of the two of us who seemed to have a clue.

"What about you? Have you got any ideas?"

"I was thinking Lennon, sort of works for both a boy or a girl." She smiled like she *hadn't* just thought about giving our unborn kid the worst possible name ever. I take back what I said. She didn't have a clue either.

"I'd rather call our kid *Ummm*." Was she serious? "We are not naming him or her after a Beatle." Pfft. Like *that* was even a possibility.

"What have you got against The Beatles?"

Jesus. She *was* serious. How much time did she have?

"Dude, they're like a hundred years old. Their music sucked and they were English. I want our kid to have an American name."

"They aren't a hundred years old." She gave me the eye-roll, head shake combo I usually got when we didn't agree.

"Their music still sucked."

Not even she could debate how snore-town their tunes had been. *I wanna hold your hand?* Can someone please give them some testicles and a different cord progression?

"Okay, so *you* think of something."

Random names pinged around my noggin with nothing sticking. Maybe she had something going with the musician thing. Nothing cooler than sharing your name with greatness.

"What about Tommy if it's a boy, Lee if it's a girl." The Mötley Crüe drummer being one of my first idols.

"Sure, let's name our kid after a coked-up drummer who has a sex tape. That makes all the sense in the world."

"Firstly, he might have been on drugs, but he was and still is a fucking kick ass drummer. Secondly, did you see the size of his cock? Mad props to him and his monster dick." No sooner had the words come out of my mouth than I realized what I'd said. The cold-day-in-hell Kenz was shooting me was also another tip off.

Okay, on second thought, our kid wasn't getting named Tommy Lee. Like ever. Now I needed to also wash the visual from my mind with about two gallons of bleach.

"Not happening," she unnecessarily confirmed. "What about something like Chance?"

"Are you fucking with me right now?" She must be fucking with me. Lennon and Chance were her suggestions? "Why don't we just cut out the middleman and steal his lunch money right now. Because that's what a name like that gets you. A couple of black eyes too. No, our kid gets a normal fucking name. Oh, and no tricked up spelling either."

Or hooker names. Or jock names. And no fucking names that sound like a bunch of letters that some sucker believes is the Hawaiian word for purity.

"I believe it's your turn." She laughed, seeming to thoroughly enjoy how easily I got annoyed.

"Shit this is really hard." Thank God we had more time because we were going to need it.

"I hope that wasn't your suggestion because if it was, I'm putting Lennon back on the table."

"Ha. Ha. You're so funny, and no that wasn't the suggestion."

God she was beautiful. Maybe it's 'cause we were talking about our kid but I swear it's like every day she just got more stunning. I had to remind myself that the fact we were having this conversation was proof I had already been there. And even still, it seemed hard to believe. Max was right to think she would never be with me. Why the hell would she? She must have men climbing the walls to get to her. Thank God our little agreement meant I didn't have to worry about that for a while.

"You want a cracker?" My silent staring obviously gave her the heebie jeebies as she angled the box toward me, the dry slices of cardboard holding zero appeal.

"And deny you your feast. What kind of heartless bastard do you think I am?" I responded, keeping it tight as to what I was really thinking about.

Not like I could spill now, could I? Not when things were so good with what we had. Besides, we had the kid to think about. No way was I fucking that up.

"The one who's still wearing no pants. You want to fix that? I really need to keep my breakfast down, I have work to do today." She pointed to the towel still slung around my waist, my lack of clothes not forgotten, especially not by me.

"Yeah, what are you doing?" I became suddenly interested in what kind of work she had to do. Far as I knew she didn't have any daytime gigs, and her band wasn't even close to laying down an album, which ruled out the studio. And call me nosey, but part of me just wanted to know what she did when we weren't together.

"I've got a song I'm working on." She brushed the cracker crumbs off her sheets before giving me a look of no-big-deal. "I've been working on it for a few days."

"So, maybe I can help. Think of it as our second

collaboration."

I had no idea what I was even suggesting. I'd contributed to the stuff we put out but for the most part it was extra window dressing. The hard yards were always done by Angie and Rusty. It's what worked and I knew better than to rock the boat. But I had enough theory to be able to put something together if I wanted to, I just never wanted to. Now, doing it with her, maybe it would be a good thing.

"Thanks, Joey but I work better by myself." She laughed shooting me down without even a second thought.

"Then look at it as practice, me doing my part for your personal growth," I offered, thinking maybe there was more I could offer than just the song.

"Right." She rolled her eyes. "It's not a color by number kind of song, Joey. Sometimes the adults need to do their thing."

Ouch. Seriously? Sure we threw names back and forth and while I knew I didn't have a fancy piece of paper on my wall like she did, I wasn't stupid either.

"You could still toss some ideas around, I'm a good listener." I tried a different tactic, hoping she'd see there was more to me than what she knew.

"It's really not ready to share. Besides, you're a *drummer*. I don't need to hit things today." She laughed, completely oblivious to the burn she'd just given me.

It's not important, internally I argued. She was going off past experience and the Joey Shaw from three months ago would not have thought sitting down and writing a song was a good time. So I couldn't be pissed at her that she hadn't gotten the message it was something I'd now consider. Which up until five minutes ago I hadn't. Clear as mud, right?

Besides, it's not like she was saying *no* to me but was sitting there writing with Rusty instead. She said she works better alone. It's not personal, just personal preference, and I shouldn't be pissed because she wanted to work solo. Hell, some songs Angie wrote she wouldn't even let Rusty play with until she was done. And those two did everything together. I should let it go, maybe revisit it some other time down the track.

"Drummers do much more than hit things, string plucker," I volleyed back, sticking to what we knew. Yeah. It was better this way.

"String plucker, really?" The *is that the best you can do*, not needed.

"Fine, I'll put my pants on and go." I threw my hands in the air dramatically, slightly annoyed I had no reason to stick around. "My talent isn't appreciated here."

"I'm going to grab a shower." She gave me a quick squeeze on the arm, her cue I was overstaying my welcome. "Thanks for staying over. Maybe call me later?" A goodbye-you-can-go-now if ever I'd heard one.

"Yep, cool. Take care," I said, like I was waving off a great aunt.

Maybe The Beatles weren't the only ones who needed

to find their testicles; I should probably jet before I made an even bigger fool of myself.

"Catch you, Kenz." I grabbed my clothes and shoes from her bedroom floor and walked out to the living room.

And after a quick redress and dumping my damp towel in her laundry hamper I grabbed my keys, my phone and headed out the door. The goodbye made easier in that she'd already moved into her bathroom. I tried not to think about her being naked in the same spot I had been. Or that a few footsteps in the right direction would put me in the same location.

Fuck.

I needed to get out. I threw my body into my truck and hightailed back home, the distance hopefully cooling the burn.

"Everything cool, bro?" Max was in his usual spot; in the kitchen with a cup of java in his hand.

"Yeah, all sorted." I tossed my keys and phone onto the counter while I got myself a cup. "We are not fucking other people. That's the rule." I took a sip of the caffeinated goodness before continuing. "Sorry for bailing on you and Rusty last night. We can do it again sometime soon."

"No need to apologize. I'm glad you worked it out." Like the stand up that he was, he didn't make an issue of it. The dude always had my back; yesterday had been no exception.

"You really did me a solid yesterday, saved my ass from making a big mistake." I didn't even want to think about how shit would have gone down if I had gone home with Rochelle. Bad. It would have been very bad. And I saw that now even if it had been Max and Rusty who had pointed it out. Thank fuck for that.

"That's what friends are for, Joe. Don't get too sentimental on me." He cupped my neck and gave it a shake.

"Seriously, dude." The words of gratitude I'd given him not even close to being enough. "Anytime you see me going off course, just hit me or something."

"Joey, you are going to be fine. Give yourself some credit; you are going to be great."

Yep. I definitely had lost my balls somewhere. Max proved how good a buddy he was by ignoring it, another reason why he was my best friend.

Thankfully my phone chimed with an incoming message before I went full Oprah and started bawling like a baby, the text hopefully being from the girl I'd just left. The preview of the message visible in screen lock.

"What the fuck?" I stared at my phone like the message was in Chinese.

"All those dick pics finally catching up with you, huh?" Max laughed, dumping his cup in the sink with no idea on what I was dealing with.

"No, it's a message from some douchebag I don't know." I reread the message again wondering if I had just misunderstood it. Or like the second time around the letters would leap of the screen and suddenly divulge some other meaning.

"Well what does it say?" He tipped his head to the phone, not having the same perspective as I had.

"Got your email. You're amazing and I'm really into it. Let's make the magic happen. Dom." I read out loud the same message I'd scanned at least ten times since it landed on my phone.

"He sounds like a nice guy, you should invite him over." Max laughed, thoroughly enjoying that my latest fan was a dude. Not that there was anything wrong with that, I just didn't play on that team.

"Why the hell won't my phone unlock." I continued to press my four-digit code but got nowhere, the shaking screen taunting me in its denied access.

"Did you forget your pin number again?"

That had happened one time, not like I made a habit out of it. I stared at the screen for a beat before I suddenly realized the answer was really fucking obvious.

Like staring me in the face.

Literally.

"Ohhhhh." I smiled; glad the mystery had been partially solved.

"What?" Max asked once again out of the loop.

"This is Kenzie's phone." I turned it in my hands to show him the screen locked picture of her and Sara smiling broadly behind the glass. "I must have picked up hers by accident." In my agitation over the message I'd completely not noticed.

"Well there you go, crisis averted. Dom doesn't want you." Max laughed like it was somehow okay that the message wasn't for me. Right now I would have preferred if the message *was* fucking for me.

"No, he wants Kenzie, and that is soooooo much better." An irrational pang of jealously washed through me. 'Cause getting territorial over a chick I wasn't dating made all the fucking sense in the world.

"Fuck, dude." Max blew out a breath, the two-and-two coming together in his melon as well as mine.

"She obviously had this guy in play before we'd had our talk."

Kenzie wasn't the type of girl to play me; that I knew. But who this asshole was remained a mystery, and what he might want with her made me uncomfortable. Shhh, you hear that? That's the sound of my mind exploding with a bunch of emotions I didn't understand.

"Well, from the sounds of things she hasn't done anything." He took the phone out of my hand and read the message for himself. "And *almost* doesn't count."

"Yep." Not sold. Not even close.

"Look, give her the benefit of the doubt. Maybe ask her when you give her back the phone." Ever the diplomat, Max tried to run interference. It's not like he didn't know I was my own worst enemy, especially when left to my own devices.

"You know what, no. And you're not going to say

anything either." I snatched the phone out of his hands and placed it on the counter. Dom could go get fucked, he had a snowballs chance in Hell before I'd let him anywhere near her. I didn't give a fuck about whatever magic he wanted to make happen. He could find his own girl. Yeah, because she was sooooo much more mine than his. *Shut up*, I screamed at my inner logic, the bastard not adding anything helpful.

"Joey, don't do anything stupid," Max warned, his eyes tracking me as I shifted on my feet; my skin feeling like it was crawling with ants.

"No, no. I won't." I tried to remain calm even though underneath I felt like a lion in a cage. "Hey, toss me your phone. I need to call myself."

Worst thing was, none of this shit made sense. We weren't in love with each other, and apart from the last twenty-four hours we hadn't made any kind of commitment to each other—whatever that commitment actually was. So all of this was way out of left field, not that I could reason with myself in my current state.

"Hello?" Kenzie answered confused, guessing she wasn't talking on her own cell.

"Hey, Kenz, yeah I fucked up and took your phone by mistake. You have mine." *Don't mention the asshole. Don't mention the asshole. Don't mention the asshole.*

"Is this just an excuse to see me again? Surely you could be more original." She gave a throaty laugh. And if I hadn't been so keyed about the asshole I was trying not to mention, I would have fucking loved it.

"Sadly, I can't. Look, I need to go out for a bit so I'll leave yours here. Max will be around to do the swap." I gave her my clipped response knowing the longer I spoke the more chance I'd say something I probably shouldn't. Or maybe something I should. *Who is this asshole,* at the top of the list.

"Oh. Okay. Yeah I can do that." She sounded surprised, like she'd expected me to say something else. Sorry, all out of happy-happy-joy-joy today.

"Awesome. Thanks. See ya."

"Bye." I'd barely let her get the word out before I hung up.

"What was *that*?" Max glared accusingly, a whole lot of explain-yourself radiating off the guy.

"I need to find out who this fucker is." And maybe kill him. Okay, so I wasn't a murderer, but I'd find a way to destroy him.

"Joey." Max warned not realizing the train had already left the station and I was well and truly on it. No stopping me now. Not until I knew either way.

"Just be a friend and do the swap." Too late. Way too late to stop this now. "Don't fucking sell me out. I've got a number and a name. I'm going to FBI this motherfucker into next week."

Whoever he was better watch his fucking back because this wasn't playtime. And like hell I'd sit around while he tried to take Kenzie.

Joey had been weird.

Actually, that was an oxymoron because he'd always been weird. But he was *weirder* than usual.

I'd stopped off at his house and did the phone exchange, but he hadn't waited around.

See, weird—because things were actually in a really good place between us.

Max had been nice enough, so I chalked it all up to my instincts being on the fritz. It would stand to reason seeing as the rest of my body was completely out of control.

I would literally cry if I had to pee again in the next hour.

Shit was getting ridiculous.

The conversation with Joey about us not seeing other people had been an eye opener, and part of me hoped it might be more than it was. The idea of maybe something happening between us not as crazy as I once thought. But then I remembered.

It was Joey.

Not happening.

So I packed all those hopes and dreams and put them on my metaphorical bookcase where they could sit for all eternity. That was the best place for them.

The days that followed were business as usual. I spoke to Joey every day, sometimes more than once and whatever *weirdness* he had going on seemed to have disappeared.

Like magic, gone. Which was awesome because he was back to being his funny self. The flirting was still there too, no matter how many times I told him we weren't sleeping together.

Still, it didn't bother me as much as I pretended. Not that I would admit it, but it was sort of nice.

"Hey, Kenz, I was working on those notes you emailed. I can't wait to show you what I've done with our song." Dom greeted me at the door with a big hug.

Big being the operative word because the dude was ginormous. His head whipped around, slightly disappointed when he saw I was solo.

"Awesome, Sara's not well so she is sitting this one out."

More like she begged me not to go without her, insisting we wait until she was no longer under the influence of NyQuil. I disagreed, wanting to get the song finished ASAP to give it the best chance of getting on the album.

And after a pinky-swear vow to tell her every single thing that happened while I was with Dom in military-precise minutes, she agreed I should go alone. Or at least, she didn't sulk too badly when I did.

"Is she okay? Nothing serious I hope."

Dom's concern for Sara overtook his interest in me as he motioned me to come in. His living room already set up with guitars and notebooks.

"Sounds like it's just the sniffles, but she's convinced she's dying." I dumped my purse and pulled out my notes. "You could always bring her some soup or something, if you want. Or an erection. Either would improve her mood."

Sara's illness not so life-threatening that she wouldn't appreciate a bedside visit by her crush.

And by bedside, I mean inside of her.

These two really needed to have sex.

Someone should be doing it considering my vagina was developing tumbleweeds. But that was another story.

"You two kill me." Dom laughed, always getting thrown off by Sara and my personal brand of enthusiasm. "Thanks for the tip. I might stop by her place later."

"Don't forget the erection; I was lying about the soup."

Dom laughed, his face flushing red before urging me to take a seat. "You want to get to work on the song now or you want to try and embarrass me some more?"

"We should work," I conceded; it was only fun for so long. Besides, the whole point of me coming without Sara was to get this finished. And today felt like it might be the day.

After discussing some ideas Dom had thought of and me throwing in some of my own we picked up our guitars and started to work through the entire song. It was easier to hear exactly what worked in the notes rather than on paper and what we had so far sounded great. Possibly even mainstream enough for radio play, without sounding like Justin Bieber.

"That's great. Sounds awesome." Dom's smile hinted he felt it too, the song a perfect mix of rock and emotion. "You've got such a good ear."

"Thanks, not so bad yourself." I smiled back, glad it was working out so well.

I had never really written with anyone other than my band but who knew where it could lead? Maybe I could get a gig co-writing songs for other people. It would be an awesome way to supplement my income and be something I could manage with the baby. Look at me being all responsible.

"Hey, you want to take-five?" Dom put down his guitar as he rose to his feet. "Something to drink?"

"Sure. I just need to empty before I fill up again." I smiled, placing my guitar on the stand. "Sorry that's probably too much information."

"Nah, you're good."

I excused myself, hopefully making my pit stop as quick as possible. I spent enough time as it was in bathrooms answering the call of nature; I wasn't interested in prolonging the experience.

The knock at the door came right when I'd taken a seat on the toilet, Dom's heavy footsteps happening soon after.

"Oh hey, dude, can I help you with something?" Dom's voice echoed down the hall. His walls were paper-thin, so it sounded like he was in the bathroom with me. Having sex in this place would be tricky, no wonder he didn't have a roommate. PS. I needed to stop thinking about sex.

"Yeah, I'm looking for Kenzie, is she here?" I heard Joey's voice and I froze in place. Huh? How did he even find me here? It's not like I'd mentioned it. Or had I? Me discounting baby brain so early in the game wasn't smart.

"Yeah she's here but we're kind of in the middle of something," Dom responded, probably not sure if I wanted a visitor or not. We hadn't really spoken about Joey since my baby confession; he was probably being cautious.

"Okay so let me rephrase it. Get Kenzie." Joey sounded pissed. Like seriously mad.

"Dude, you might want to watch your fucking tone. No way am I letting you talk to her like that."

I willed myself to pee quicker so I could leave the confines of my bathroom prison and find out what the hell was going on.

"Fuck off, King Kong, I'm not interested in what you think." Joey's aggravation rose, as did his voice.

"Do yourself a favor, take a walk and chill out. I'm not looking to hurt you." Dom was keeping his cool despite being justified in losing it. Joey wasn't exactly being complimentary.

"Do you know who I am?"

"As in a dick who plays for Black Addiction? Yeah, I think I've heard of you."

I quickly finished on the toilet, opening the faucet a crack so I would still be able to hear the conversation over the water, trying to speed up the hand washing process. My wet hands forwent the towel as they rubbed the front of my jeans in an effort to hurry up and get to the front door.

"I didn't mean like that, asshole. I mean, that Kenzie is carrying my kid."

My heart stopped. There is no explanation why I didn't at that point go to the door with a big ta-dah reveal. *Hi, it's me. The girl you wanted to see.* But part of me was so shocked that Joey had apparently lost his damn mind, while another part genuinely didn't want to see him acting like that.

"She's mentioned, doesn't change anything as far as I'm concerned." Dom refused to budge, his large body blocking the door as I walked from the bathroom back down the hall.

"Doesn't change anything? Is your Godzilla brain really

that small? You really want to mess with that?"

My heart started to thump louder as I got closer, my feet moving slower than they should.

"Bud, lay off the insults. They aren't helping you right now."

"All I'm hearing is wa wa wa, Big Foot. For a big motherfucker, you really are a pussy."

Something inside me snapped. It was like I'd woken from whatever trance-like state I had been in when I walked out the bathroom and finally my brain had kicked into gear. And thank God it had or I was pretty sure Dom would quickly run out of patience.

"What the hell, Joey? What are you doing here?" I slipped into the spot between Dom and the door, most of my body being obscured by his monstrous frame.

"Taking a walk, randomly knocking on doors and seeing if I can find any freaks of nature. Oh look, I found one," Joey spat back, his eyes mixed with emotions I couldn't read.

"You want me to get rid of him?" Dom turned to me, completely ignoring the madman on his doorstep.

"No, it's fine, I'll talk to him." I nodded, signaling he could open the door a little more. Whatever was bugging Joey, I doubted he would ever hurt me.

"I'm right here," he said to me but didn't take his eyes off Joey, slowly backing away from the doorway to give us some room. No doubt sticking close by in case he was needed.

"Joey, what the hell has gotten into you?" I moved into the now-vacant space but stopped short of inviting him in.

"I read the message. *Let's make the magic happen.* I thought we had an agreement?"

Oh.

And then it all made sense.

The day of the phone swap, Dom had sent me a message saying he liked the suggestions I emailed him and that he was anxious to get started. I suppose out of context it didn't sound great, but it wasn't a smoking gun. In any case, he had no right to come to Dom's house and start throwing around accusations. Especially when Dom had been nothing but supportive and was providing me a much-needed opportunity.

"You think I'm sleeping with Dom?" I almost exploded, wondering how the hell Joey of all people decided it was okay to be judgmental. Oh, and also he was calling me a whore in a roundabout way. And not in a joking you're-a-whore-I'm-a-whore way.

"No, I know you're not sleeping with him. You said you wouldn't and I believe you," he fired back, shocking the hell out of me.

He *didn't* think I was sleeping with him, but he was here acting like a jealous boyfriend. Yeah, because that makes all the sense in the world.

"Then why the hell are you acting crazy right now?"

"Because you're working with him, yet you won't even

consider working with me."

The true motivation for his visit was revealed. He was pissed because I was working with another musician? It was my job—I wouldn't get upset if he suddenly started working with someone else.

"Joey, you're not a song writer. It's not personal."

"You think because I'm a *drummer* I can't write? Sure, Angie and Rus do the heavy lifting but I'm in there too." And past the anger I saw some of the hurt, possibly rejection, having dismissed the opportunity to work together so easily days before. Ironically on the same day as the phone swap. That day was just awesome all round it seemed.

"I thought you were joking. You're a drummer. We're both guitarists; I just didn't think you were serious."

"When I saw that message initially, Kenz, I thought maybe he was an ex-boyfriend trying to hook up. You gave me your word and I knew you wouldn't go back on that. But even though it made no sense, it pissed me off some asshole would just call you for a booty call." He lowered his voice as he tried to explain; on his face the look of defeat.

"You mean like you tried to so many times before we actually did it?" I reminded, though his text messages hadn't been so innocent.

"That was before I really knew you. Look, I was a dick I'll admit that, but if you are going to be with a guy then he better treat you right. So I did some digging. Found out who he was and then heard through the grapevine you guys were working together."

Like when I had first spoken to Dom about Joey, the industry was a gossip pit, and it wouldn't have been hard for him to find out about me working with him. It wasn't like I was trying to hide.

He took a breath. "You blew me off. Wouldn't even give me a fucking chance. And it's more than just about the music. How the hell is that going to work when we are having a baby together? You just going to assume I'm a fucking loser who can only drum? That I can't contribute because I'm stupid."

"I didn't—" I stopped midsentence, the words getting stuck in my throat.

I guess when it came to Joey, I often joked about his intelligence level or his lack of college education. Not because he was stupid but because it was easy. We made fun of each other, that's what we did. I'd never meant it to be hurtful.

"I'm sorry. I don't think you're stupid. I never thought that."

"Ah, fuck. I'm sorry. I have no idea what is going through my head right now, but it's a mess. I guess I feel sort of left out like, you're calling all the shots. And I get it, I totally understand but I just need to be a part of this."

He did it again.

Completely flooring me with his kind, sensitive side very few people saw. The man who would be an amazing father.

I swallowed.

Hard.

"You're part of this. I promise. I won't freeze you out."

"That's all I'm asking." He reached out and squeezed my hand.

"You guys want to come inside or you happy to stand in the doorway some more? Pretty sure every single one of my neighbors is looking out their window right now." Dom appeared back at my side, obviously hearing the whole conversation. Not that he seemed overly annoyed we had commandeered his stoop to get talk-show crazy. All we needed was the paternity test results, and it could have been an episode of *Maury*.

"Hey." Joey tipped his chin hello, about twenty thousand levels calmer than when he'd met Dom a few minutes earlier. "I think I'm just going to take off. We can talk about this later."

"Can I call you later?" I didn't want him to leave, but asking him to stay didn't seem like a good idea either.

"Of course you can call me, you know my number." He gave me a nod and then turned around, walking down the stairs onto the sidewalk before he turned a corner and was gone.

I could have gone after him but I didn't.

"You need anything?" Dom put his arm around me and pulled me into his side.

"Yeah, a lobotomy." I tried to force a grin.

Thirteen
Joey

"**H**ey, can I come in?" I could count the number of times Kenzie had ever come to Max and my place. There had been a few parties but that's about it, so seeing her on the other side of my security door wasn't what I expected. Especially not three hours after our last encounter. Not my finest hour.

"I thought you said you were going to call?" I opened the door and stepped to the side. "Come on in."

I didn't give a fuck what people thought of me. None. And I really didn't give a shit if people thought I was stupid, I knew different. And I didn't live my life with something to prove. But now with Kenzie—it fucking mattered.

We wandered through to the living room, my hand gesturing for her to take a seat.

"I hate how we left things." She paced nervously,

declining the offer of the couch.

"You're right. It was bullshit. I should never have come down there and spoken to you like that. That was a bad call."

There were better ways to have handled it; unfortunately I didn't choose the other options. Pissed, not because she was blowing me off, but blowing me off because she didn't think I was good enough. Which is why I acted like a sixteen-year-old girl.

"No, you were hurt. I get it. I think you're great." She continued to pace, her hands twitchy at her side.

Awesome. Now she was nervous to be around me too. Just another layer of BS to an already shitastic day.

"Can you sit down, you're making me edgy." I eased up to her and ran my hands along her arms, moving her closer to the couch.

"Okay." She smiled, her ass lowering onto the two seater.

Not much better. Her hands locked into place in her lap as she took her seat and waited for me to do the same on the opposite armchair.

Silence.

Fucking great.

"I don't like seeing you like this." I leaned forward, knowing we had to somehow fix this shitty situation.

"Like what?" She shrugged, like she had no idea how uptight she was.

"Nervous around me. Quiet. It's not you."

"I'm not nervous. You want me to be loud?" she asked with a slight look of confusion.

"Yes, it will make me feel better. Feel free to get crazy," I offered, hoping it would tease us from this no man's land we were currently in.

"Fine." She slowly rose to her feet and started to stomp around dramatically. "Fuck," she screamed out randomly and picked up a pillow and threw it across the room. "Fuck. Fuck. Fuck." The later ones slightly louder than the first.

"That's you being loud? You need more bass behind the fucks if you are going to get serious. And one pillow? Really?"

"FUCK." My voice boomed, echoing off the walls, as I grabbed the stash of Sports Illustrated chilling on my coffee table and pitched them against the wall. The flap of pages rained through the air before falling into a messy heap.

"Impressive." She smiled. "I can probably do better." She looked around for something to throw, her eyes falling to the television remote.

"Not that." I warned and pointed to the shitty thrift store lamp that sat on the end table beside her. "That."

"Are you sure?" She looked between the lamp and me like she was convinced I meant something else.

"As a heart attack." I smiled and watched her unplug the piece of shit lamp and grasped it in her palm.

"FUCK." The lamp catapulted through the air with a

satisfying smash as it hit the wall, the globe shattering on impact.

"What the fuck?" Max stormed into the living room. The front door left wide open, his keys still in his hand. "What the hell is going on in here?"

I assumed the question was directed at both of us even though he was looking squarely at me. The bastard assuming I was the reason furniture was being thrown. And in this instance, he would be correct.

"Kenz wants to moonlight as a quarterback." I nodded toward Kenzie, her hand still raised in the air from the arc of the throw. "She's got a great right arm, wouldn't you say?" I gave her a big smile.

"Yeah, because I believe that." Max's face all I-wasn't-born-yesterday as he eyed us both for an explanation.

"It's true." Kenz played along trying not to laugh. "It's always been a fantasy of mine." Her hand lowered to her side as she smiled, nodding to me in a show of support.

"You *both* are full of shit." Max shook his head, disappearing momentarily to take care of our still open front door. "I'm going to go hang in my bedroom away from the crazy that's happening in here." He waved his hand dramatically in the air. "If you could not destroy any more of the living room, that sure would be nice too. Peace." He gave us a wave before taking off down the hall.

"Wow, I would have expected more questions. If that had been Sara, I would have had to give a three-page account with a PowerPoint display." She looked skeptic-cally at the hall like Max might reappear any minute and demand more info.

"Yeah, Max doesn't give a shit. I'm sure once he realized they weren't angry *fucks* and we weren't trying to kill each other, he lost interest pretty quickly." I moved from my place across the room so that I was directly in front of her.

"Hey." She smiled, her eyes meeting mine.

"Hey." I grinned back, the urge to touch her too great as I gave in and pulled her in for a hug.

"We can do better." She didn't fight my hold, if anything moving closer against my chest.

"I agree." My mouth unconsciously brushed against her forehead and gave her a kiss. And fuck me, the contact was not nearly enough. "You want to do something? We could go see a movie?"

"Like a date?" She pulled back slightly so she could get a better look at me. "We've never dated before."

"Sure, Date Joey is so much fun. You've completely been missing out." My hands lowered a little, settling on her waist.

Hmm. That felt really fucking nice, exactly where I wanted them and her. The rise and fall of her chest caught my attention as I tried to regulate my own breathing. Had we been this close before without having sex? Not to flirt, but just to touch each other? It pissed me off that I couldn't recall, the curve of her hips absolutely perfect for my hands.

"I don't know, Joey." Her fingers played with the fabric of my T-shirt and if I wasn't so sure she'd freak the fuck out, I would have kissed her.

God, I wanted too. Kiss away any hard feelings; hold her close to my chest.

I wanted *her*.

Not just to take to my bed, I wanted something else as well.

More.

Whatever more was.

And just like she got a brain scan of what I was thinking, she pulled away a little further. My hands slipped from her body as she gave us more distance, the silence threatening to come back.

"Or we could fuck. You know I'm good at that." I slipped back into the Joey she remembered, hopefully lightening the mood. Praying to God she didn't think I was a jerk off and was actually suggesting we fuck.

She jabbed me in the ribs with her elbow. "You had to go ruin it." She rewarded me with the laugh that I had wanted.

"I'm just keeping it real, babe."

●●●

You would think we hadn't played in years with the amount of practice Angie had scheduled. It was like we were recording again, days spent holed up in a room. At least we had the convenience of her makeshift home studio this time, her new house boasting a soundproof basement. I guess it beat spending hours at my own home twiddling my thumbs.

"Just a head's up." Max loaded his bass and amp into the back of his car. "I'm doing a stop-and-drop at home and then heading out. I'll probably have company tonight."

"Whatever, dude. I might go see Kenzie, it's been a few days." I lifted the last of my kit into the back of my truck.

My plans for the night had already been set regardless of Max's agenda. Him and *company* just made the choice a lot easier, giving the dude some extra room while getting what I wanted. Everyone won.

"Yeah, you do that." The bastard laughed as he finished packing up his ride.

There was no need to pretend. Max had known me so long, half the time he knew me better than I knew myself. And while I was still wading my way through what it all meant, my interest in Kenz was no longer purely as the mother of my child.

In what I can only describe as sick twisted perversion —that I would never repeat, not even to Max—I was glad I'd knocked her up. Pleased beyond measure it was my kid that was inside of her. And since we'd gotten those ever-important paternity test results that confirmed it, I was strutting around like I'd just been given a key to the city. As far as I was concerned, getting her pregnant was the best thing I ever did.

Of course shit was still in a weird sort of limbo between us, but she'd finally caved and went out on a date like I asked. I had been the perfect gentleman, keeping my hands and my dick to myself the entire time. Not even a sly brush of the ass when I put my hand around her waist. Nope, my mitts were above the belt the entire time much to my dick's disgust.

And because I'd been good and hadn't so much as kissed her, we'd done it again a couple more times. Sure, we weren't doing anything super exciting; keeping the outings pretty PG, but it was cool just to relax with her. And that laugh of hers was making my world go round.

The hard-ons weren't as much fun. My balls ached like no other and I was jerking off so much I was sure I was going to be rocking epic chafing. Not like I had an alternative, at this point I doubt I could have fucked anyone else even if it were an option. Which was another thing.

Since I'd taken a hiatus from the ladies, I had more pussy thrown at me than ever. No shit. Pussy for fucking days. I'm talking random pussy just turned up when I least expected it, for no good reason. It was like the big man upstairs was testing me, seeing if I would crack and I wasn't even breaking a sweat.

I gave them the thanks-but-no-thanks and kept it polite, because the other thing I was working on was dialing down the asshole. All part of the plan in being a better man. Not just for Kenzie, but for our kid too. Besides, it was time I did more than throw on a new coat of paint; I wasn't fucking eighteen anymore.

My truck pulled up in front of Kenzie's apartment like it had driven itself. My braining zoned out on the miles as I thought about seeing her. Every time it was just a little bit better.

"Knock, knock." I drummed on her front door, the old lady who lived next-door giving me a look of disapproval for my loud announcement.

"Did we have plans?" She opened the door, her blonde hair piled on her head in a messy bun.

"Nope, was in the neighborhood and thought I'd stop by." I leaned on the doorjamb and waited for the invitation. "Did you want me to give you a minute so you can sneak out your boyfriend? I can turn around, pretend I didn't see."

She laughed, throwing her head back as her eyes lit up.

"He left an hour ago, why do you think I'm ready for bed? He completely wore me out." She cracked open the door wider to reveal her favorite sleepwear, a pair of shorts and T-shirt combo made me harder than anything in a Victoria Secret's catalog.

Don't let the game fool you. If there was even the *slightest* possibility there was a dude she was seeing, I'd probably hunt him down and rip his balls clean off. Clean. Off. Then I'd probably feed them to him just so he got the message. Lucky for me—and the general male population—she had shown no interest in other dudes. Thank you and hallelujah.

"You wanna do something tonight?" I walked into her apartment trying to keep my eyes off her ass as she walked in front of me. The hard-on-of-death already pitching a tent in my jeans.

"As in . . ." She sunk her ass down onto her couch and motioned for me to do the same.

And wouldn't you know, the T-shirt she *loved* to wear to bed had gotten a little tighter since the last time I'd seen it. The curve of her tits being showcased like a brand new car on a game show. *I'll take blue balls for one hundred, Alex.* It was going to be a rough night.

"I don't know, something. We've been practicing for this gig like day in, and day out and I'm about to climb the walls. You wanna come hang out at the bar?" I suggested the first thing that came into my head, my ass coming down onto the seat beside her.

Trying to keep my eyes nailed to her face took most of the effort; the fact the sentence even made sense a serious fucking bonus.

"You want to take me to the bar even though I can't drink?" She tilted her head to the side like I'd suggested we go skydiving. I guess it hadn't been my best work.

"Sure, think of how much fun it will be. I'll drink and you make sure I get home okay. We can even get burgers on the way." I leaned back into the couch and rested my arm around the back, my hand just brushing up against her neck. See, model citizen, I didn't even try to touch more.

"As exciting as that sounds—" She picked up her remote and brought the box to life. "—I'm going to have to take a pass. I have a hot date with *Vikings* and Dunkin Doughnuts. Nothing works up my appetite like a good raid." She smiled and then slowly licked her lips.

Jesus. Fucking. Christ.

I wasn't going to make it.

As the opening sequence burned up the screen, my dick sent out an SOS of epic proportions, signaling this was not the shit he'd signed up for while I tried to remember what Ron Jeremy looked like naked.

"You want to stay and watch? I have a dozen original glazed." She taunted as she lifted the lid of the cardboard box on the coffee table. The box and the contents of absolute zero interest to me.

"Sure," I coughed into my fist as I watched her bend forward and grab a doughnut from the box.

"There's like a billion calories in these, you want to get fat with me?" Her fingers lifted it to my mouth as her lips spread into a grin.

Two things.

She could eat about five hundred boxes of doughnuts and still not even be close to being fat.

Annnnnnnnd if I ate that doughnut from her fingers I was probably going to throw her down on the couch and *eat* like a savage. And I didn't mean the fucking doughnut.

"Nah, I'm good," I mumbled through my locked jaw, genuine fear washing through me on what would happen if I opened my mouth. "You go first to make sure they aren't poisoned."

"Who said chivalry was dead." She laughed and took a small bite. "See, perfectly safe. Delicious too. You are totally missing out." She licked the glaze off her fingers and it took everything I had not to pass the hell out.

"Awesome." I grabbed one of those bad boys and shoved it in my mouth, praying its sickly sweetness would send me into a sugar coma. Nothing fancy, just a few hours out cold so I could regain some of the feeling in my lower legs. Hopefully give my dick a reprieve because as it stood now—*stood* being the operative word—I wasn't sure the thing wasn't going to snap off.

"You're such a pig." She giggled taking another small bite.

The comparison to pork not nearly as offensive as the distance between my mouth and her body.

"I can't be good looking, charming, a monster in the sack annnnd have perfect manners, babe. We have to give the rest of humanity a chance." I moved my hand a little lower, coming to rest on her shoulder. Still acceptable without breaking my PG rule.

"True." She leaned into me, her head resting on my shoulder. "If I fall asleep, don't eat all the doughnuts," she whispered against my chest, the tiny vibrations making my dick punch out against my fly.

"Trust me, Kenz." I gave her a quick kiss on the top of her head. "Doughnuts are the last thing on my mind right now."

Fourteen

Kenzie

I had no idea why, but I was nervous.
Maybe it was because I still hadn't told my parents, just wanting to live in my bubble a little longer. Or maybe it was something else.

Butterflies were flapping wildly in my stomach and I couldn't stand still. I had gone completely overboard, spending hours obsessing over clothes and hair was something I hardly ever did. But tonight was special; it was Joey's big night and I wanted to look amazing.

Of course it was because I hadn't gone out in a really long time, and *not* because he had been so absolutely amazing in the last few weeks. That had nothing to do with the fact I was flipping between excited and I-am-going-to-pee-my-pants.

"Can you tell I'm pregnant? I probably can't pull this off anymore. I swear my tits are like three times their usual size." I poked at the top of my dress, my ample boob-age straining against the neckline. I'd always assumed it would take months before I looked any different, but small changes were starting to happen. The biggest one—my breasts.

"You look hot, I'd totally do you." Sara waved off my concern with a flick of her wrist, her eyes coming to settle on the topic of conversation. "And your tits are definitely bigger."

"I should have changed." I tugged the hem of my dress, the length against my thigh sacrificed to compensate for my growing assets. "You'd tell me if I looked ridiculous, right?"

I was nervous enough tonight with just the Joey component, fussing over my outfit choice was a stress I didn't need. Goddamit, I should have worn something else.

"I just offered to sleep with you and I'm straight. If that isn't a ringing endorsement then there is no hope for you. The dress is fine." Sara folded her arms across her chest, annoyed I didn't believe her. She was right; the dress was fine. *It was fine. It was fine.* I repeated in my head.

"So that's how it's going to be tonight? Talk about tits and whether or not we'd fuck each other?" Becca wandered over, her hands straining with three bottles of beer and a water contained within them.

"Only *Kenzie's* tits, and probably because they need their own zip code." Abbey grabbed a bottle as her eyes also took up residence in my chest region. "Wow, do you think they are going to get much bigger?"

"Okay, you can all stop now." I rolled my eyes, twisting the top off the water wishing it was something with a little more kick. Sure as hell could have used it right now to take the edge off whatever it was I was feeling.

"Just putting it out there but I prefer dick, girls aren't my flavor." Becca's grin hidden behind the bottle as she lifted it to her lips.

"Like I'd sleep with any of you." I scoffed, glad I had the kind of friends who would even indulge this kind of conversation. "I know where you've all been."

"Wow, kettle black much pot?" Abbey laughed, her eyes twinkling with mischief. "And who are we here to see again? Oh . . . that's right, the dude whose baby you're carrying."

"She has a point." Becca nodded as if seriously weighing Abbey's words. "If anyone is displaying whore-like behavior, it's you, Kenz."

I laughed, the word *whore* often being used by one or more of us as a term of endearment, something most people didn't understand. The power and sting being removed from something all of us had been branded with for most of our adult lives.

"You're all whores." Sara agreed, sipping her beer with enthusiasm.

CJ's was packed to the brim, as it was every night—but tonight was special. Wall-to-wall people from varying walks of life had all gathered in the same place of worship to celebrate a common god. Music.

We'd waited two weeks for the night to finally get here. Black Addiction had been working their asses off if the amount of rehearsal was anything to go by, and I was excited I got to share it with Joey. The girls were along for moral support.

Nestled away in what used to be a bad part of town, was the iconic bar-come-club that for most of us was the Holy Grail. Legends were made and Goliaths tumbled, all on the same simple wooden stage. And through it all, the dirty red-bricked building exterior had remained unchanged.

Unlike standard clubs, CJ's didn't separate the talent from the mortals. All of us were thrown together as equals until someone stepped up onto the stage. The mingle that happened before and after, just as important.

"Ladies," Rusty, Black Addiction's talented guitarist greeted us. "I didn't think they let your kind in here?"

"You mean incredibly talented?" I laughed, wondering where the rest of his band was. More like just one member in particular. "We're here in case someone needs to show you how it's done. Just give me a wave Rus, if the playing gets too complicated."

"The wave won't be happening, Kenz." The assurance Rusty gave wasn't necessary. He was an amazing guitar player.

"So, where's the baby daddy?" Sara's head whipped around, noticing no other members of Black Addiction.

While I had been wondering the same thing, subtlety wasn't in her repertoire.

"Yeah, I have to congratulate him. Seems all this time I was wrong and he *did* actually have a penis." Becca laughed, enjoying herself even if it was at my expense and Joey's. Thankfully he wasn't around to hear her.

Abbey nodded in agreement. "Got to hand it to our girl for finding it, she's a regular *Magellan*."

"I hate you all." I shook my head reminding myself it had been me who suggested we all come to CJ's. "Ignore them, Rus, it's what I do."

"You girls are sick and twisted." Rusty's eyes moved slowly between each of us before breaking out into a smile. "And I fucking love that, we should tour together."

"Name the time and place," I said even though I knew it was a bullshit offer, allowing myself to indulge the fantasy. Being on tour with Joey would be a dream come true. *Funny how not so long ago I wouldn't have even considered the idea, and now I would give my right arm for it.*

"Time and place for what?" Joe appeared behind us, the man of the moment gracing us with his appearance.

And holy shit.

Wow.

Just hearing his voice made my heart start beating a little faster. I didn't even have to see him, with just those words enough to make my panties wet. While I'd always had an attraction to him, it had somehow amplified. Now

I was a walking talking homing beacon whenever the man opened his mouth.

My skin prickled as I turned around, my eyes getting wider the minute I saw him. Which was ridiculous, because I'd seen him only a few days ago.

But tonight it was different.

He looked *good*.

Really good.

He was stage ready with a pair of dark-blue torn jeans, heavy black boots and black fitted-Tee. His colorful tattoos poked out from underneath the snug fabric, looking every inch the rock star. Irrational jealousy spiked inside of me, wishing I could be that shirt. Or at least, touch what was under it. What the hell was I saying? It was hot, the temperature in the club playing with my internal biology.

"Gang bang, Joe. You want in?" Rusty threw out the line, ready to reel him in.

Had to admit I really respected Rusty. Not only because he was amazing at what he did on stage, but also because he was really pulling my ass from the fire right now. Saving me from looking like an idiot while I stood there gaping like a goldfish.

His efforts infinitely helpful at the moment considering I was warring with some conflicted emotions. The ones where I was more interested in whether this club had bathrooms that locked rather than what was about to go down on stage.

"What?" Joey's smile slipped as he turned to his guitarist. He hadn't even taken the bait where sex was mentioned. Perhaps he hadn't heard correctly. Not that *I* was interested. No, of course not.

"Hey Joey/loser/douchebag/dumbass," polluted the air. His actual name only spoken by me. I tried to make it sound normal, even though no part of me actually felt that way.

"Rus, you should have told me the circus was in town." Joey grinned, looking and nodding toward the girls.

While he may have initially been thrown off his game, he was back in standard form. His joke earning a few middle fingers from the girls much to his delight.

And thank God for that. Funny Joey, I could deal with—sexy Joey, not so much.

"Actually, Joey, we have an opening for the bearded lady." I internally cheered I was able to keep it together. "Wait. That's not right." I paused before leaning in closer to him. "You're too pretty for that."

Bad idea.

A waft of his aftershave hit me, the scent dazzling me for minute. I probably shouldn't do that again, making a mental note to maintain a safer distance. A mile or two should cover it. Anything closer and I was putting myself at unnecessary risk.

"Yeah, yeah, you ladies laugh it up." He shrugged, completely unaffected by our light-hearted teasing, or my body's apparent silent inferno. "But prepare for greatness, we're going to explode on that stage tonight. I didn't come all this way to choke."

I coughed, clearing my throat and tried to remember that the words had been unintentionally sexy. The *explosion* was for the audience, and not for my own personal enjoyment. Pity my body hadn't gotten the memo.

Not that any of us doubted he had earned his success, but we each had our reasons to poke fun at him and pretend like he wasn't ridiculously talented.

For me, it was so I didn't ask him to strip off his shirt and trace the curve of his torso with my tongue. Everyone else's reason really didn't matter at this point.

"Guys, I'd like to have a band on stage with me." A nervous looking Angie joined the group, Max not far behind. "Twenty minute warning."

Awesome, more reinforcements. There was safety in numbers and the bigger the buffer between Joey and I, the better. Considering I was having thoughts about his chest and my tongue, I needed all the help I could get.

"Ladies." Max tipped his chin hello, Angie followed by giving us a wave in greeting.

"Looks like it's show time." Rusty nodded to Angie who was clearly about to hyperventilate. She wasn't the only one. "And the spotlight waits for no one."

"Seriously, Rus. Not everything has to sound like a fortune cookie." Angie shoved Rusty as the two of them and, Max ambled toward the stage.

Which left just one member of Black Addiction.

Ah. Crap.

"We'll give you some space, let you have your awkward moment privately." We were treated to another subtle segue courtesy of Sara. It was a talent always delivered with a smile and one I didn't appreciate right now. Being alone with him wasn't smart. In fact, it was downright stupid and I had to fight the urge to beg them not to leave.

Be sarcastic, I reminded myself, anything else is a trap.

Joey and I watched as the girls made a hilarious display of trying to discreetly move to the bar. They needn't have bothered. I was happy to have my awkward moment with an audience—encouraged it in fact—but they weren't to know that.

The consideration they'd shown was enough to make my heart swell, even if it had left me hanging out to dry. *Sarcasm*, I recited, and *don't look at him too much*.

"You feeling all right?" Joey asked when we were finally alone. The question offered with what appeared to be no hidden agenda. Or at least I hoped he hadn't suddenly developed mind reading abilities or that awkward moment was definitely going to happen.

"Aren't I supposed to be asking you that?" I deflected, and praise baby Jesus I still had some fight in me. It hadn't been easy.

Despite what *I* was feeling tonight, things hadn't changed between us. We were happily planning to stave off the weird and keep it friendly between us. It wouldn't be worth tossing it all away purely for instant gratification. Or would it? No. No it wouldn't. Why was I struggling so much tonight?

"You can reach down and feel for yourself if you want." His eyebrow rose suggestively as the outer edges of his lips curled into a grin.

So. Not. Helping.

My hand jerked at my side, ready to volunteer as tribute as I nervously laughed like an idiot hoping to God he didn't ask again. I wasn't sure I'd be so strong, especially when he was offering. How much trouble could I get into just by touching?

It was just Joey, I rationalized. Talking about his penis and sex was normal. Making me laugh like he always did. Ha. Ha. Ha. This was so *not* funny.

"Dream on," I responded between giggles. My hand locked to my side so I wouldn't be tempted as my libido mocked me—the son-of-bitch determining now was a good time to come back online.

"Joey, ten minutes," a voice called from the distance. My silent thanks were offered to the owner of the mysterious voice and their random act of kindness. Their intervention saved me from making an ass of myself.

"You going to stay after the show?" Joey raised a hand in the universal signal for hold-on, his attention not leaving me. "Hang out with us."

Not good, I didn't need any extra encouragement.

"Sure. Someone needs to keep you grounded." I had no intention of going anywhere. Not sure I could at this point.

"Good. I'm glad." The tension in his shoulders seemed to ease, perhaps not expecting me to stay. "I need to go. See you later."

And with a wave he disappeared, dissolving into the crowd of people until I was left standing by myself.

Panting.

Like a moron.

"Aww you guys are so cute, I threw up in my mouth a little bit." Sara threw her arm around my shoulder and pulled me into a hug. Becca and Abbey returned as well, this time they had more drinks.

Mentally I checked myself, shaking off the crazy as I concentrated on my friends and not the sexy drummer who'd just walked away.

"I'm glad you swallowed. Spitting is for quitters." I hugged Sara back, metaphorically getting back in the saddle.

Becca laughed, handing me a second bottle of water. The first one only half consumed. "Thanks guys, like I don't already need to pee every five minutes."

At least it might help put out the flames I had going on, the forced sobriety also contributing to my hands not doing what they wanted.

"You need the hydration. It's hot in here," Becca answered, being serious for the first time since we arrived before giving me a wink. "We've got you."

Well. Shit.

An entirely different emotion overwhelmed me as I looked at my three best friends.

The act of caring done gently because they knew I hated when anyone made a fuss. A lump tightened in my throat as my eyes started to blink rapidly.

"Don't cry," Sara warned, her finger pointed at me accusingly. "Your makeup is too perfect to be ruined by tears."

"Agreed." I nodded, thankful for the mood swing but wondering if I would ever be off the hair-trigger I seemed to have.

"Let's all objectify Black Addiction instead." Abbey nodded to the stage that had started to darken. The suggestion not needed, considering it had already been my plan. Hopefully the music would also offer a distraction, it sure as hell couldn't get worse.

"And heckle, because I'm jealous," Becca added with a laugh.

The overhead lights were killed as the crowd turned their attention forward. The only illumination coming from the spotlights mounted to the ceiling truss, showcasing the still empty stage.

Other shows, other venues, usually had a build up. An Emcee who revved up the crowd or introduced the act. Sometimes a low-key intro thrown out by the DJ, but this place had none of those things.

It didn't matter if you were an ensemble or a soloist, you were expected to walk out, pick up your instrument and play.

Like an audition.

With Satan.

I was terrified for them.

My heart was in my throat as I watched them step on the stage, the nerves I felt obviously not shared by them as they readied themselves in their positions. Air popped as amps were turned on while the tap of Joey's drumsticks echoed through the boom mic. And with a silent count-in, they exploded into their first song.

Unlike a usual gig, the crowd didn't immediately break into applause. Tonight they would have to earn every single cheer, clap and whoop they got.

It didn't take long.

Slowly heads started nodding in time and bodies started to move. Next were the smiles, the noise building as Black Addition went seamless into the next song.

No showboating. No ego. Just the music.

Usually at gigs I focused on the guitarist, checking out their form and watching the magical dance of his or her fingers across the fret board. But tonight Rusty's prowess wasn't even a blip on my radar, my eyes locking on Joey.

And that is pretty much where they stayed, watching as he played through the set, each movement of his hands sharp and deliberate. The crack of the snare harmonized with the ring of the hi-hat in a ballet of noise that drove the music.

The pulse.

The heart.

The foundation.

It was so fucking hot.

Like a bear waking from hibernation, my skin tingled as the feeling spread through me. Different parts of my body checked in as the warm sensation tumbled over me in a hot wave.

I don't know why I hadn't seen it before. Why I had blown him off as just a drummer while we were all musicians, but it was arrogant at best and completely ignorant at worst. He was sensational.

I'd hoped the show would distract me from my earlier feelings—the ones where I wanted him to take me home and make sweet, sweet love—but watching him play only *stoked* those embers.

"I hate to admit it but they are pretty good," Sara shouted; the crowd louder and fully committed to the band on stage, the tide well and truly in their favor.

"Agreed," Becca shouted. "But if anyone tells them I said so, I'm denying it." She smiled, her goodwill apparently only going so far.

There really wasn't much more talking. The noise both on and off the stage drowned out the opportunity, while the talent demanded attention. My appreciation went a little further as I strategically mentally categorized every inch of Joey's body.

Arms. Hot.

Abs. Hot

Chest. Hot.

Okay, I'll admit it wasn't an adequate filing system but I was enjoying it.

"Thanks everyone, you've been great." Angie's voice signaled the end of their show. The beaming smile she wore reflected in the faces of Max, Rusty and Joey as they left their instruments where they were and took a collective bow.

The audience gave them their applause, as whistles and shouts of adulation welcomed them off stage.

It was just the heat and the playing I rationalized, I was carried away by the excitement. This stupid feeling inside me would stop now the show was over. But it didn't, the tug in my lower belly intensifying as I watched Joey climb off the stairs and mingle with the crowd. The need in me *more* than the high-fiving and hand shaking he was dishing out.

I was so fucked.

This is a really inconvenient time for me, body. Did you not get the memo? We are not sleeping with him. I tried to rationalize, but no one was listening.

"Let's go over and tell them they sucked." Becca sighed, reminding me I wasn't alone. She and I both knew she wasn't that good an actress, but I wasn't giving away a viable excuse to get closer. Because really, keeping away wasn't an option.

"I'm going to go find a bad decision to make." Sara smiled at a tall, grungy-looking, dark-haired man who was strangely missing his shirt. "We don't want Kenzie feeling lonely in her irresponsibility."

"Thanks, Sar. Just don't be an over achiever." I gave her arm a halfhearted squeeze as she headed like a heat-seeking missile in mystery man's direction.

Her departure gave me less of an audience, and I wasn't sure if I was grateful or concerned she wouldn't be around to stop me. Seemed like I had some bad decisions of my own I was contemplating.

No. I can't.

Stay focused.

Becca and Abbey decided against making their own bad decisions, instead following me to mine, the three of us heading to the bar where Black Addiction had stalled. Their progression any further into the club stopped by the sea of people looking for face time. It was a good problem to have. Meant the chance of me doing anything stupid was minimized, there was no way I could be trusted.

"So, tell me how awesome I was." Joey grabbed me from behind, pulling me close to his body and squeezed. "How many times did you almost come? Be honest."

His hand on me was like a lightning rod, electrifying each nerve as he touched me. He had no idea what he had done. I swallowed hard as I begged my body not to betray me.

"Not even once. You weren't that great." I lied as I feigned a yawn, praying to God he bought it. "Glad it's over actually."

"Hmm." He turned his head to the side as if to consider. His dark eyes smoldering as he looked into mine.

I couldn't breathe.

Every part of me short-circuited as I focused on his face, completely distracted.

Which is why I didn't realize until it was too late that he'd moved closer, his lips covering mine as he sealed them in a kiss.

Oh. My. God.

Now I *really* couldn't breathe.

There would be no coming back from this.

I didn't care we were in public or that he hadn't even asked to kiss me, his tongue teased through my lips as he explored my mouth. His hand cradled my head as he brought me closer, kissing me harder as every cell in my body exploded like a fourth of July firework.

"So," he whispered against my lips, separating his mouth from mine. "That's what lies taste like." He was unable to hide the satisfied grin as I blinked back in silence.

Do. Not. Sleep. With. Him.

My mouth opened and closed wordlessly, as I tried to think of something to say.

Nope.

Nothing.

"Joey, don't eat Kenzie." Rusty thankfully broke my catatonic trance, giving Joey a stern look. "And it's rude to talk with your mouth full."

"Kenzie, did he break you?" Becca asked concerned as to why I hadn't taken a swing, either verbally or otherwise. I rarely let anyone have the last word, especially Joey. And I'd been doing so well. Did he really have to kiss me? He might as well have laid down naked and offered himself to me, because essentially that's what the kiss felt like.

"I need the bathroom," I mumbled and turned before anyone had a chance to stop me. The bodies in front of me not making it easy for me to hurry the hell up.

"Kenzie, wait." I felt an arm stopping me and pulling me back. The bathroom door only a few feet away, and yet still too far.

"It was a joke, I'm sorry." Joey spun me around, his fingers wrapped tightly around my arm. No intention of letting me go. "You were supposed to tell me to go to hell, or go jerk off. I wasn't trying to be an asshole." His face remorseful.

Although I had torn out of there like a bat-out-of-hell, it hadn't been my feelings that had been hurt, quite the opposite actually.

I wanted that kiss, desperately. And what's worse, I wanted it again.

I was pissed off.

At myself mostly.

And at him too, for looking like that.

"No, it's fine," I lied, trying to brush it off. "It was just the heat and then you were on me, I couldn't breathe. I felt sick." The only truth to that statement was I couldn't inhale air, and that had nothing to do with the temperature.

"You want me to take you home?" Joey's hands didn't move, locked on me as bodies bumped into us. Our presence not important to them other than we were currently in their way.

"No. You should stay." My head shook, hopefully convincing myself it was not a good idea. "I'm just not feeling great. I'll get a cab."

"Like hell you are." His tone sharpened, reinforcing he had no plans to slink off into the darkness like I so desperately wanted. "I'm not putting you in a cab when you just admitted you don't feel well. Look, be pissed at me for being a dick but let me get you home."

Trouble.

That's exactly where this was heading.

"Okay but if you kiss me again, I'm throwing up on you." I summoned every ounce of bravado I had as I forced a smile, the crazed exaggerated grin hopefully far from sexy.

"See, now that's what I was expecting." He gave me a hug and pulled me in closer. *Not helping* my brain screamed as I returned the hug.

"Just let me tell Max what's going down and we'll get out of here. He'll take care of my kit." Joey grabbed my hand pulling me back in the direction of the bar.

The opportunity for me to run came and went.

It was too late now.

Well done, Kenzie.

Welcome to the dark side.

Fifteen
Joey

I'd kissed her.

It was exactly what I had wanted to do from the minute I saw her. Walking up to her and seeing her talking with Rusty was like a kick in the balls and not the kind she'd been threatening me with.

Her hair hung loose around her shoulders like a golden mess of cotton candy, highlighting her bright blue eyes that refused to stay still. The hot pink lips also did me in, sending up a flare that if I didn't kiss them tonight, someone else would.

It was enough to drive me motherfucking insane.

And that was just her face; her body was another story. That dress she was wearing had wrapped her curves like a sexy birthday present. Just begging to be unwrapped and there wasn't a man alive who would have been able to resist. Well, certainly not this one.

Not that my cock didn't harden almost every time I

saw her, but for the past few weeks I'd pushed all that aside and tried to be good. Not because I didn't want her, but because I wanted it to be about her.

I would have happily been used as an instrument of pleasure if she'd wanted it, fuck, even if she just needed me as a distraction. That's how fucking far-gone I was. And I didn't give a fuck how pussy whipped that made me sound, I welcomed it. Happy to give her whatever she needed.

Tonight, however, I was a little ashamed to admit it wasn't about her. She looked different, and it wasn't just the clothes. Hell, I had no idea what it actually was, but I had used up my reserves of polite.

In any case, playing nice wasn't what I wanted to do. My adrenaline had already been jacked up just with the thought of being on stage, getting a look at her—the extra shot taking me into the danger zone. *Sorry Goose, but it's time to buzz the tower.*

I'd fucking given it a red-hot go at keeping it nice, moving the conversation along and tried to be my usual charming self. The to-and-fro with sexual banter was par for the course with us, so I had to throw that in there too. If I suddenly stopped talking like I usually did she would have immediately known something was up. Like hiding in plain sight, I kept the dick jokes coming and ignored that my own was as hard as stone.

Great.

Fucking.

Plan.

In an act of God—or possibly the Devil, I hadn't decided which—I'd gotten the call to action to jump on stage and take care of business. You know, do what we'd actually come here to do. Which I did, walked away and sat behind my kit even though my primal instinct was to kiss her first. It was a feeling that overrode sanity and I knew if she happened to be sticking around after I got off stage, neither of us would stand a chance.

So I let fate decide.

And *fate* had fucking spoken.

I took the chance the first opportunity I got and I didn't even give a fuck I had to play it off as some kind of joke. However I got there didn't matter, I claimed those lips like they'd always been mine, and kissed her so fierce there was no mistake about what I was doing.

Unfortunately I had been the only one who'd felt it.

I figured it could have gone two ways. She would either cuss me out and possibly take a swing, or she would take what I was offering and let the sexual healing commence.

Neither of those things happened.

Instead she stared back at me like I was the Apocalypse and his four horsemen, and then pulled a duck-and-run.

Kenzie never ran.

Ever.

So I knew that I'd fucked up, and I'd do whatever I

needed to do make it right. The drive I'd offered her, the least I could do.

She sat in silence, staring out the windshield at the road in front of us like it was suddenly going to start handing out divine guidance. With one hand in her lap, the other white knuckled the passenger door handle as she barely made eye contact the whole ride home.

Answering every single one of my *are you okay's* with a generic *fine*.

I was such a dick.

"You can yell at me if you want," I offered, selfishly preferring her to call me a fucktard rather than sit there in further silence. The car eased into a parking spot in front of her apartment.

"I don't want to yell." She stared out the window like she hadn't realized we'd stopped moving. "I said I was fine."

"Let me get you in and settled then." I opened the car door and ejected before she told me she didn't want me to come in. The chance of leaving shit like it was, not an option.

"This isn't necessary." She was out of the truck before I'd reached her side, my instincts fired up being so close.

"Since when have I ever done what was necessary? Come on, Kenzie, you know I'm not a practical kind of guy."

No response.

Nada.

Zip.

Instead she turned and trudged to her door, resigned that I was following her and pretending to ignore me.

Not sure which was worse. The silence or the indifference. Both pissed me off as she opened her front door and walked inside like I was a ghost behind her. Her keys tossed on the side table, leaving me to close the front door as she disappeared down the hall.

What the fuck? Was she avoiding me now?

"You want some crackers or something?" I followed her into the bedroom ignoring the five hundred I'm-fines she had fed me since we'd left the bar. The offer of Saltines, partially because I knew they made her feel better and partially because I wasn't letting this go.

"No, I'm fine."

Make that five hundred and one. She sat on the bed and kicked off her shoes, reaching down to rub her bare feet, the action of bending down treating me to a big eyeful of cleavage.

Oh. Hell.

"Maybe I should stay here tonight," I said a little too quickly, sitting down on the bed beside her before she got a chance to look up and see the bulge in my pants. "In case you need something."

Yeah, because *that* was the reason, you lying sack of shit. The chance of my dick being that *something* was also not fucking likely. Were we having fun yet? I really wished she'd snap out of whatever the fuck was going on and call me a dick.

"Joey, really. You can go I'm—"

"Yeah, you're *fine*. You've said." I cut her off, not needing to hear that word again.

"Well, if you'd listened the first time, maybe I wouldn't have to repeat myself," she snapped back, meeting my eyes for the first time since we'd walked in.

Jesus Christ, finally!

"Maybe I like hearing you talk, ever think of that?" I cracked a smile knowing it would probably piss her off, which was better than the lack of emotions I'd been dealing with.

Her eyes stayed on me but her mouth clamped shut. Her lips twitched like they were begging to say something but still she didn't cave.

"What, no come back? That's twice tonight you let it go, Kenzie. So either you are sicker than you are letting on, or something is wrong." And I was going to find out which because let's face it, I had nowhere else to be.

"I'm just tired of arguing with you. You're exhausting," she spat out, the fire returning to her eyes and I'll be damned if I wasn't going to push a little further.

"Bullshit. You love it." I smirked back. "So what gives? It was the kiss, wasn't it? Too far?"

Ha, not far enough if you asked me but then again, we already knew where I sat on that debate.

"No, the kiss was fine."

Five hundred and two.

Two things. I did not expect her to say she was cool with it, and that kiss I'd given her was soooooo far from fucking fine. In fact, if it was only *fine* then I wanted a do-over to prove she'd been mistaken. Because that's why I wanted to kiss her again, not because the first time I had done it tonight hadn't been nearly long enough.

"Really, the kiss was fine?" I waded into dangerous territory and I cupped her face in my hands and moved in closer. I waited for *fuck off* to come.

Any minute now.

Still waiting.

It didn't happen. And because I was a selfish asshole, I saw it as a green light. My mouth moved closer, not stopping until it was on her and not in a way that meant anything *friendly*.

Hungry.

My lips devoured hers as my tongue filled her mouth, my hands bringing her face closer because I couldn't get enough.

She whimpered but I didn't stop, her mouth moving against mine gave me all the encouragement I needed, gently biting her lips as I prayed to God this wouldn't be the last time.

"Still fine?" My mouth moved away from her lips, desperate to touch more of her, getting familiar with skin before she came to her senses and called time out. The thought it could be over at any minute pushed me a little further, moving my hand up her body and palming a tit, the gentle squeeze under my fingers teasing out a strangled "yes" from her lips.

"Fuck." I couldn't stop as I moved back to her mouth, the moan muffled by my tongue that was desperate to get inside of her. My hands completely rogue as they moved over her body, wanting to touch every inch, and it still wasn't enough.

I had no idea what we were doing, if she wanted this or if I hadn't fucking fallen into a coma and was somehow imagining this whole thing. Parts of my brain misfired trying to slow me down, the roar in me to keep going, fucking out of control.

"Do you want me to stop?" I asked, hoping like hell she wouldn't say yes but needing to give her a chance to walk if she wanted it. My dick punched against my fly, its shut-the-fuck-up protest ignored while I waited for her to answer.

"No." Her hands bunched the sides of my T-shirt and pulled me down on top of her. The hard-on that had been so desperate to get noticed hit her right in the sweet spot between her legs. The moan it earned made me push my hips in harder.

"This fucking dress is killing me." I groaned against her throat as my hands slowly traveled down her sides, following the contours of her body. "Driving me insane." I stopped for a minute to admire the view. And, Jesus, if I wasn't already worshiping her with my mouth, I'd have started a new religious order.

"It's too tight, my tits look huge." She pulled me back down, her fingernails grazing me as she tore off my shirt. My assist needed to toss it to the floor. Clothes were not our friends tonight.

"It's fucking perfect, and don't you dare trash talk your tits." I lowered my head and kissed between them to prove the point. "I fucking love your tits."

As much as I liked the dress—seriously, well done—I needed it off. Like yesterday. My hands got busy peeling the fabric from her body while my mouth welcomed the newly-exposed skin. It was a good system. Efficient.

The dress didn't stand a chance, joining my shirt on the floor, which with any luck would hopefully be reunited with my pants. I couldn't be sure how far Kenzie would let it go, but any stopping wouldn't be coming from my side.

"Joey, remember the agreement we made?" She grabbed my face forcing me to look her in the eyes, her chest heaving up and down as she tried to suck in air.

"Kenzie, I've got a hard-on right now that could cut glass. I can barely remember how to talk and breathe at the same time." My hand smoothed the strands of hair that had covered her face. "You're going to have to spell out *exactly* what agreement you're talking about."

My mind tried to do a quick inventory of the past couple of weeks.

Nope.

No dice.

"The one where you said if I wanted to have sex, that you would do it." Her hands moved up and down my arms that had been caging her in.

There was some sort of debate that had gone on in her head. One that moved her from I-never-want-to-see-your-dick-again, to okay-show-me-your-dick. I hadn't been a part of the conversation and honestly, I didn't really care but I was very, very glad of the outcome. My dick was too.

"Babe, right now I'd probably eat my own cock if you asked." My mouth moved to her throat, my tongue and lips alternating as to which was getting the action.

"So . . . that's a yes then?" She laughed, tilting her hips against me, working up the friction between us, a satisfied mewl spilling from her lips when she got what she needed.

That noise was enough to snap whatever sanity I had left, pissed off we weren't completely naked yet and that she'd be only using my length to get herself off. That wouldn't do. My hand, my mouth—all of it would have to get a turn first and then when I was satisfied she had come hard enough, I'd give her my cock.

I grabbed her, pulling her close and wanting to get closer. That bra that was doing a sensational job of framing her tits needed to burn, *burn* right the hell off her so I could get at what was underneath. And I would burn right along with it because my hands on her skin weren't getting enough.

"Fuck, Kenzie." I tore at the snap at the back, the piece of shit clasp not strong enough and coming apart in my hand. The damaged scrap of lace getting tossed to the floor as I moved my mouth to her naked tits. "I'm so fucking hungry for you, I can't see straight."

"I want . . . I want . . ." She tried twice unsuccessfully to finish her sentence as my tongue swirled around her tits, her pink peaks getting extra attention as I sucked on them hard.

"Anything, tell me. I'll give it you." My car. My house. My balls. All were on the table ready for the taking.

"Touch me, everywhere." Her hand moved between her legs, sliding in between her panties. The show-and-tell not needed as I made quick work of destroying that piece of lace too.

"Shit." She moaned as I tossed what was left of her panties on to the floor.

My hands fumbled with my fly like a virgin with zero motor skills, my finger coming off second best against the bite of my zipper. Care factor remained zero as I toed off my boots and wrenched off my jeans. The whole process only took two minutes, which was exactly two minutes longer than I'd wanted.

"Touch me," she moaned reaching out and palming my cock through my boxers, the bastard getting harder in her hand to show his appreciation.

Like a blind man trying to read the word of God, my hands were all over her like my life fucking depended on it. Which was partially true, because if I stopped at this point I wasn't sure I wouldn't stroke out. My fingers at war as to which place they wanted to go. Her tits got the attention first.

"Joey." My name on her lips with a desperation that almost made me come.

While my hands and mouth had been on her before, my brain kicked into overdrive that the playtime hadn't been long enough. Nope. She needed to be appreciated and I didn't think I'd properly proven my point. My mouth suddenly annoyed that it had to leave her tits in the first place went to them in a dead run, my lips wanting to curl around the tight pink peaks that were calling to me like a fucking beacon.

I wasn't gentle, my tongue hitting her skin drew out a moan and a shiver, I wasn't sure I hadn't already got her there. Not that I would stop, continuing my assault on her skin until she was liquid. Her hands locked around my head were the only encouragement I needed to keep going as I continued my little tour south.

"Yes." Her back bowed off the bed as my hands and mouth moved over her stomach, the rounded warm skin goose pimpling under my touch. My journey not even close to being finished.

"God, I want to go down on you so fucking bad." I barely recognized my own voice as I caught sight of the soft pink skin between her legs.

"Do it." She arched, throwing her head back.

Her legs parted, welcoming my mouth as I booked my one-way trip to the Promised Land. Her hot core was already drenched by the time my lips reached it, my fingers begging to be part of the tag team.

It was too much.

All it took was one pass of my tongue, her heat coating me instantly as I lapped her. Like she'd suddenly jammed pins into an electric socket, Kenzie's body jacked up off the bed, bringing the action closer to my mouth. The constant streams of "yes" all I needed to hear.

I couldn't stop. I wanted more, needed more, her taste on my tongue magic as I stretched her out with one of my fingers. It wasn't enough, her body bucking against me as I added another, her breathing becoming so rapid I wasn't sure I should keep going.

My cock strained against my boxers, trying to find the ejection handle, no longer happy at being contained. My free hand reached down and pushed the boxers down past my hips, my legs doing their best to help the cause as I kicked my way out of them. My dick jerked as the cold air hit my exposed skin.

Blood roared in my ears as I tried to slow down and be gentle, but it was no use. The unrelenting assault of my mouth and fingers made her explode within minutes, her core contracting around me in tiny pulses. Her back hit the mattress, sated and lax as the satisfaction of a job well done sent a shiver right down to my cock. The bastard was desperate to take over, disappointed he hadn't been in the first string.

"Kenzie, I need to be in you."

No shit, Sherlock.

I'd barely got the words out as I scrambled up the bed, her body underneath mine still shaking as the last echoes of her orgasm rang through her. My length filled her in one, long stroke. My intention to make it slow obviously got lost in the translation as I pulled out and pushed into her again. Her slick center so ready for me, I had to fight the urge to come.

Oh, hell, no. I gritted my teeth refusing for it to end in forty-five seconds, no matter how fucking good it felt. There was no way I would finish, at least not before I made her come again.

"Yes." She grabbed my ass and thrust me forward; getting me in so deep that every inch was buried inside her.

Her fingernails bit at my skin, digging into my ass. The sting juiced me up further as I thrust into her as hard as I could.

"Like that?" I gritted out through clenched teeth, hoping like fuck I wasn't hurting her. If she had wanted gentle, I had failed miserably. My body pistoning as she continued to squirm underneath.

"Yes, harder. Yes like that." Her voice halfway between a shout and moan as she clawed at my back.

"I can't get enough." My hips continued to thrust as my arms locked on either side of her body so I wasn't crushing her. My weight on her frame obviously not a concern for her as she tried to pull me back.

"God, you're beautiful." I gave up trying to fight her hands, grabbing her knees and got just a little more leverage. The slight change in angle enough to send her into orbit one more time, her pussy gripping me like a fist as she screamed out my name.

"Shit, Kenze. I need to come."

It wouldn't have mattered how much I wanted to prolong it; I had lost all control. Chasing me down like a motherfucking typhoon, the force knocking me so hard my arms and legs gave way under me.

"Holy shit. Yes, yes." I couldn't stop, pumping into her as my cock jerked, filling her with my load as I smothered her with my body.

"Yes, that feels so good. Yes." She held on tight, stopping me from pulling out, her legs wrapping around my ass in case I hadn't gotten the hint.

Which was when I realized.

No condom.

"Ah, fuck." I cursed out a breath as my head fell into the crook of her neck.

"No, no it's fine." Kenz's fingers knotted in my hair, a small chuckle traveling up her throat. "We weren't weird after sex the first time; we will be totally fine this time too."

Yeah, not what I had been worried about.

I lifted my head, her beautiful eyes completely devoid

of any concern. "That's not what I meant. Kenzie, I'm not wearing anything." My head tilted down toward our bodies in case she needed a visual cue.

"Oh." Her mouth formed an O as she got up to speed. "Condoms seem to be a problem for us."

"Yeah, we don't have the best track record." More like fucking terrible. "I'm sorry, I should have asked."

There wasn't a doubt in my mind I had a clean bill of health. I kept myself checked out and other than with Kenzie, I'd been wearing condoms religiously for years. Which is a conversation we probably should have had a while ago, but it got pushed to the side. I didn't expect her to know all of that, or trust that shit was all fine and dandy. It was a dick move—literally—to go in bare without her permission.

"You can only get me pregnant once, Joey." She laughed, shifting below while I was still semi hard inside her. "I think most of the damage was already done."

"That's not what I meant." I grinned, thankful she didn't go all *Call of Duty* on my ass. Let's face it, she was entitled. "I want you to know I don't make a habit of this. I mean, other than you. That had been a first for me in a really long time and tonight, well I obviously lack any sort of control whenever I get anywhere close to your pussy."

Honestly, I was powerless against it. The stats didn't lie.

"Joey, it's no different than anyone else's." She rolled her eyes, completely clueless as to what she was saying.

"Kenz, you saying that proves you have no idea what you're talking about." Seriously, fucking clueless. "I could fucking live in there, buried in its magical treasure forever. So, no it's *not* like anyone else's."

"That's really creepy." She screwed her face up in a grimace not appreciating my pussy worship.

"Just embrace it, babe. There's no fighting it, trust me." I laughed, slowly pulling out of her and rolling to my side. My cock was already limbering up in case there was a round two.

"Also," I cleared my throat not wanting to throw a spanner in the works now she was acting normal. Last thing we needed was for her to go back to ignoring me. That wouldn't fly a second time. "We need to address the elephant in the room."

"I overreacted." Kenz rolled to face me, her cheeks still pink from the sex "I don't even know why I did it." Her words came out in a rush before I'd had a chance to respond. "But I saw you, and you were being all sexy. And then you *kissed* me and threw me off. I was trying to stop myself from being weird because it had been my idea to keep it platonic." She continued to babble barely pausing for a breath. "See, stupid. I don't know what came over me. Maybe I was wrong about the hormone thing because tonight I felt like a cat in heat."

Silence.

"Yeah, that's not what I was asking about." I grinned, happy to hear what had been on her mind but not really needing the run down.

"You *weren't* going to ask me why I gave you the cold shoulder?" Her eyebrows arched like it would have been the only logical question.

"Well, no." I admitted, praying I didn't stick my foot in it. Honestly, it could go either way. "Not because I don't give a shit, but because you seem fine now, so obviously my cock fixed whatever the problem was. He's good like that."

"God, Joey." Kenz's fingers squeezed the bridge of her nose. "You really are making me rethink this." Her head shook slightly before it turned back to me. "So. Tell me. If it's not about me being weird . . ."

"No."

"And it's not about us having sex even after we agreed we wouldn't . . ."

"No."

"So, what?" she asked, completely bewildered.

"I mean the bet, which you obviously lost."

Not to be an asshole, but I had sort of said she would cave before me. Which she did when she begged me for sex. Not to say it wouldn't have been me. Lord knows I'd been tempted to beg before, and after seeing her in that dress—I would have spent the night on my knees.

"Um, I don't recall saying anything *remotely* close to the agreed term." She narrowed her eyes; probably annoyed I'd called her on it.

"Fucking semantics, Kenz and you know it." I pointed

at her, unable to hide my grin. "*You* wanted sex. *You* lose."

"You started it, *you* plied my body with all of *that*—" She waved her arms in front of my chest. "So there was no way I would do anything but ask for it. This was your plan all along so it doesn't count." She tipped her chin defiantly.

"I did no such thing." I scoffed, wondering how the fuck she was pinning it on me. "And what the fuck does all of *that*—" I mimicked her hand action over my chest. "—mean? I didn't hypnotize you with my cock." Pretty cool trick if it were possible, but it wasn't. I knew this because if it *were* true, we would have had sex the day I met her, and *not* months after.

"So we have a stalemate then." She folded her arms across her chest, which pushed up her boobs. I tried not to look because if I did, I would have agreed to anything.

"Which means, what?" *Keep your eyes on her face, keep your eyes on her face.* "We're still allowed to jerk off, right?"

"Would you have had sex with me if the answer would have been no?" She tilted her head as she waited for me to answer.

"I would have given up jerking off just to kiss you tonight."

The words came out of my mouth before I'd had the chance to change them. Call me a pussy, but it was the absolute truth. That kiss would totally have been worth keeping my hands off the snake for a week.

"Why do you have to go and be so sweet?" Her face softened into a smile before giving me a pop in the arm with her fist.

"Sorry." I shrugged, the punch—if you could call it that—more of a tickle than a hit. "I'm still high from the buzz. Give me a few minutes and I'll say something inappropriate." I grabbed her waist and brought her closer.

"You want to stay over?" She bit her lip as her hands ran down my shoulders—the sensation really fucking nice.

"Is that so you can hear me say something inappropriate?" Wanting to make sure I wasn't misreading the situation.

"No, it's so we can do *that* again."

Situation had *not* been misread.

"Oh, yeah?" I shot her a grin, wondering how many times I was going to be able to make her come tonight. "You just can't keep away from all of *this* huh?" I grabbed her hand and ran it down my chest.

"It must be hormones because I don't remember it being this good the first time."

"It's not the hormones." I brought my face closer, my lips inches away from hers. "I am just that good."

"And . . . he's back."

Sixteen
Kenzie

It was hot.

My body was overheating like the internal furnace had been turned up to maximum. But it wasn't a freak fire consuming my bed whole, it was a Joey blanket that had wrapped itself tightly up against my skin.

"Too hot," I whispered in his ear, loving the feel of his hands on me but hating the sensation of dying. Perhaps I was already on my way to Hell, I wouldn't be surprised of anything right now.

"Ah, babe. You want sex again?" He kissed my shoulder and moved his hand to my breast. His erection already awake and poking me in the hip.

"No, I just need some air." I was finally able to breathe as he loosened his grip, still maintaining contact while allowing me my freedom.

"And then sex?" He laughed in my ear as the kissing moved to my neck. "You know we denied ourselves too long. That wasn't healthy. Whose stupid idea was that anyway?"

"Um. Yours." With my free hand I poked him in the chest, the same chest I spent the better part of the night licking.

"No, *mine* was the no sex with other people. I'm pretty sure you're the one who didn't want this."

Who remembered anything any more? It seemed like we'd made a whole bunch of bad decisions. The first being that I didn't want this as much as I had. Or that what had happened between us was just sex. Maybe it had been just sex in the past, but it wasn't anymore. I had feelings for him, and while I admit it was the ones that tingled in my girlie parts that were running the show tonight, it had been the others that had asked him to stay. The hours when he'd held me, a calm I hadn't felt in weeks.

"Clearly I was crazy." I nestled up closer to him, ignoring that my body was still an inferno. The need to touch him was greater than my personal comfort right now.

"And I was crazy to agree." He nipped at my shoulder, his teeth grazing my skin. "I like this situation a whole lot better."

"Because you had sex?" I turned, wondering how much of this was because he was sex drunk.

"No, because I have you."

It would have been easy for him to say something silly.

An innuendo. But he didn't. Instead he locked eyes with me and kissed me slowly, his hands sliding over my body.

"It's not the sex I wanted, it was you," he whispered between kisses.

Oh hell.

I was either going to cry or launch myself at him, and I wasn't sure which would be better at this point. My emotions went into overdrive as I tried to process what he was saying.

There had been a change. One I didn't think was possible so hadn't even hoped for and now I was holding my breath that it would last. That this latest infatuation with each other could be something more. Because it wasn't just about us anymore. It was bigger than that, with the little person inside of me relying on us not to fuck up the only chance for this baby to have two parents that got along.

"We need to take this slow, Joey." I swallowed hard, hoping I wouldn't cry. "No matter what happens with us—"

"Shhh." He put his finger against my lips, silencing me. "If you think I would let anything bad happen to you or the baby, you'd be mistaken. I know you're scared. I'm freaking the fuck out too. But when I say I'm all in, I'm all in."

He was so sure. I don't even know how because I had no idea what the hell we were doing. I knew that he'd been kind and considerate and that I wanted to be around him. I knew that I could be myself and he'd never once asked me to change. And I knew he made me laugh more than anyone.

"Just don't ask me to marry you again." I laughed, for the first time not really sure if I wouldn't want to in the future. The idea might not be so crazy.

"After the last time I'm still nursing my ego." He kissed me, his lips teasing me from the place where I doubted this. Where I doubted us.

"Go to sleep," he mumbled against my hair, his finger gently trailing along my shoulder.

"I thought you wanted sex?" I yawned as my eyes slowly closed. My lids had already decided they'd been open long enough.

"Yeah, I do. Always." His husky voice filled my ear. "Which means I'll still want it in the morning. So sleep."

I didn't fight it.

I couldn't.

Every part of me content as I floated away.

●●●

"Aren't you going on tour soon?"

It was weird to see Joey in my kitchen, even stranger to see him wearing only boxer shorts waving a spatula around the morning after he'd slept over. But he'd decreed he was making breakfast and I wasn't telling him no. I was fairly sure I was done saying that word to him.

It was better for all involved when I just said yes. It certainly made me a lot happier if the smile I was wearing was anything to go by.

"Yeah, which is why I need to get things squared away." He dug around in my kitchen looking for a skillet with the box of Bisquick in his other hand. "I'm setting up a bank account for you and the baby. So if you need something while I'm gone, you'll be taken care of."

Ugh. Reality check.

"Joey, I don't want your money. I'm fine." I slid off my seat at the breakfast bench and pulled out the skillet he'd been unable to find. "Just call me lots so we can have phone sex."

"Unless you want to reconsider my offer of coming on tour, the account is happening. Just for once don't be a hard ass," he said as he swatted my ass with a tea towel.

"Fine." I threw up my hands in defeat, knowing it wasn't worth the argument. "Open the account, and I'll drain every last cent on hookers and Colombian blow."

"That's the spirit." He gave me a wink as he pulled out a mixing bowl, ready to make pancakes. "And I will *still* call you for phone sex because I'm that much of a giver."

"This kid is completely screwed with us as parents, you know." My hand unconsciously went to my belly as I laughed.

Joey stopped with his all important breakfast preparation as he watched my hand, his eyes locked on my fingers before they came back to mine. I quickly pulled my hand away feeling a little stupid that I'd been caught. I wasn't even showing really, other than looking a little softer around the edges, I still looked mostly the same. Except for my boobs. But they'd always been on the larger side.

"I beg to differ." Joey set down the bowl and walked up behind me, his hand flat against me where mine had been. "Our kid is going to be the coolest kid in the universe."

With his other hand he brushed my hair to the side so he'd have access to my neck, his lips pressed on my naked skin the minute the path was clear. His kiss so gentle, yet sensual my nipples pebbled against my shirt.

He didn't stop with just one kiss; his lips moving up and down the curve of my neck slowly yet deliberate.

"I thought you were making pancakes." My body melded against his, loving the feeling of his hand on me.

"I will, but I have something more important to do right now." He continued to kiss me while his hands decided to take a world tour across my body.

"And that would be . . . ?" I closed my eyes as he sucked on my neck, hoping like hell his answer was get me naked. Even if it wasn't, I would still be ending up that way.

"You're a smart girl, I'm sure you'll figure it out." He spun me around in his arms so my body was now facing him. "I'll even give you a clue." His lips came down on mine hard, kissing me so fiercely I couldn't have answered him even if I'd tried.

Not that I tried.

Instead, some primal desperate groan worked its way out from between our mouths, my hands doing their own world tour.

He was so hot. It's what had attracted me to him in the first place. The perfect balance of sizzle and cool that most rock stars strived to achieve, he had it all without even trying. His just-been-fucked brown hair was just a few shades darker than his eyes, like they'd been paint-matched at The Home Depot for maximum impact. All of which played second fiddle to his blinding, devilish smile. That face of his was a menace, guaranteed trouble, which was only helped along by his body. That was something *else* that got my attention.

He was solid, toned and athletic. And while he wasn't bulked like a body builder, his muscles were no less clearly defined. He was a modern day work of art—absolutely beautiful—paired off with a complete goofball personality. It was *that* contradiction which finally won me over, which had taken me from daydreaming about him as a fantasy to wanting him as a lover.

But even with all of that, it still didn't even come close to how much I was attracted to him now. The well of feelings I had for him multiplying with each new day. It was amazing, and I was terrified.

"God, I want you." He pulled off my sleep shirt, the one I had barely been wearing an hour, and kissed my newly-exposed skin. "I don't think I've ever wanted anything as much as I want you."

My eyes closed as his lips wrapped around my nipple, my brain trying not to derail with all the stimulation—his mouth only part of the problem. The hard-on pressing against my stomach, the bigger concern.

"I want you too," I mumbled back like an idiot, unable to think of anything more original or intelligent to say.

"Thank fuck we're on the same page." He laughed as he palmed my breast and rocked me against his erection, the sensation making me giddy.

"Actually, I don't think we are." My hands moved down his back and gripped the waistband of his boxer shorts needing to get them off. My fingertips paused only for a second from tugging them violently down past his hips.

He didn't seem to notice; a mission of his own taking up most of his time as he pulled a similar maneuver on my shorts, the thin cotton tumbling to the floor.

"No panties," he murmured with appreciation as his fingers swept my core. "Damn, you're so wet."

As much as I had been enjoying his talented fingers, I pulled away knowing in another minute they'd own me. Not that it was a bad thing usually; the idea of losing myself in the screaming orgasm I knew they'd provide was actually really nice. But I had other plans right now and they involved my mouth and his cock, and watching him come apart before I did.

He resisted, trying to pull me back as I sunk to my

knees in front of him, pushing him against the cold, hard granite counter top.

"Fuck," he growled as I slid his length into my mouth and sucked. My hands wrapped around his shaft and twisted toward my lips before making their way back down.

"Kenzie." My name was all he managed to say, his fingers twisting in my hair.

My mouth was busy, alternating between sucking him hard and swirling my tongue around the head of his cock. My hands gripped him tight as I continued to play.

"Babe, you keep that up and I'm going to need to come." He looked down on me as my teeth grazed the sides of his girth, my intention not to stop or even slow down.

"Seriously, Kenzie." He squeezed his eyes shut trying to resist the orgasm I could feel building in his cock, his hands moving to the counter top where they white-knuckled as he gripped.

"I'm not stopping." I slipped him out of my mouth long enough to say the words before going back to licking him, my tongue working every single inch of his length.

"Babe, I want to be in you when I come." His hands reached down and grabbed my arms, pulling me to my feet. A pop came from my mouth as the suction was broken which seemed to send him wild.

"I wasn't done," I protested as he captured my mouth with his own and shoved down his boxers the rest of the way.

"No, you weren't." His lips moved to my throat as he guided himself to my entrance. "And I'm not being done until you are." With one swift thrust he was inside, filling me completely as my body tried to adjust.

"Joey." My arms wrapped around him tight as he moved slowly out and then quickly back in, the mixture of the push-pull making me insane.

"I need to be in deeper." One of his hands reached down and cupped my ass pulling me closer, the angle hitting me just right so that I had started to pant in anticipation.

"Yeah, that's better." He smiled, pleased with his effort. "So. Much. Better." He thrust in deeper after each word.

"Yes." The word had come from my mouth but was in a voice I didn't recognize as I met each of his rocks with one of my own, my body primed for the explosion.

"That's it, baby." Joey kissed me hard as I splintered, my legs feeling like Jell-O, barely able to hold my weight. I wasn't worried about falling though, with his strong arms gripping me as he had his own detonation. Our bodies fused together with heat and sweat as they pulsed through the wave of euphoria.

"Mmmm." He went back to the soft slow kisses that had started this escapade, his hands holding me tightly against him. "You're more delicious than pancakes."

"I hope that doesn't mean I'm not getting breakfast because I'm still hungry." I nibbled at his lower lip only partially telling the truth. Food could wait, but I wanted more of him.

"Then I'll feed you." His hands wandered from my ass, pressing gently as they moved up my back. "Pancakes, my cock—whatever you want, baby."

Seventeen
Joey

"Holy shit." **Rusty let out a low whistle. "That** looks like it could be Joey, I'm not sure though. It's been a few days since anyone has had visual confirmation."

By a few days, Rusty meant five. Which is the exact amount of time I spent wrapped around Kenzie, both in and out of bed. It wasn't all sex—although it seemed like we were making up for some lost time—we did lots of normal stuff too. Grocery shopping, a movie, dinner—respectable stuff with our clothes on. Of course most of the time I was imagining them off, but I'd had a lot of practice in waiting so the slow burn was worth it.

"I've been busy, asshole, and Max has kept me in the loop so I know I haven't missed anything important."

As much as I didn't care if the world fell apart around us—seriously, who gave a shit if it ended right now as long as I was with her—I wasn't going to be totally irresponsible. Max knew where I was and what I was doing and filled me in on any band stuff that was going on. Which lucky for me wasn't much so I hadn't had to tear myself away from her, that was, until today.

"How's it all going?" Angie was multitasking with her son in one hand and a stack of papers in the other. The little dude giggled, giving his mom a hard time as his little fat fingers tried to grab at stuff. Jase was busy with his own band's biz so the little guy was joining us today.

"Really good. Things are really good." I couldn't have hid my shit-eating grin if I'd tried. "You want me to hold him for you?" My head tipped to the kid who was squirming in her arms.

"Um." Angie looked between me and Zack—the little guy a perfect mix of his father and mother. "Sure. That would be great." She tentatively handed him over in a move I knew wasn't easy for her. She was like a lioness with her cub when she was with him, and I was starting to understand why.

"I'll be careful, Angie." My arms wrapped around his little body and brought him in close. His wriggles tapered off as I rocked him slightly against my chest.

"I know you will." Angie smiled, her eyes staying on her boy as she sat down in her chair, something she hadn't managed since we'd started this meeting.

"Well, fuck me." Rusty shook his head in utter disbelief. "Max, you feeling okay, buddy? Because the other two members of this band have been abducted by aliens or something."

"Not sure, Rus. All of you guys pairing off and procreating, I'd say I'm the only one unaffected by this epidemic." Max laughed as he leaned back into his chair. "Not that I mind, it's kind of badass to see everyone happy. Might have to look into it for myself."

"Just wait for the end of the tour," Angie warned. "It's going to be hard enough juggling dates around doctor's visits for Kenzie, we don't need any other complications." Angie took a sip from her coffee cup, something else she'd been unable to do since we'd walked in.

"Kenzie isn't coming." The three heads of my band-mates snapped around to face me like it had been a forgone conclusion.

That had been another thing we'd discussed during our five-day reconnection. And each time I suggested the possibility of her taking some time and joining me on the road, she shot me down—flat out refusing. "Trust me, the idea of leaving her here and taking off is fucking killing me but she's hell bent on staying. And short of tying her up and taking her at gunpoint, I can't see it happening."

"If she's worried about us, I can talk to her," Angie offered, her eyes went from me to her now settled son in my arms. "I'd love to have another girl on tour. Alison will even be there sometimes."

"She won't budge, saying that she won't desert the Beauty Queens. I get it, they have a residency happening and that's a tough gig to walk away from. I'm not back-flipping over it but I can't ask her to give up her career because of mine."

The big silence that bounced off the walls was the sound of me being reasonable. It wasn't in my usual bag of tricks and to be honest, I wasn't sure I liked the way it felt but I wasn't going to be an asshole either.

"Aliens *have* taken Joey." Angie smiled, a little too pleased that I was stuck between a rock and a hard place.

"Yeah, well fuck you." I smirked, unable to flip them off on account of my hands being occupied.

"All right, let's go over the rest of this stuff. Tour starts in two weeks and I'm already having a panic attack over being stuck on a bus with all of you."

Zack fell asleep in my arms as Angie went over the particulars of what our first headline tour was going to be like. The venues were a fraction of what we'd played when we were Power Station's support, but we didn't care. It was our gig and we were proud that we'd gotten to the point where we could sell out an arena solely off our own name and reputation.

The big time was right at our doorstep. So freaking close I could smell it, taste it and yet part of me felt unfilled. *Aliens.* Maybe Angie and Rusty were right.

After all the T's and I's had been dotted or crossed—whatever that meant—I opted to forgo hanging out at Angie's with the crowd and headed back to Kenzie's. After all, in two weeks all I was going to be seeing were those fuckers every single waking moment and I needed to soak up as much time with my girl as possible.

My girl.

And would you look at that. I somehow fell into a relationship. What's more is that I could never remember being so hardcore about a girl as I was about this woman. I liked the way it felt—me and her being together. Not because we'd made a human, but because somewhere in my head and heart I believed it would have happened all along. Someone that fucking awesome had been under my nose this whole entire time and I hadn't locked that down?

Fucking idiot.

World-class moron.

Biggest dumbass of all mankind.

And thank fuck for whatever shit was going on in the universe for hooking that up for me, considering I'd been too blind to do it myself.

Yep. My ass was owned.

"Hey Jo—"

I didn't let her finish the sentence, preferring for my greeting to be a little less verbal. Talk was so overrated.

"Well hello." She laughed when my mouth had finally let go of hers. "How was your meeting?"

"I missed you." My lips got cozy with her throat, wondering if I was being a complete asshole but not wanting talk. Not when we had so little time.

"Hey, what's got into you? You're not dying are you? Because if you've knocked me up and leave me, I'll kill you." She laughed realizing how little sense she was making. "And death will hurt so much more the second time, I assure you."

"Look at me." I cupped her face and tilted her chin so she could look at me. "Not even the Grim Reaper stands a chance at taking me from you. Nothing is going to stop me from being here to raise our baby with you."

Flat out it wouldn't happen. I'd dig my heels in and tell that fucker to suck my dick before I'd abandon either of them.

"Joey, you're scaring me. What's wrong?" She raised her hands to my face and swear to God, I felt like my life was flashing before my eyes.

"Nothing, just for the first time everything is really right." I swallowed the urge to cry because it would A: Probably make me look like pussy and B: I didn't want to worry her.

"O-kay." She nodded completely unconvinced. Not that I blamed her, I wasn't doing a really good job of selling the it's-all-good. "You're still coming to see me play tonight, right?"

"Hells yes I'm coming." Like I would be anywhere else. "Rusty and Max are coming too. Angie is trying to work Zack into a routine so is out and Alison already had plans."

"Cool, let me go see what I can still squeeze into." She wrinkled her nose as she tried to pull away from me.

"Not yet." My hands moved from her face to her hips,

stopping her from leaving. "I'm not done kissing you."

•••

Kenzie and girls AKA *The Beauty Queens from Mars* had continued their usual gig. They had a standing spot at the Alley Cat and packed the place two nights a week. And an opportunity like that was more than a secure paycheck, it was a chance to build a fan base. Not easy to come by, especially in New York City where every dickwad with a hard-on had stars in his eyes wanting to be a rock star.

Max and Rusty had met us there, with Kenzie and I showing up a little earlier so she could sound check. Plus, I'd been pretty much monopolizing her time of late, for which I made no apologies.

It was nice to sit back and chill for a while as the girls warmed up, reminding me how much I missed it. We used to be regular fixtures on the bar circuit, checking out other bands—most of which were our friends—but like all things, shit had changed.

"Sperm donor," Becca called from behind her kit, her smiling hinting that she would be giving me shit for most of the night. "What's the chances you have a drum key in your truck? I can't find where the hell mine is."

"What are the chances if I hook you up, you let the insults slide tonight?" I walked across and handed her the one hanging off my car keys. I'd learned early on I couldn't be trusted to remember the fucking thing unless it was attacked to something important.

"Steady on, homeslice." She accepted the key and started tightening the lugs. "You see a halo above my head? Unlikely." She went about tuning her drums as I laughed.

"What's so funny?" Kenzie asked, walking over to where Becca and I were standing.

"Your boy here is chasing miracles, and there ain't no saints hanging around this lot." Becca grinned, warming up her double kick and hitting her crash.

"It's a drummer thing, I'm convinced." Sara weighed in, her short skirt barely within the confines of being legal. "All that banging makes you aggressive. It's evolutionarily proven."

"How about I *evolutionarily prove* your ass into next week." Becca tossed a stick narrowly missing Sara. She'd found a new target to hang shit on.

"Stick to beating the skins, Becca. Your aim is fucking terrible." I laughed, expecting a stick to come sailing toward me at any minute.

"Be grateful Kenzie likes you, daddy-o. You're in my blast radius." She spun her stick taunting me.

"Infinitely glad Kenzie likes me." I slung an arm around my girl and brought her in close for a hug, the angle of her guitar almost clocking me in the nuts. "But not 'cause I give a shit what you think."

"Who said I liked you?" Kenzie said as she pulled me

across to her part of the stage, giving us no more privacy but at least a small buffer against flying projectiles.

"I sort of assumed." I bowed my head so I could kiss her. "Good thing is, I like you too."

"Seriously, if you two are going to kiss and talk about liking each other I'm going to barf all over the stage," Sara shouted from behind us as I flipped her the finger. "And Kenzie just stopped doing that like maybe a week ago, so we'd like to keep it vomit free."

"I'll let you do your thing." I gave Kenz another kiss despite the protests from the others, my girl giggling as I left her on stage.

She looked beautiful tonight.

Her hair pulled away from her face but left loose in the back, so it fell like a crazy dark-blonde waterfall. She'd bitched about her clothes being too tight so I gave her my Stone Temple Pilots T-shirt. She'd cut off the sleeves and somehow by tying knots in it at the sides she'd made it into a dress, topping it all off with a pair of biker boots.

And there wasn't a girl on the planet who was hotter.

"You're gonna get in a lot of trouble tonight, my friend." Max came up from behind and slapped me on the back.

"What are you talking about? I'm not interested in trouble." I kept my eyes locked on Kenzie despite my best friend standing beside me.

"I'm talking about this territorial look you have going on while staring at her. I hope for all our sakes no one is stupid enough to go anywhere near her tonight. Not in the mood for a bar fight."

Fuck. I hadn't even thought about that. My eyes scanned the room for anyone paying a little too much attention, my fist ready to lay anyone out who even breathed in her direction.

"All good, Max." Rusty walked over carrying a couple of icy-cold beers, big shit-eating grin on his face. "I roofied his drink. He'll be mellow and ready to be Kenzie's bitch by the time she gets off stage." A longneck thrust into my hand.

"I'm already her bitch." I took a long pull and let the brew wash down my throat. Maybe this wasn't going to be as fun as I'd anticipated.

"At least he's honest." Max laughed, taking a swig of his.

"I've got nothing to say." Rusty shrugged. "My balls are happily under lock and key." He paused before taking a big long breath. "The perks are freaking sens-a-tional."

"Dude, that's my fucking niece." Max smacked him across the chest, the old joke about Alison and her family ties working its way into the conversation.

"I keep forgetting." Rusty laughed, the two of them clinking their beers and taking another drink.

Background music was piped through the PA until the girls were ready to start. The lights dimmed but didn't go completely black, allowing people to move around the room if they needed to. Not that anyone did when the

Beauty Queens finally took the stage.

Four hot women who could legit sing and play? Yeah, no one was going anywhere. Unless it was the bathroom to pull one out. God, I didn't even want to think about it.

I'd always thought they were talented, but watching Kenzie on stage playing and harmonizing Sara's vocals gave me a whole new appreciation. It wasn't just that she didn't drop a note, or that her playing was flawless, it was that she was perfect on stage. Doing her thing without the unnecessary theatrics, the crowd being drawn in a little further with each bar she played. It was sexy without being slutty, hot without being over the top, and smooth beyond freaking measure.

Even Becca was on point, keeping the sound tight. I couldn't fault any of them—and neither could the crowd. Their applause shook the foundation as the girls took a bow, the loudest cheer from yours truly.

"Just keep your dick in your pants; this is a nice place and we don't want to get tossed out," Rusty whispered as Kenzie stepped off stage, her face shiny from sweat.

"Did he just growl?" Max laughed from the other side, the bastards thoroughly enjoying the fact I needed to nail my feet to the floor so I didn't attack her the minute she got closer.

"Shut your mouths, I need to kiss my woman." I grabbed her the minute she was in arms-distance and planted my lips on her so fast she'd barely realized what was happening.

"Thank God he can only get her pregnant once." Someone laughed from behind us. I'm pretty sure it was Rusty but I didn't care enough to turn around.

"I guess you liked the show then?" Kenzie pulled her mouth away from mine. "How many times did you almost come? Be honest." She grinned giving me the same bullshit line I had given her not so long ago.

"My dick is so hard I could drill for oil right now." Understatement of the fucking century.

"Ewww." Sara la-la-la'd and plugged her ears. "Some-one needs to make them stop."

"Hey, guys." The meathead who'd been working on a song with Kenzie appeared from nowhere. His big Sasquatch body taking up like half of the bar.

"Hey, Dom." Sara launched herself at him like a battering ram, the man mountain not seeming to mind. Well then. I guess we know where his interests lie and thank Christ for that.

A bunch of hi's-how-are-you's were thrown around and introductions were made, the dude being as polite as can be as he did the rounds. His eyes only detoured south when he looked at Sara, keeping them face-level when he spoke to the others. Just as well. And not that I gave a shit about the behemoth, but if he was a friend of Kenzie's then I'd try and play nice.

"Hey, I owe you an apology." I pulled him aside and stuck out my hand, offering it to him. While I was happy to play nice, I didn't need a freaking audience.

"It's cool dude, that's between you and your girl." He clapped my palm and gave it a shake. "If she's cool with you, we've got no problems."

"Yeah, shit is more than cool now." I nodded toward Kenzie who was laughing with her band oblivious to our secret squirrel meeting. How the hell she'd missed the shift in the Earth's atmosphere was beyond me.

"Good, because Kenzie is a good friend and anyone who messes with her, messes with me." The dude squared off his shoulders, in an I-mean-business kind of way.

"Unnecessary, dude. I'd rather rip my own arm off and beat myself with it than hurt that girl." And I meant every fucking word. Which is why I was going to say the next bit even though I'd rather swallow glass than ask this guy for anything. "Look, I'm heading out of town soon." Seriously, was I going to do this? "And not that she needs looking after, she's one of the strongest chicks I know. But it would make me feel better knowing someone with her best interest at heart was keeping an eye out for her."

"It killed you to say that right now, didn't it?" He eyed me intently, trying to get a read on me.

"Every fucking word." I nodded, wishing there was a way I could tear myself in two. "But I need to do what's best for her and I can't cancel the tour. I can't be in two places at once, and if something happened to her or the baby while I'm gone . . ."

"It won't. And you didn't need to ask. I was planning on

it anyway, but the fact you were man enough to say something has earned you a heap of my respect." He put out his hand, offering it to me.

"Look at you making new friends." Kenzie nestled into my side as I finished shaking Dom's hand. "Either of you want to tell me what is going down?" Her eyes shifted between him and me waiting for one of us to start singing.

"Coke deal, I'm trying to get a better price on the Columbian blow." I kissed her neck without missing a beat.

"No, seriously." She jabbed me in the ribs with her elbow, not satisfied with what I thought was a perfectly good answer.

"I can admit when I'm wrong and apologize when I've acted like a tool. He seems like a decent enough dude, even if he creates a fucking eclipse when he walks out of his door." I grinned, fully aware the dude was standing right there.

"You guys have fun." Dom smirked, making a beeline for Sara. How that even worked out for them was beyond me. She would definitely have to be on top.

"You know." She wrapped her arms around my neck smiling up at me. "We never really officially got together."

"Babe, if you think we are anything *but* together then you're delusional." I bowed my head and kissed her. This time a little less intense.

"No, I get that." She snuggled in closer, the feel of her

against me—the greatest thing in the fucking world. "But it just sort of happened."

"Well consider this me making it official." I wrapped my arms around her and lifted her off the ground. My lips on hers were a given.

"Okay, we're together." She sighed, her head resting against my shoulder. "Now take me home so we can have sex."

Joey had left exactly forty-four hours, thirteen minutes and fifty-three seconds ago. Yes, I was now one of *those* girls.

Our goodbye had been bittersweet. We'd spent almost every minute together until he got on that bus and said goodbye. Every gig I played he was there in the audience. Every night, he was in my bed. We hadn't decided to be in a relationship, it just sort of grew into one. One day I was single, pregnant and thinking about raising this baby largely by myself, and then all of those things changed. There was no discussion that this was more than just about raising our child together; this was about wanting to be with each other. *Needing* to be with each other.

"You're not going to be lonely on the road? There will be a million girls who'd be more than happy to help you with that," I whispered against his back, not liking the insecurity that had crept up from nowhere.

"You're right, there will be a million. Maybe even more. And none of them will be you. So how will any of those millions of women help me if I'm lonely?" He twisted around and pulled me against him. "Trust me, no one is more surprised at this than me, Kenzie. But I don't want anyone else."

That smile.

It had always been my weakness. The way he looked at me like I was the only person in the world. In the past I knew it wasn't mine permanently but now, things were different and he wouldn't give it to anyone else. He just wouldn't.

"Stop smiling at me like that." I playfully shoved against his chest. "It makes it too easy to believe that everything is going to be okay."

"Look at me." He tilted his chin so I had no choice but to look him in the eyes. "It's not so easy to leave you behind. I'm battling my own demons on whether this is the right thing to do when my instincts are telling me to stay here. But I know there aren't enough miles in the world to change the way I feel."

He kissed me.

Not like he usually did, it was slower, deeper—like he wanted to capture the memory. His hands moved over my body with the same deliberate intent, each sweep of his fingertips making me tremble.

"Yes." I breathed, though I had no idea what I actually wanted him to do.

"*I want you to remember how I touch you, Kenzie.*" *Slowly, painfully slow, I felt him across my skin.* "*Remember, so when you touch yourself while I'm gone you feel my hands, not your own.*"

Everywhere. My arms, my legs, my feet—places that shouldn't be erotic yet were now driving me insane. My neck, my breast, in between my legs—the insanity rose to a new level.

"*Remember this, remember how this feels.*" *His fingers slowly moved against my core, the sensation alone threatening to undo me.* "*I want my hands on you every single night.*"

I nodded because words didn't have a hope of coming out of my mouth in any way that made sense. My body ached for him to let me finish while my heart never wanted it to stop.

"*I want to touch you too.*" *My hands reached for him, my palms flattening against his chest.* "*This is what I'll think about, not just your hands on me but how I'd touch you.*"

"*Yes,*" *he moaned as my fingertips glided down his torso and gripped his already hard cock.* "*Fuck, that feels so good.*"

My hand moved up and down his shaft, feeling him thickening with each stroke.

"*Joey,*" *I pleaded; the two fingers that had been circling my entrance were pushed inside of me as his thumb continued to rub against my clit.*

"*I love to watch you come. I love it against my hand,*

against my lips but most of all against my cock." His fingers continued to pump inside of me while my hand worked his length.

"That feels so good . . . So good . . ." I couldn't finish the sentence.

Hot breath against my skin as I panted, desperate to get closer to him even though it didn't seem physically possible. And as if he understood, he kissed me; his hands moved from between my legs right as I was about to come and he filled me with his cock. Wrapped in his arms I shattered into a million pieces, feeling him do the same in our private whirlwind.

It was everything.

And I knew I could never say goodbye.

That feeling carried me through the hours since he'd left, hoping it would be enough until he got back.

There were other things that also needed attention before he got back. Things I had put off for far too long.

• • •

"Kenzie." My mom wrapped me in one of her trademark hugs as soon as I'd walked into the kitchen.

I'd finally decided to tell my folks. Honestly, it was well past due and while I had skated through to this point with a few baggy tops and clever wardrobe choices, I wanted them to know. Hopefully the fact I had waited so long didn't add another level to the freak out, but whatever fall-out happened, I'd deal. I was standing behind my decision.

"Hey, Mom, where's Dad?" I looked around wanting to get it over without having to repeat it. I still had no idea how either of them were going to react to the news their *baby* was going to be having a baby.

"Right here, sweetheart." My dad emerged from the backroom, his magnifying glasses still fixed to his forehead. "I'm building a destroyer." The gunmetal gray paint still on his fingers as he pulled me in for a hug of his own. Two parents, two hugs—it was time to get this show on the road.

"Soooooooo." I swallowed, wondering how the hell to soften the blow. Yep, I had nothing. "I'm pregnant." I blurted out like almost every time I had made the announcement. You think I'd be better at it by now. Apparently not.

"What?" Both of them answered in unison like they hadn't just heard their youngest child was knocked up.

"I'm pregnant," I repeated knowing it didn't sound any better the second time around. "But this isn't a bad thing, and I'm in love with the father."

Wow.

Did I just say I was in love with Joey? Probably should have told him first, not that I was taking it back now. I *was* in love with him. Completely, and it had taken me up till this moment to realize.

"Sweetie, we didn't even know you were dating

someone and now you're telling us you're pregnant? This is all a bit sudden." My mother fluttered her hand at her throat like she always did when she was nervous, the news harder to take because she hadn't even met the man in question.

"I know, Mom, and I didn't want to tell you right away because I thought you'd be disappointed in me. But I love this baby, and I love Joey and we're going to be a family." The L word was getting a workout now that I'd finally said it, and I wasn't holding back. I wouldn't apologize for how I felt and no matter what road we took to get here, this felt right.

"Well, where is this Joey?" My dad's eyes shot to the closed front door. "You think he'd be standing here beside you instead of sending you here to tell us by yourself."

"He wanted to be here but it was my choice to come alone. Trust me, he isn't happy about it either."

It had been my decision to wait, to tell them alone. While he had spilled to his folks we were expecting, I had yet to tell mine.

It had been so easy for him. Hopped in a car and told his parents they were going to be grandparents. He'd even invited me to go with him but I just couldn't. Worried their reaction might be lukewarm or subjecting us to disapproving stares. And rejection wasn't something I could take right now.

Of course none of that happened with both his mom

and dad being thrilled he was settling down, and begged to meet me as soon as possible. I'd almost cried when he told me, which just got me more nervous about telling mine. What were the chances they would also be so cool with it? And as much as I didn't admit it, I didn't want to subject him to that.

"You know we love you, Kenzie." My mother slowly lowered herself onto the kitchen chair. "But a baby is a big deal. It's not something you can take back. We just want to make sure you are doing the right thing."

It was weird hearing them ask if I was doing the right thing, because for me there was no choice. Not because I didn't think I had one, but because I hadn't *wanted* it. Joey, the baby, my future—none of those things was mutually exclusive.

"If by right thing you mean having this child and being with the father, then yes, I'm doing the right thing." I'd never been more sure of anything in my life. I just wished I'd had the opportunity to tell Joey before he'd left.

"We weren't suggesting you not have the baby, or not be with him." My dad who refused to sit gave me a second hug. "We just want to make sure no one is pressuring you. We will support you no matter what."

"Good, then prepare to be grandparents."

Next came the inevitable follow up conversation.

How far along was I?

Are we getting married?

Was he going to be gone for the entire duration of my

pregnancy?

Why I didn't move back home to make things easier?

Why hadn't I taken out medical insurance like they'd asked?

I knew they meant well but it would have been easier without the inquisition. In the end, they'd resigned themselves that I would be doing it my way—as I'd always done—but reminded me that their love and support weren't far. Something that Sara had told me to expect when I'd first found out.

"Hey." I answered my phone without checking the caller id, my hands being tied up trying to open the car door. My parents still at the window while I tried to wave and balance the phone with my ear.

"Hey, babe." Joey's voice filled my ear. "I've missed you."

"Joey." It hadn't been that long since I'd heard him and yet I struggled not to get 1D fangirl crazy as I said that one word. My heart did a summersault in my chest cavity as I tried not to dance in the street. It was a decent neighborhood; they wouldn't appreciate my crazy.

"So," his voice rumbled through the phone. "My hand is on my dick." His sexy laugh told me he probably wasn't joking.

"It's two in the afternoon, don't you have something more important to do?" I laughed as I successfully unlocked my car door and slid into the driver's seat. It wasn't easy, especially given I had already pictured him naked, his dick in his hand just as he'd described. I made a mental note not to lick my lips.

"Sure, I'd rather be doing you, but you're back in New York and I'm in Connecticut sooooooo that just leaves my hand. Unless you want to drive up here—" He deliberately left his sentence trailing.

"I can't just drive up there." *Really? It wasn't that far, two hours tops. I could be there and back before bedtime. No. I couldn't.* "It will make it harder to say bye when I have to leave. I can't do another goodbye so soon."

It had been hard enough a couple of days ago, a piece of me leaving on the bus with him. And as amazing as it would be to see him now, that elation would be short lived when I would have to get in my car and drive home. I'd probably cry too this time, having managed to successfully not cry the first time, and that was *not* happening.

"Fine, just my hand then." He didn't sound surprised, knowing full well I'd probably refuse. "You want to talk dirty to me? You should touch yourself too, that's so hot."

"I'm driving, I can't have phone sex and drive." My hand hit the ignition bringing my engine to life. If there was any doubt I was operating heavy machinery, the rev of the engine would help put that to rest. I probably hit the gas a little harder than was needed as I pulled out into traffic.

"You are just shitting on all my ideas today." He puffed out a breath seemingly exasperated before chuckling.

"Okay, I'll compromise. Don't touch yourself but tell me what you would do if you could."

Ironically, if I had him in arms distance, sex would be the last thing on my mind. He could get me from zero to a hundred with just that sexy smile but right now, I wanted something else.

"I'd hold you Joey, and then ask you to hold me. And fall asleep listening to your beating heart knowing that you would be right there when I woke up."

I didn't even care how desperate it made me sound, I was done hiding my feelings and while our first *I love yous* wouldn't be done on a telephone, I couldn't hide how much I cared. How much he meant to me.

"Baby, you're killing me here." He cursed softly into the phone. "Maybe I can borrow a car and come to you."

Yes. Is what I wanted to say. I wanted him to grab a car and meet me at my apartment so we could be alone in our moment. Not deal with my parents, or his. Not deal with work, or bands, or tours. Just us. But I couldn't say those words and make it harder than it already was.

"You need to do this tour, and I'm just moody and emotional. It will get easier." Or at least that's what I had to believe. "I told my folks." I hoped the change in conversation might stop me from wanting to cry and make the drive home a little easier.

"Yeah, did they think I was a deadbeat for letting you tell them by yourself?"

While Joey had supported me in telling my parents my

way, he hadn't liked it. Not that I'd ever really given him the choice.

"No, I told them it's what I wanted. And they know me well enough to know that I do what I want."

"Well, no arguments here." He laughed quietly into the phone. "So I'm guessing phone sex isn't going to happen." Once again he didn't sound surprised.

"Not right now but you can talk to me while I drive and keep me company. Maybe I'll get inspired when I get home." Or maybe I'd just listen to his voice and pretend he was right there with me and it wouldn't be months before I'd see him again.

There was silence, its weight filling the air and I knew he was thinking about it too. The distance. The time. And how were we going to survive four months when we'd barely survived a couple of days.

"Can I still jerk off or is that going to be creepy?" he huskily whispered into the phone, breaking the moment and making me laugh.

"Joey, if you need to ask . . ."

"Okay, I am not doing anything then." I heard the smile in his voice, pleased that his diversionary tactics had worked.

"How can any of this even be remotely sexy to you?" I asked seriously. Somehow I had gone from strong and independent to clingy and needy. I couldn't think of anything less attractive. And thank God he couldn't see me because I looked really ordinary as well.

"Because it's you on the other end of the phone," he said with zero hesitation. "And anything to do with you turns me on. You could be doing my taxes and it would still give me the biggest hard-on."

"You are such a romantic." I laughed, knowing he was probably telling the truth.

"All for you." He sighed into the phone.

I could tell this was just as difficult for him and I didn't want our last moments on the phone to be sad so I started telling him about my drive. It was boring and monotonous but he listened, asking questions until I finally pulled up at my apartment.

Then he took over and told me about his current reality. About the band, the bus—his words filling my time while I unlocked my door and entered my apartment and then finally when I collapsed on my bed.

"Kenzie?" he asked when he hadn't heard me answer in a while, my body completely relaxed as I listened to the cadence of his voice.

"Yeah, Joey." I waited, the silence stretching out a little longer.

He let out a long deep breath like he'd been holding it for a while, seeming to stall on whatever thought he was going to vocalize.

"Nothing, babe. I just wanted to hear you, make sure I hadn't sent you off to sleep."

I wasn't sure what he was going to originally say but whatever it was, the moment had passed.

"You can do a lot of things, Joey Shaw. Sending me off to sleep not at the top of that list."

"Does that mean you want phone sex now?" he asked, hope brimming in his voice.

I bit my lip desperately trying not to laugh as I dropped my voice seductively low. I'd never been good at saying no to him.

"Guess where my hands are?"

Nineteen
Joey

This had been my dream.

Traveling the country with my three best friends playing our songs to thousands of people and having them sing them right back. It was what I had laid awake dreaming about as a sixteen-year-old, when I wasn't dreaming about girls. Just the road, the band and our songs. And now it wasn't enough.

I wanted her with me.

Kenzie.

The girl who'd knocked me on my ass and completely claimed my heart.

And as much as I wanted to enjoy what was happening for me, it was just empty without her.

To top it off, while her folks had been relatively cool with the situation—or so she told me, I had yet to see their it's-all-fine with my own two eyes—her older brother Brandon was another story.

The tough-talking bastard—or as I liked to call him, meathead—wasn't so happy his little sister was knocked up. Not that I could say I blamed him—he was obviously protective of her—but I hated that he was giving her a hard time. Thankfully he hadn't returned from his deployment yet, which meant any displeasure he had about the situation was delivered via phone, text or email. Oh, yeah, I also forgot to mention the dude was also a fucking hero, serving his country with the National Guard, so I couldn't even legitimately hate him. Just one more thing to add to my already fucked up resume. Left pregnant girlfriend to go on tour and wants to beat up her salt-of-the-earth-patriotic brother. My week had turned from suck to blow.

And, if all of that wasn't enough to convince me to find a fucking car and drive down to see her, news of Kenzie's pregnancy had started to filter through.

Around the New York scene it had been the worst kept secret ever, but as long as it stayed in our little circle, we didn't really give a shit who knew. Now, it seemed that's all anyone wanted to talk about. The dude from Rolling Stone had even asked Rusty about it and I hadn't even been at the fucking interview. It was making me edgy. And I hoped like hell she wasn't dealing with her own shitstorm.

"Hey Joey, it's Rich here. How are you?"

I stared at the laptop in front of me, the Skype call I *apparently* had to take.

Rich Steer had come on board after we signed the new record deal. He wasn't with Power Station or the label but was some dude that we supposedly had to keep on retainer. In case one of us did something stupid, because apparently now we were a target for legal action, blah, blah, blah. Fucking bored me to tears. Just put some sticks in my hands and let me play. I don't want to deal with any of that shit.

"I'm good, dude. Any reason why you wanted me and not the band?" Or why the fuck I need to talk to you in the first place considering I'm not in jail or some shit.

"So the label mentioned you were going to be a father, is that true?" He leaned forward, his eyebrow cocked waiting for my answer.

I really didn't like this douche but it wasn't up to me, and as long as he kept our shit in order, we didn't need to be BFFs.

"Yeah, I am." No point denying it, pretty sure it had been printed in at least three different publications, it was hardly a state secret.

"And I'm to assume that you are sure this is your child?" he asked while I stared blankly at the screen. My mind wished technology had evolved enough that I could have give him a beat down remotely.

"Not trying to be improper here, but it wouldn't be the first time a girl has claimed to be pregnant by someone for a settlement. You are looking to make quite a sizable fortune on this album." He went on to explain, my silence taken the way it was intended—he'd pissed me off.

"Kenzie isn't like that." Lord knows she could have fucked me over a million times by now and hadn't, there wasn't a chance she was chasing dollar signs. "And we took a paternity test already. The baby is mine." Not that I needed to justify myself to this asshole, but I was hoping if I answered his questions we could run this shit along and be done. I already didn't like the guy, now we were moving into another territory of distrust.

"Well that's good. And what are your intentions regarding the child?" He asked like we were discussing what my plans were for the weekend.

"Not really sure how any of this is your business, buddy." No seriously, was he intentionally being a dick or was this usual demeanor because I still had no idea why the fuck I needed to be talking to this asshole and not doing something more productive, like talking to the fucking woman that I loved.

Yeah. That.

And wasn't it just the fucking kicker that I had come to this realization when she was fucking miles away from me so I couldn't tell her. Just another level of blow to add to my already shitty mood.

"I'm the band's lawyer, Joey, you're paying me to make it my business." He snapped like I was inconveniencing him. "Are you marrying her? Moving in together? Has child support been discussed? Visitation?" He fired questions at me like I was some kind of a suspect on a murder trial.

"Dude, hold on, the kid isn't even born yet." And I still didn't know why the hell we were even having this discussion. "We're not married or living together at the moment, but that's all going to change once I get off the road."

Or at least I hoped it would, Kenzie and I hadn't had the talk yet but you could bet your ass it would be happening. Of course I wasn't about to suggest either of those things when I was about to leave, was I? No, it had to wait and when I asked her to marry me again, this time it would be for the right reasons. The one that she had asked me about the first time I'd gotten down on one knee. Did I love her? Hells yes I did, and I didn't want to be without her.

Rich waited for me to continue, drumming his fingers on the desk, I guess needing a more detailed answer.

"But we don't need all that shit. We had agreed from the get-go that we were raising the baby together, it's always been the plan and it's not changing now." Especially not once I got back and told her how I felt.

"So shared physical custody?" He looked at me like those words should mean something to me.

"Of course we're sharing custody. I just told you we're raising this baby together." I shook my head wondering why this idiot hadn't heard me the first time.

"Okay, well good. I needed to know your intentions so I knew how best to proceed, and as you already have the paternity test it will make this a whole lot easier. If you can forward me the paperwork, I can make sure everything is in order on our end." He started writing notes on his notepad while I tried to make sense of everything he had said. Nope, still just as clueless from when we started the conversation only now I had wasted a good twenty minutes of my day I wasn't getting back in a hurry.

"You just need the results?" I repeated like an idiot, barely catching the mention wading through all the shit that had come out of his mouth.

"Well yes, that would be very helpful." He nodded, making more notes. "I'll take care of the rest of the paperwork so it's all neat and tidy and you don't have to worry." He looked up from his notepad and gave me a smile. Now I really didn't trust him.

"Alrighty then, if we're done, I'd like to get going." I rubbed the back of my neck; glad I could end this fucking conversation and hopefully never have to deal with him again.

"Yep, all done Joey. Enjoy the tour. If there are any foreseeable issues I'll contact you but I think it's all standard from here on out." Another smile accompanied by a wave.

"Great, goodbye." I killed the Skype call and leaned back against my chair.

Kenzie had told me our lawyers would want the paperwork from the paternity but I'd never bothered to file them. As far as I was concerned the only reason we'd taken the damn test was because she'd been so insistent. But if them having that piece of paper made them feel warm and fuzzy, and reassure them that Kenzie wasn't a gold digger then what was the harm? And honestly, I didn't give a shit what the asshole wanted as long as he left me the hell alone and did what we paid him for i.e. for us not to get screwed.

"Hey, brother." Max wandered in from his connecting hotel room. "What's shaking, you look like shit." He took a seat next to me on the couch without the invitation.

"Nothing. Just wished Kenzie was here." Did I sound as pathetic as I thought I did? Pity at this point I didn't care.

"So what did Rich want? Why the sudden urge to talk to you?"

The request for the meeting hadn't been private, in fact Angie and Rusty would probably be giving me the exact same what-the-hell the minute they saw me too. It wasn't every day legal representation wanted a private meeting with a band's drummer. Even more of a head-scratcher was why whatever he needed couldn't wait until we got back to New York, of course now, I knew.

"He heard through the grapevine Kenzie and I are going to be parents, guess he was pissed he didn't get a personal announcement or something." It still irked me that he needed to know in the first place. My business was my business, and no signing on dotted lines changed that.

"So, he just wanted to confirm the news?" Max's brows bunched as he tried to make sense of it.

"No, he wanted to make sure Kenzie wasn't going to use it to sue me or something. Asshole has no idea."

Even saying it to Max annoyed the hell out of me. Kenzie had never asked me for a thing, she barely let me pay for the doctor's stuff and she hadn't even touched the account I'd set up for her. Not that I expected her to go nuts and hit the mall, but I would have thought she might have caved once I was gone. Nope, not a fucking dime had been withdrawn and I assumed that was the way it was going to stay.

"Did you tell him she wasn't like that?" Max was definitely on Team Kenzie; knowing her almost as well as I did. "Jesus, she's the last person on earth who'd sue your ass."

"Yeah, I told him. Hopefully now it's all a big non-issue." I waved him off; already annoyed Rich had taken up too much of my brain space today. "Besides, I've got bigger problems. GI Joe gets back soon and he'll probably be bringing with him a shitload of judgment. I don't give a fuck what he thinks of me, but I don't need Kenzie dealing with all of that."

From what she'd said he was getting in today or tomorrow at the latest and I bet the minute his combat boots hit the ground he would be heading right for his sister. The fucking honeymoon was over and there was so much shit flying from every direction, I had to fight the urge not to toss this whole tour aside and go do what my instinct was screaming at me to do.

Of course if I did take my ball and go home I would be fucking over three of the most amazing people in my life. My friends. My family. Here's a rock, here's a hard place and here I am wedged between both of them.

"She's stronger than you think, Joe." Max thumped his hand on my shoulder. "If she says she's got it, you got to trust her on that."

He just didn't get it.

Kenzie was one of the strongest chicks I knew.

A fucking gladiator.

She could deal with any situation without even batting an eye, even my shenanigans. So when she told me she missed me and wished that I could hold her, it broke my fucking heart. Because she'd never asked me for anything, and the one time she did, it was something I couldn't give her.

"It's not about not trusting her, it's about me wanting to do anything I can to make it easier for her. Dude, I love her. And believe me that it fucking cuts me deep that I'm saying those words to you instead of her. I'm completely gone, she owns me. And every day that I don't tell her is killing me."

It didn't get more real than that, and I could tell by the look on Max's face he knew I wasn't playing.

I don't think I'd ever told a girl I'd loved her. I loved her ass, I loved her rack, I loved the way she sucked dick—but never an *I love you.* So his wide-eyed oh-shit expression was perfectly justifiable given the circumstances.

"Pick up a phone and do it." He grabbed my cell from the side table and handed it to me. "Alexander Bell did the hard yards, all you have to do is dial."

"She's worth more than that." I tossed the phone onto the couch beside me. "I want to be able to see her face when I say those words to her. I want to be able to hold her so she knows I mean it. I'm not giving her a half-assed effort."

She was going to get more than that. I promised her every single night before I closed my eyes, pity none of those times she'd been around to hear.

"We've got solid dates for the next two weeks. No breaks between shows. If I can just hold out until then, I'll fly to her and tell her. I don't care if I only get to see her for two days, I'll do it. I just need to get through."

Two weeks. It should be a blink of an eye in the scheme of things but I was going to curse every single grain of sand that was going to have to pass through the hourglass.

"Okay, Joey. You know what's best but if I was you, I wouldn't be waiting." Max didn't agree with my need to wait but he wasn't going to ride me either. He never did which is why things with us were always cool.

"Hey, when we get back." I took a swallow before continuing. "I'm going to move out. I want to get a place with Kenzie, something new for the both of us. I don't want either of us to be fighting ghosts of past relationships in our space."

"Yeah, I totally understand." Max nodded. "And I think it might be time I get something a little closer to the city. It will be nice to get a clean break."

The two of us had lived in that same house since we were eighteen. We'd pay the rent and the bills and then spend the rest on beer, sometimes food. First few months we'd lived there, we'd had a mattress each on the floor—no box spring, and a couple of lounge chairs in the living room. Max's parents had hooked us up with a refrigerator and television, which summed up pretty much all our worldly possessions. It was a much different story now.

"You with me, brother?" Max punched me in the arm, my zoning out catching his attention.

"Yeah, just thinking about shit when we were younger. I swear living in that house with you, I thought it was the best time of my life."

"It was good times, my friend. Some of the best." Max smiled, the reminiscing probably conjuring some happy times in his own melon.

The band, Kenzie and the baby. It was a hat trick I wasn't sure I deserved, but I sure as hell wasn't handing it back.

"I'm thinking while those times were awesome, the best is yet to come."

"Yeah, I think you're right."

Twenty

Kenzie

"**I** can't believe you were so stupid, Kenzie. Really?"

Brandon was home from his deployment. He hadn't even gone and seen our parents yet, instead landed on my doorstep and gone off the deep end. For twenty minutes he'd been giving me varying degrees of his disappointment, mixing it up once in awhile by making threats against Joey. Of course that meant I had been yelling too, which made for an interesting conversation.

"I'm not fifteen, I'm twenty-five. Lots of people have children at my age, you're making it sound like it can't be done."

I was tired and if it hadn't been my brother—someone who I knew loved me deeply—then I wouldn't have bothered justifying myself. He'd hated almost every boyfriend I'd ever had. As far as he was concerned, no man would ever be good enough.

"If everyone was jumping off the Brooklyn Bridge, would you be doing that too? Kenzie, I know I'm hard on you but it's only because I love you. When Mom and Dad told me about this I freaked out." He paced in my kitchen, his feet threatening to wear a hole through my linoleum.

"I know you are trying to protect your little sister, but I'm not a kid anymore and I don't need protecting. Not from Joey anyway."

Brandon had been gone a lot when I was in my teens; he'd joined the Air Force straight out of high school and dutifully went wherever the US Government sent him. My dad had a mild heart attack right before he was due to reenlist, which is why he switched to the Guard, so he could be home more. And while I loved having my brother around, he ran his life like a military operation. I, on the other hand, did not.

"Sis, he's not even here. He left you alone. How do you know what the hell he is doing out there? He could have a different girl in every city and meanwhile you're here pregnant with his kid." He gave me every possible worst-case scenario because *obviously* I wasn't capable of thinking them up all by myself. That was sarcasm in case you didn't catch it.

"Would you stop?" I shook my head trying to remember if my brother had always been this high strung. "I trust him, okay. I don't believe he would cheat on me just because I'm not there. Besides, he could just as easily cheat on me here if he wanted to; I'm not with him twenty-four hours a day. I love him. We're having this baby together."

Now I had come to the realization I couldn't stop saying I loved him, unfortunately I still hadn't said it to him. That was going to change though. I didn't care if it was on the phone or via carrier pigeon—I was telling him. The longer I kept it down the edgier it made me, and if he happened to not feel the same way, then at least I'd know. Not that it was a real concern. He must have those feelings; there was no way this could be one sided.

"And does he love you?" Brandon tossed in, bringing up doubts if I'd had any. "Has he said what he wants to happen after the tour? Is he going to stick around? Or is he going to go live the highlife in a big-ass house while you are at home raising a child."

I couldn't help it. My voice rose as I waved my arms like a lunatic wondering what it was going to take for him to see that this was the real deal. That we were two people in love and that maybe it wasn't a typical situation, but we weren't typical people.

"We're going to be together. We haven't worked out everything yet but we'll be together. I'm sure we'll move in together. Maybe we might even get married."

I was purely speculating but I assumed we'd move in together. Joey hadn't asked, but neither had I. And while previously I had completely shot down his idea of getting married, it wasn't something I would immediately discount. I mean, maybe it could work. No, it would work.

We would be happy and if I was going to marry anyone it would be him. It was just my stupid insecurities coming to play, because even if we hadn't talked about this stuff, I knew he loved me and the baby. He would want to be with us.

"Kenz, I just don't want you getting hurt. That's all. I know you said you don't need protecting, but those habits die hard." He stopped pacing and looked at me, it was hard for him to accept I no longer needed him to chase the boogieman out of my closet.

"And I love you for it, but please. Back off."

He opened his mouth to continue when my phone started to buzz, my screen lighting up like a Christmas tree with a number I didn't recognize. It was local, the number displaying a New York area code.

"Hello?" I pressed my phone to my ear fully expecting some random wrong number.

"Hello, is this Ms. Kenzie Clark? My Name is Rich Steer, I'm Black Addiction's attorney."

The mention of Black Addiction immediately made me panic. What if something happened to them on the road? When was the last time I spoke to Joey? I tried not to hyperventilate as I answered the man who'd been patiently waiting for me to respond.

"Yes, I'm Kenzie. Is everything okay with Joey and the band?"

"Yes, yes, of course," he assured me with a smooth laugh. "I just spoke to Joey yesterday actually. He was kind enough to send me a copy of your paternity results."

"Oh? He did that? Oh, okay then."

What? Paternity results? We had those results weeks ago and he had been in no hurry to file them. If it hadn't been for my insistence he wouldn't have even bothered with the test in the first place, happy to take my word. So why this was all an issue now was beyond me.

"I'm sorry, Ms. Clark, does that surprise you?" The lawyer—I couldn't remember his name—probed like I was somehow on the stand. He might sound polite but I could tell it was an act.

"No, I mean I told him he should. I just didn't think he'd done it, that's all." Or he hadn't mentioned it to me and I assumed he would. I also assumed that if he hadn't done anything with them at this point, he probably wasn't going to. It seemed a weird thing to do while he was on tour.

"Good, I'm glad we're all on the same page." His assurance made my skin crawl. "I assume you have your own representation?"

Hold on. What was happening here? How had this conversation moved from paternity to him questioning me?

"What do you mean, my own representation? Why do I need a lawyer? I'm not suing him for support." I immediately got defensive.

"No ma'am, he mentioned you weren't." He slithered about politely but I knew it was to buy time. "But we'll be filing for joint custody for the child after the birth, so you'll need someone to represent you for those proceedings." He waited to let it all sink in. "I can recommend someone if you like? As you both seem to have the best interest of the child at heart, it shouldn't take very long at all. I expect you aren't going to contest his right to custody?"

It was as if the air was pushed out from my lungs and no matter how hard I tried, they wouldn't expand. The heat flooded me in a light-headed rush and suddenly I had to grab a hold of the kitchen counter in front of me just to stay vertical.

"Wait? What?" I coughed out, the words burning their way out of my throat. "Why would he need to file for custody? We're together."

"Ma'am, in the state of New York, without an existing custody agreement, there could be disputes regarding the child at a later date."

It felt like my heart stopped beating, the breath in my lungs slowly exhaling as he continued.

"While you *state* you have a relationship, you aren't dwelling at the same address, nor are you married, so from a legal standpoint it's better to have this in writing."

He kept talking, ignoring my silence as the world crumbled from under me.

"It's as much for your protection as it is his." A laugh bubbled from his throat like he was doing me a favor.

"This way all parties would need to be agreeable on

the terms and conditions of the child's upbringing. For instance, if the child was taken out of state for extended periods of time, it would need the consent of both parents. It's all very typical and procedural."

There was so much in that, I didn't even know where to begin. *While you state you have a relationship.* What the hell were we doing if it *wasn't* a relationship? And don't even get me started about *all parties would need to be agreeable on the terms and conditions of the child's upbringing.* Our baby wasn't a fucking contract that was going to be negotiated. What the hell was Joey thinking?

"And you spoke to Joey about this?"

"I asked him what his intentions were and he said he wanted joint custody, yes." The asshole cleared his throat. "Listen ma'am, no one would try and take the child away from you if that's what you are thinking."

It was like a bomb had gone off and I had been tossed out of my body, the impact making my ears ring as my vision blurred. And then just as suddenly, I was thrown right back in, the jolt literally making me step back.

"Are you fucking kidding me?" I fired back, not giving a shit how crazed I sounded. "Like I would let you take *anything* away from me, let alone my child."

Brandon grabbed my arm, reminding me he was there—honestly, he was not my primary concern right now—as I went right back to yelling. I was doing such a great job of it, why stop now.

"You have some fucking nerve trying to muscle me

with fucking legal talk. Do you think I don't know what my rights are? I haven't asked for a thing and now you are throwing this at me? Go to hell, I'll find my own damn lawyer." I hung up before he had a chance to give me more of his bullshit posturing. Seriously, who did he think he was talking to? Did he just expect me to listen quietly while he explained his intentions of filing a court order regarding custody as soon as my baby was born? Who even does that? Was Joey motherfucking insane? He can't have honestly asked for this? Why the hell hadn't he spoken to me about it? I had never even implied that I would withhold his rights as a parent; it had been my fucking idea to get the paternity test in the first place. What the hell just happened?

"What the fuck was that?" Brandon exploded, getting enough from the one sided conversation to work out it wasn't good.

"Joey intends to file for joint custody after the baby is born and that was his attorney advising me to get representation." I tried to calm down knowing the stress wasn't good for the baby. "I don't know . . . I need to talk to him."

There was something about this that didn't add up and before I went off the deep end—okay, continued to go off the deep end—I needed to have a serious conversation. He couldn't honestly believe that I would stop him from having a say on how we brought up our baby. We'd always agreed we were doing this together.

"Wait a minute here, the asshole abandons you, and then sics his lawyer onto you? Are you fucking kidding me right now?" Brandon's attention was no longer directed at me as his face turned red.

"He didn't *abandon* me, he's working and this must be a mistake. This wouldn't be him." It couldn't be, he just wouldn't. This wasn't the Joey who held me before he left; this wasn't the Joey who called me constantly just to hear my voice. It didn't add up.

"Sure, Kenzie, it's a mistake and how did this lawyer guy get your information?" Brandon slurred sarcastically. "He just randomly called women and hoped it was someone the asshole got pregnant?"

"No, he probably got my details from the paternity results. Obviously I'm listed as the mother. It has my contact information on them since I was one who asked for the test. It was my doctor who organized it." I tried not to yell even though inside I was screaming.

"Why the hell would he even file those unless he wanted to start something?" Brandon grabbed my hands, forcing me to look at him.

I hated the he was saying the exact things I had been thinking, dragging up any doubt I had tried to bury.

"I don't know, I know what he said. We were raising our baby together. He told me that there was nothing that was going to stop him from being with me and the baby." Yes, that was my truth. I needed to believe that.

"Yet there's no fucking ring on your finger, you're not

living together. You have no plans to do either of those things and he's filing for joint custody. Yeah, sounds like he is doing *everything* to make sure he is in both your lives for a very long time."

"Stop talking, you're confusing me." I put my hands to my ears not wanting to hear another word as I sunk to my ass on the floor. "It's not him." I hiccupped, the tears I had tried to stop welling in my eyes. "I know him, and he wouldn't do this. He just wouldn't. I just need to talk to him." My head fell into my hands as a tear rolled down my cheek.

"Kenzie, listen to me." Brandon dropped to his knees beside me. "Please, you need to speak to someone first. You have no idea what you're dealing with and anything you say right now could be used against you for their case." He put his arm around me as I tried not to lose what little composure I was hanging onto. "You lawyer up before you talk to that asshole again. If this is a big misunderstanding, then I'll be the first to say I was wrong. But if it's not, then you need to make sure you and the baby are protected. You can't honestly tell me I'm being unreasonable now, can you?"

"No, you're not being unreasonable. I just don't want to believe he would do that. And as for a lawyer, I don't have that kind of money." I shrugged, knowing I was probably going to have to give up eating just to get a consultation.

"I'll pay for it; you're my sister and I'm not letting

anyone mess with you." Brandon hugged me closer. "Just do not call him until we've got this sorted. And if he calls you, let it go to voicemail."

That was going to be hard when all I wanted to do was pick up the phone *and* talk to him. Ask him why? I needed to hear it from him, that he genuinely wanted this. And then I needed him to explain how he could just crush my heart.

"I can't just stop answering his calls; he will think something is wrong."

"So. Fuck. Him." Brandon gritted out. "Did he come to you like a fucking man and tell you about all this stuff or did he send one of his people to do his dirty work? He sweats it out for a day or two, too bad. That's the least of what he deserves."

"Please stop being so angry; I'm at my limit of what I can take and I can't stand the hostility even if it's not directed at me." My head fell back into my hands as I once again lost the battle with my tears.

"I'm sorry, Kenzie. I just . . ." He stopped midsentence and kissed the top of my head. "I'm a hot-head. Runs in the family, but you're right. Nothing is more important than you and my little niece or nephew in there."

"That's the first time you referred to the baby as something other than a mistake." I lifted my head, the tears coming a little harder now.

"Yeah, well I was an idiot. Older brothers are allowed to be from time to time." He laughed.

At least something good had come out of this mess, even if it was just a sliver of a silver lining.

My phone rang obnoxiously from on top of the kitchen counter, its vibrating body gyrating across the surface.

"I should get that." I slowly rose to my feet, Brandon joining me at the counter as we looked at the display.

Joey.

"Kenzie, please don't."

I looked as it buzzed, the screen lighting up, calling attention to itself as my hands stayed by my sides.

I wanted to answer.

Desperately.

But I didn't.

And finally the screen went dark.

"He didn't leave a voicemail." I watched as the notification that no message had been left flashed across the glass.

"Maybe it's easier that way, Kenz. Just for now."

I'm not sure I agreed with my brother, in fact it made it harder.

"Call someone, find me a lawyer. I need to know where I stand."

It felt like my world had been turned upside down and inside out, and I wanted things to go back to the way they were. But what I wanted wasn't important anymore. It was about the little person inside of me whose heartbeat I'd heard for the first time.

As I tried to rein in my breathing, I felt a flutter inside

my stomach, a strange sensation I wasn't sure wasn't my imagination.

"What's wrong?" Brandon asked as my hand flew to my belly.

"I'm not sure, I think I felt the baby." I waited and sure enough, another flutter.

"Like a kick?" Brandon's eyes dipped down to my stomach like the baby would suddenly rip through it alien style.

"No, it's too soon to feel a kick." Or so I'd been told. "But it was something."

Ironic that it would be *now* that I would feel the baby move for the first time. Crap. Now I was going to cry again.

I'd never have this moment again. There would be other movements, kicks, heaps of other milestones—but this one I'd never get to share. And I think that's what hurt the most.

While I knew I could do this all on my own, I just didn't want to.

Twenty-One
Joey

Another call rang out, diverting to her voicemail. "Hey, Kenzie, it's Joey. Ummm haven't been able to catch you the last few times so I guess you're busy doing something. I'm getting ready to get on stage so I won't be able to check my phone." Why did I sound like such a fucking loser? "Anyway, I was just checking on you. How you're feeling, how everything is, the baby. Yeah. So. I guess we'll talk soon then. Okay, bye."

If that wasn't the worst voicemail in the history of voicemails then I'd be fucking surprised. I hated talking to a stupid machine, and I really needed to hear her voice.

"Hey dude, you almost ready?" Max gave me a nod as he pointed the way to the stage.

It was the last thing I wanted to do right now but there weren't a lot of other options. Our name on the banner meant I pretty much had to turn up.

"Yep, good to go." I switched my phone to silent and

slipped it into my pocket.

Even though I knew I wasn't going to be able to answer on stage, I wanted it close by. At least if she called back I'd feel it vibrating, giving me some peace of mind. Or maybe she'd send a text and I could read it during one of the bits Angie was talking or when Rusty or Max were doing a solo. No one would even notice if I pulled it out to check while I was behind the kit.

"What's up?" Angie and Rusty were already standing beside the side of the stage, just killing the last few minutes before we had to step out into the spotlight.

"Kenzie isn't answering her phone." I didn't even try and bullshit my way out of it. They knew me well enough to see through when I wasn't honest and I didn't have the energy to front.

"Maybe she's hanging with the band, or maybe she's just wiped and getting some sleep," Rusty offered, trying to be helpful no doubt.

"Joey, I remember when I was pregnant and sometimes I would switch my phone off and just forget about it." Angie injected her version of what she thought was happening. "Sometimes it was intentional, just to get some peace and quiet but other times, I'd just forget. I'm sure she's okay."

"Yeah, we'll play this gig and by the time we get off the stage she will have called you back," Max added, all of them probably wondering why the hell I was freaking out over of a couple of missed calls.

"You're all right, I'm overreacting. It's nothing. We spoke yesterday, it's only been a day." I tried to shove down the instinct that was telling me something was wrong.

"It will be fine, dude. Don't stress." Max wrapped his arm around my shoulders as we walked out to a deafening crowd.

It was show time and I had to sideline any other BS that was weighing me down and do what I needed to do. These people weren't paying to see a half-assed effort, and I wasn't going to give them one.

I sucked it up and pulled it together, taking out some of the frustration and punished the hell out of the skins. Everything I had was funneled into the songs, the distraction my ultimate saving grace as I played one the best shows of my life. I almost didn't notice when Angie raised her hand in the final goodnight, Max calling for me to step back from behind my kit.

Shit, we were done. I raised my hands and tossed the sticks I'd been playing with into the crowd as I joined the guys in front of the stage. A final bow, a bunch of waving and we were heading back through the corridor toward the dressing room.

My phone hadn't shown any signs of life the entire time. No messages, no calls—nada. I fished it out of my pocket just in case I had missed something, but the black screen confirmed that there'd been nothing to miss. Then I did a full power down and restart, because that was going to suddenly make a difference. And yet I was surprised when my cell didn't immediately start singing with activity the moment it turned back on.

I didn't even care how desperate it made me look—I was desperate—as I dialed her number again, my heart thumping through every second she didn't pick up.

Nothing.

Voicemail.

"Hey, Kenzie, it's me again. Listen, I know you're probably tired but if you can give me a call back or a text I'd really appreciate it. Okay, miss you. Bye."

Wow. I'd hit a new low, because that message was even worse than the last.

"Dude, you going to come into the dressing room or hang out in the hall?" Max stuck his head out the doorway realizing I'd stalled in the corridor.

"Yeah." My feet managed to get me inside the room even though my mind was still lingering outside.

"Still no answer?" He pulled off his shirt and kicked off his shoes, and collapsed into an armchair.

"She could be sleeping, right?" I started rationalizing; maybe she hadn't seen the missed calls or the messages and then went to bed. It was eleven o'clock, not late but if she was tired? "Or forgotten her phone on silent like Angie said."

"Exactly." Max nodded. "Last thing she needs is you getting crazy because she missed a few calls. I'm sure there is a perfectly good reason for it and she's going to think you are a complete tool."

Yeah, well she already knew that so there wasn't much danger of that now, but he was right about needing to cool it.

"Okay, I'm going to let it go. Shower, get on the bus and head to the hotel." Just hearing the plan out loud made me feel better. Besides, by morning all this shit would probably be a non-issue.

So, I went through the motions. Let the spray of the water wash off the grit and sweat from the show, toweled off and got into some clean jeans and a T-shirt. Max did the same and we headed for the bus with Rusty while Angie took a little bit longer. And with the band all together, the bus dropped us off at our hotel for the night.

I said my goodnights and went up to my room, the idea of crashing not even entering my mind. As tired as I was, my brain still churned a million miles a minute, so closing my eyes and getting some shuteye probably wasn't going to happen.

Instead I took another shower—for no other reason than I felt antsy—and ordered room service. With enough carbs to send Dr. Atkins into cardiac arrest, I sat up watching cable and drinking beer. And God help if anyone monitored the channels I was spending my time with. No, not because it was porn—that would have been acceptable—I was chilling with The Disney Channel.

The thought of watching porn bored me and at this point, I wasn't even sure I could get hard. That right there should have been a problem, and yet I couldn't make myself give a shit, happy to let the beast have a night off as I watched reruns of *The Wizards of Waverly Place*. Honestly, I had no idea what I was watching, it could have easily been some other overacted kid show and it would have done just as nicely.

Of course not to be outdone by my earlier stalker behavior, I sent Kenzie a few emails and Facebook messages. It not only helped balance out the crazy but also meant I'd covered all bases of communication, just for a little extra something to do in between my food coma and mind-numbing television watching.

And so was my night, the half eaten pizza shoved to one side of my king-size bed—too lazy to even put the tray outside my door—while the glow of the screen lulled me into some weird catatonic trance. I assumed at some point I fell asleep because when I peeled open my eyes the sun was streaming through the drapes I had neglected to close. Like a big asshole alarm clock, hitting me over the head with its morning cheer, the daylight also highlighted that it had been almost two days since I'd heard from Kenzie.

Like a kid on Christmas morning, I grabbed my phone and commenced my game of phone tag. I didn't even give a shit how pathetic it was, I just kept calling. Of course, I gave it an hour between each because obviously anything more would be bordering on stalking. As it stood now, I wasn't sure that by the time she did *eventually* call, she wouldn't demand a psych evaluation. Once again, care factor was zero.

Voicemail.

Again.

This was one of the rotations where I actually left a message, as opposed to the few times before where I didn't. Not like she wouldn't have seen the missed call even *without* the message, but common sense wasn't rating high currently.

"Babe, look I'm kind of freaking out a little. Trust me, sanity left the station about seven hours ago, so whatever you're thinking is probably right on the money. Pick up the phone and tell me what an asshole I'm being and how you are allowed to have one day where I don't call. Text me and tell me how pathetic I sound. I don't give a shit if you think I'm a loser; all I know is right now I have no idea why I can't get in touch with you and my hands are fucking tied. Kenzie, call me."

If she had any doubt on where my mental status was at, that message was the final nail. And to top it off, I was so frustrated I threw the fucking phone across the room, the shiny piece of Steve Jobs' legacy skirting the carpet like the useless piece of crap it currently was. Which sent me into a whole new set of panic as I rushed to see if I hadn't broken the fucker.

Still in one piece. Thank you, Jesus.

I sunk my ass back on the mattress, the phone—which I had little hope would actually ring—beside me and closed my eyes. Had I forgotten some kind of date or something? Did I accidentally say something stupid and now she was mad? Did I sound too excited about being away from her? What the hell was it?

And around and around we went. The party trick where I tried to recall or remember every fucking interaction I'd had with her in the last few days to try and pinpoint the moment where it could have potentially gone downhill. And with nothing to do today until the show tonight, I had all the time in the world to let every bad thought marinade and get good and festered. I didn't even leave my room, ordering more shitty room service as I sat pondering every worst-case scenario.

Had I been smart, I would have asked for her friend Sara's number. But I hadn't anticipated needing it, and didn't want anyone thinking it was for the wrong reasons. Was I desperate enough to call Dom XXXL? I still had his number from when I'd recon'd him when he and Kenzie were working together. And we did have our little gentleman's agreement where he'd keep an eye out for her. Lord knows if shit had gone down, he wasn't doing much of a job. Ah, fuck it. Who am I kidding? I should have called him hours ago.

I scrolled through my contacts till I got to his name— Big Ass MoFo—and let my fingers do the walking.

"Dom here." He answered after only the second ring. If only my girl would do the fucking same, we'd all be a lot happier.

"Hey, Dom. It's Joey." I wasn't sure if he needed more of an introduction. Not entirely sure which one I'd go with, Kenzie's boyfriend? Drummer from Black Addiction? Dude who showed up on your doorstep and acted like a lunatic? Take your pick.

"Hey, Joey, how's the tour? You guys still in New England?" The extra intro not needed as he threw back his hello-how-are-ya.

"We're actually in Philly at the moment, tour is going well. Listen," I'd done pleasant chit-chat for as long as I was going to. "I'm having a hard time catching Kenzie and I'm getting a little concerned. Nothing I should know about going on back home is there?" Translation, do you have any idea what the fuck is going on with my girlfriend? Of course he might not have gotten all of that from what I'd actually said, so I was fully prepared to fill in the blanks if needed.

"I saw Kenzie last night actually, just briefly. She was hanging with Sara and they had gone out to pick up some takeaway. Ran into them getting my own chow. She looked fine when I saw them."

So she'd been out with Sara, I started to piece together the information like a forensic detective.

"Did you talk to her? Do you know if she had her phone with her?" Yeah, because the dude would have noticed shit like that while he was waiting for his order of wildebeest or whatever the fuck the dude ate.

"I don't know, she didn't really say much. Sara did

most of the talking." The laugh at the end meant it was probably not to be repeated, not that I gave a shit what those two got hot over.

"Can you think of anything? Anything that might have been weird?" Like a neon sign above her head that spelled out what the fuck was going on, although that probably wasn't even in the realm of possibility.

"She was wearing sunglasses inside, I guess that was sort of weird. I didn't think that much of it at the time, but Sara had pulled hers off when she said hi and Kenzie kept hers on."

"Like what? You think she was hiding something?" I didn't even want imagine a possibility where she needed to hide her fucking eyes.

"Dude, I honestly don't know." The big guy proved to be not very helpful. "She didn't look like she was nursing a shiner, if that's what you're thinking."

"I have no idea what to think, but something is fucked up and if I don't talk to her some time today, you're probably going to be seeing me on the evening news."

Turn on channel five, Joey Shaw burnt down his hotel room in a fit of hysteria when he couldn't get a hold of his girlfriend. No one wanted to see that, least of all, me.

"If it makes you feel better, I can give her a call and see how she is?" he offered, his voice wavering like he wasn't sure he wanted to.

"YES!" I said probably a little too enthusiastically considering I was talking to a dude. "Give her a call and then at least we'll know if there's any issue with her phone."

Seriously, was this what girls went through every time a dude blew them off? Maybe I was being punished for all those times I said I was going to call and then didn't. Or avoided calls from girls I was no longer interested in. I had been a fucking asshole, and if there was a way I could repent for the sins of my past, I'd do that in a freaking heartbeat. Just as long as it didn't cost me Kenzie, because there was nothing worth that.

"No probs, I'll give her a call. Talk soon." Dom said his goodbye and then hung up.

Meanwhile, I was still pacing the carpet like the thing was on fire. Even though I should be halfway fucking relieved I would hopefully have some answers soon, it hadn't done anything to calm me down.

He'd call and either not get through, in which case we knew it was a service issue, or possibly get the 4-1-1. I wasn't sure which one I preferred, both really sucked.

Any minute now.

Any. Minute. Now.

No, seriously, were they discussing the global warming crisis? What the hell was taking so long?

I hadn't taken a look in the mirror but I was sure I had probably gotten older sitting by my phone. No shit, I couldn't even remember the last time I did something else, other than obsess over the fucking thing.

Still nothing.

This was getting ridiculous.

So, like I had done a million times before, I dialed Kenzie. Voicemail. There's a fucking shocker. Then I dialed Dom, expecting the same prompt pick up. Voicemail.

Are. You. Fucking. Shitting. Me. Right. Now?

And not the kind of voicemail where it could be someone is already on a call, where it doesn't even ring. No, this was fucking deliberate. The fucker sounded off until exhaustion before I got the sorry-I-can't-take-your-call.

I had either fallen into the twilight zone or this was the most elaborate punk'd stunt ever because there was no way that asshole didn't have his phone with him. We'd spoken ten minutes ago. I don't care who you are, you pick up your fucking phone. The text message I sent that spelled out exactly that probably didn't help my cause, but at this stage, I was too far gone.

"Dude, you in there?" Max knocked at my door, interrupting my mental breakdown.

"Yeah." I made my way from the bed to the door and pulled it open; he was going to see me sooner or later.

"Jesus Christ." His eyes widened as he walked into the room.

Oh, good. So I did look as bad as I felt, nice to know.

"No, actually but if you have his number maybe we could ask him what the fuck is going on because no one else seems to know."

Again with the pacing, I guess I would find out soon enough how durable the floor was.

"Still nothing?" Max's eyes scanned over the half-eaten trays of what had been last night's dinner and today's breakfast and lunch.

"Not even a peep. I even called Dom." I went on with the retell not sure if it was for Max's benefit or my own. "He saw her out with Sara last night but of course knew jack about anything. And then offered to call her and see if we could get a bead on what was happening but now he's stopped answering. I swear, I'm a step away from ramming my head through the drywall because right now nothing is making fucking sense."

All jokes aside, my mental grip on sanity had well and truly slipped and unless I got some kind of answer soon, we were going to be dealing with some very real problems. And by we, I meant everyone. For the first time in forever I had literally no idea what I was capable of.

"Joey, take a breath." Max grabbed me by the shoulders, forcing me to stand still.

Yeah, because taking a breath solved any problems.

"Something is wrong. Whatever it is, it's bad. I know it, Max. I feel like a caged fucking animal. If something happened to the baby, I swear—"

Max cut me off before I had a chance to finish. "If it was the baby, don't you think she would have called you by now? Or at the very least got someone else to call?"

God, you'd think so, but currently I had no idea what to

think. And it was fair to say anything I thought was a given, sure as fuck wasn't at this point. Assumptions were useless, and my biggest mistake, that I had made some of my own.

"I shouldn't have waited. I should have told her that I loved her when I had the chance. I should have done more." The what-ifs pounded in my head like an unrelenting marching band.

"Whatever it *is*, you will work it out. I barely recognize the guy standing in front of me, man. You haven't even looked at another girl, your playing is only getting better and you have been nothing but responsible lately. If I hadn't seen the transformation myself, I'd have guessed it was either an alien abduction or an Oscar winning performance. She would have noticed that too, Joey. It's not easy to miss."

"I've never felt like this. I'm fighting blind and I need to know what is going on now."

That was the biggest issue. I had literally no idea. I couldn't even start to fix whatever it was because unless I'd done something in my sleep, there wasn't a thing I could even remotely speculate it could be.

"Okay, so we find out. I'll try calling her, give me her number." Max held out his phone so I could input her digits.

With a bunch of whispered Hail Mary's we waited as the call connected, praying that she would answer an unknown caller. If this didn't work I was going to systematically go through every person I knew within a five-mile radius of her and try to find answers. And just when we thought the call was either going to end or get diverted to voicemail, the noise stopped. Max and I looked at each other wondering if we'd been disconnected when we heard her.

"Hello?"

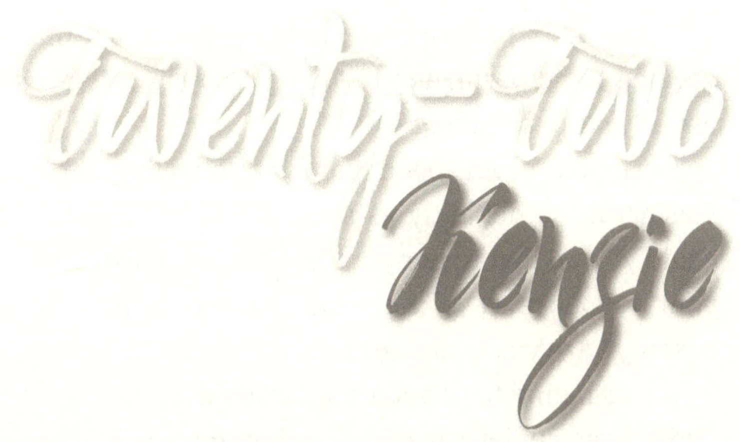

"Hello?" Sara had grabbed my phone and decided to answer the unknown caller. I, on the other hand was going to ignore it. I didn't have the best track record with phone calls especially in the last few days, so was going to let it go to my about-to-explode mailbox. Sara had other ideas.

"No, it's Sara." There was no need for confirmation, the wide-eyed look she gave me spelled out it had to be Joey. Or someone connected to him.

I wasn't surprised. We'd gone from talking and texting constantly to radio silence, and I couldn't keep doing this.

Avoiding him was killing me slowly, the ache in my chest just seemed to widen as the hours went by, but what was the alternative. I wasn't ready to talk to him yet. Unless by talk you meant yell, cry and basically spit out random fucks because that's probably all I was capable of right now. Too many emotions swirled in me to be objective.

"Hang up," I whispered, fighting the tears that had seemed to be permanently falling. Too late. My eyes had already started leaking.

Sara had never been good at following directions, staring at me defiantly as she opened her mouth. "How could you do that to her you, asshole. She trusted you and your response is to tell your lawyer to file for joint custody? Are you brain dead or just stupid?"

It was bound to happen sooner or later.

She was my best friend, so when my world tilted, she was the first person I turned to. At first she'd been on Joey's side but with Brandon's spin and the legal advice I'd received, she had quickly turned.

She might have mentioned bodily harm once or twice, which is why she ignored my explicit instruction that no one talk to Joey.

The opportunity proved too great a temptation as she let it fly. Like regular Sara with Tourette's, every single thought she had about Joey and/or the situation came flying out of her mouth with no filter.

Any other circumstances it would have been entertaining to watch.

"No, fuck you!" she yelled into the phone before ending the call. "That went well." She smiled before handing me the cookie dough we'd been medicating with. There weren't going to be any actual cookies baked, not that either of us gave a crap.

"Yeah, it sounded like it did. What did he say?" It shouldn't matter, and yet, here I was asking.

"Acted like he had no idea what I was talking about, denied the whole thing." She rolled her eyes in disbelief. "Like *we're* the dumbasses. Seriously, he had me fooled. Brandon is right, you need to keep away from him."

In the last few days, everything had unraveled. I went through and systematically analyzed every detail of our relationship. While it seemed out of character, there was no denying that we'd been thrown into a pressure cooker, going zero to a hundred in such a short time. It killed me that I couldn't be sure of his intentions, that I couldn't laugh the whole thing off as a joke. What evidence did I have either way? Just because he said he cared for the baby and me didn't mean he'd be there forever, which is why I agreed to see an attorney.

Brandon had called in a favor with an old military buddy. He had hung up the uniform and was now working with a law firm in town. His boss—Moira Feldman—had been only too happy to slot us in-between appointments so we could have a consultation. What she told us didn't make me feel warm and fuzzy.

"Yes, the father is well within his legal rights to seek joint legal custody once the child is born. Legally, paternity has already been established, so this would safeguard him if you decided to flee or later down the road wanted another man to adopt the child as his own." The leather of her worn office chair creaked as she leaned back.

"But we had a verbal agreement, I had no intention of stopping him from being a part of the baby's life. In fact, our relationship had sort of progressed where I assumed we'd be together for it." I tried to explain.

Things had been the best they'd ever been before Joey had left, and it made me realize how much I cared about him. Okay loved him. I was in love with him and hoped that us becoming a couple was more than just us being together because of circumstances. I had assumed those feelings were reciprocated, and even if he didn't love me like I loved him, he still cared deeply for me. He'd been nothing but incredibly sweet, gentle—nothing to tip me off that he didn't want to be with me.

"Perhaps the distance gave him some perspective and he got cold feet. You mentioned he's a musician who is currently on tour?" She waited for me to nod.

"It could be possible that he was reminded of what he would be giving up, I assume long term relationships hadn't been part of his original plan. It also wouldn't be the first time a man has promised something and didn't follow through. No offense, Mr. Clark." She smiled at Brandon, who had insisted on sitting beside me. I didn't even try and fight him; concerned I might miss something important.

"None taken. It's exactly what I've been trying to get Kenzie to see." Brandon sat up a little straighter in his chair. "The scumbag has decided he doesn't want to stick around, but also wants to have his cake and eat it too."

"We don't know that, this is all speculation, right?" I

looked to Moira, hopeful.

I didn't want to believe that a few short days back in his old lifestyle would erase what we had built, but if I was honest, it was entirely possible. Like giving an alcoholic a beer, maybe those old feelings of temptation would return. It wasn't even about sex; it was the freedom that he would inevitably have to give up. He'd said he wanted me, but had he been really ready to settle down? The grass might still look greener on the other side, especially since that's where he was currently mowing his lawn.

"Sure, Ms. Clark. There could be a million explanations as to why he would want to start legal proceedings, but I'm not a fortuneteller. The law is one thing I do understand and usually when a man files for joint physical custody of a child, it is either the dissolution of a union or the intention not to pursue a relationship with the mother." Moira didn't bother with the sugarcoating. Possibly she was getting impatient with me, or had become extremely jaded with years in family law but I didn't doubt that she knew what she was talking about.

When I walked into her homey, beige office, I'd hoped for something different. Reassurance that I was worrying needlessly, and that the paperwork was standard for all couples who weren't married. I'd hoped she'd give me a warm smile and soothe my fears, not add fuel to an already kindling fire.

"You're right. What are my options?" My fingers threaded in my lap as I listened to all the possibilities and

scenarios.

It was extremely sobering, hearing words that sounded so clinical used to describe my baby and our situation. It showed me how incredibly naïve I'd been to assume we could have just worked things out ourselves. I guess Joey had come to the same conclusion. I just wished it didn't have to be that way.

"Dom said he called earlier too?" Sara's voice snapped me back to the present, the unpleasant thoughts about my future being pushed to the side.

"Yeah, I gave him the condensed version and asked him to keep it to himself for awhile." I shrugged, utterly exhausted.

Last thing I wanted to do was share my tales of woe with anyone else, but Joey had taken matters into his own hands when I hadn't answered his calls. Honestly, part of me was impressed that he kept Dom's number and swallowed his pride long enough to call him and ask. If this had been another situation, I'd be high-fiving his resourcefulness. We weren't so intricately woven in each other's lives that he had a lot to go on. But it wasn't another situation, it was this one, and to think he was surprised that I had the reaction that I had, was almost offensive. Not that I had a lot of experience with this sort of stuff, but if the guy you saw as your *boyfriend* suddenly gets his lawyer to call, it doesn't mean good things. The intention to file a lawsuit; well that was just another nail in the coffin.

"So, is Brandon going to kill him?" Sara popped a piece of cookie dough into her mouth. She had taken over from Brandon this afternoon, the two of them taking turns on Kenzie watch in case I "broke down" and called him. Like I wasn't going to eventually.

"No one is killing anyone." I stole back the cookie dough, only half hearted about our quest to eat my feelings. "But you both need to stop treating me like a child."

What they failed to understand was they were only currently part of this because I allowed it. Which I still wasn't convinced had been the smartest thing I'd ever done. And the talking *at* me was really starting to piss me off. It's not like I was sixteen and stupid. I'd done fine up until this point without anyone's input.

"It's all because we love you and we're mad *for* you. Aren't you angry?"

"No, I'm hurt," I said quieter than I'd meant to. "How can I be mad at him for wanting to be in the baby's life? I'd have been mad if he all of sudden wanted to have nothing to do with—" I felt another flutter. Almost as if the baby had heard we were talking about him or her and wanted in on the conversation.

"You need to go, Sara." My head felt like it was going to explode, and I didn't know what I thought anymore. Somehow what I wanted was getting lost in the voice of everyone else's opinion.

"Kenzie, don't do it." She put her hands on her hips, not

making an effort to leave.

"If I do anything, it will be *my* choice. Last time I checked, I didn't give up that right because I was having a baby."

I hadn't intended to yell—but like all things with me— it didn't always go to plan. But I couldn't regret it.

"Maybe I was wrong about Joey." I sighed, verbally and mentally trying to sort through the mess. "Maybe all we're going to be are shared names on a birth certificate, but I refuse to hate him. I refuse to listen anymore; whatever happens from here on out is what I want to do. Brandon wanted me to seek legal advice, that's been done, the rest is up to me."

Wow, that felt good.

Like I was suddenly gaining some control from the spiral that was currently my life.

"I'm sorry. You're right. It's your choice." Sara shifted uncomfortably on her feet. "I just hate to see someone hurt my friend. Believe me, this thing shocked the hell out of me too. I really thought you guys were going to be together."

Huh, well I guess we'd all made that mistake.

"I love him, Sara. I still do. I just can't turn those feelings off even though I want too. That's the reason why I'm avoiding talking to him right now. Not because that's what anyone else wants. It's because my heart is breaking and hearing his voice will just make it shatter all over again."

I hated hearing my own vulnerability, but I wasn't ashamed of it either. Those feelings had been real for me regardless of what Joey had felt. And even if it had been for a short time, we'd shared something amazing. If that was over—if we were over—I needed to be able to speak to him without falling apart. We were going to be forever tied. There was no walking away and despite every instinct in me wanting to run away, I couldn't. Not this time.

"I'm sorry, Kenz. Last thing you need is extra pressure. I'll go and make sure your brother lays off. If he doesn't, I'll call Dom." Her lips slowly curled into a smile. "He can be very persuasive."

"It's okay." I tried to return the smile, it didn't work out so well for me. "I'll handle my brother."

She gave me a nod and then showed herself out, the silence that came with her departure, comforting.

I stopped; the quiet wrapping me up in a blanket as I stood still in the moment.

I was alone.

And it wasn't the worst thing in the world.

My hand swept across my belly, something I had been doing a lot lately and I absorbed the feeling.

No matter what happened between Joey and me, this baby would be loved. That was one thing I knew hadn't changed, and right now, that's what I needed to concentrate on.

I picked up the phone, my finger hovering over the

contacts and then I finally did it.

No. I wasn't calling Joey.

"Hey, little sis, what do you need?" Brandon's voice filled my ear.

"I love you, Brandon, but I need you to listen to me." I took a deep breath. "I know what I want and how to live my life, and you can't bully me even with good intentions." This is who I was, this is who I needed to be right now.

"Kenzie, I wasn't bullying you, I was—"

I didn't give him a chance to finish. "It's not a debate. I know what's best and right now, fighting Joey isn't it. So until you accept that I'm an adult capable of making her own decisions and that I know what I'm doing, I'm going to need you to stay away."

"Sis . . ." He took a breath. "I think you're making a mistake."

"You're wrong, Brandon. None of this is a mistake, and I won't let you or anyone else try and make me believe it is. I love you."

I didn't wait for a response or a goodbye; I didn't need any of those things. The mental fog that had weighed me down over the last few days was starting to lift and I finally felt like I could breathe.

I was alone.

And it wasn't the worst thing in the world.

Twenty-Three

Joey

"**What the fuck did you do?**" I was barely able to spit out the words through my clenched jaw. My anger level, so far in the red I couldn't see straight.

"Joey, calm down." Rich laughed nervously, "Why don't you take a breath and tell me what the problem is."

Take a breath? He'd be lucky if he was still breathing after I got through with him. Of all the fucked up things that could have been wrong, this was not something I could have ever imagined.

"The problem, you low life piece of scum, is you calling my girlfriend and filling her head with fucking lies. Who the fuck do you think you are?" I gripped the phone so tight, the POS squeaked in protest. My anger level so far off the chain, I felt completely out of control.

"Joey, I'm going to have to ask you again to calm down." Another worthless piece of advice from the dickwad in the suit, and I was really tired of hearing it. "I can hear you're upset, but yelling isn't going to fix the problem. Now, I'm assuming you spoke to Kenzie?"

"No fucktard, I haven't," I snapped back, wondering how anyone could be so stupid. "Funny how she stopped taking my calls after you told her *we* would be filing for custody. I never once told you to contact her and I sure as hell didn't agree to a fucking lawsuit against my girl-friend. How does that even make sense?"

While I hadn't gotten a chance to speak to Kenzie, Sara had only been too happy to get on the horn and tell me exactly what kind of shithead she thought I was. It was an enlightening phone call, hearing about how I'd betrayed the woman I loved and threatened her with fucking legal action. And someone needed to call fucking Guinness because the first time in my life, I'd been speechless.

"Joey, we spoke about this." The condescending ass-hole showed zero signs of remorse. "I *asked* you what your intentions were, you said you wanted to raise the child with Kenzie. I *asked* you if you wanted joint physical custody, you said yes. Any part of this conversation jogging your memory?"

Right now I was thankful. Strange in a situation like this, but I raised my eyes up nonetheless. And thanked God that this piece of shit was in a different state because if he wasn't, I'd be sitting in a jail cell right now.

"You twisted my words around, asshole. I wanted to raise our kid, together *with* her. There was no need for fucking paperwork, I never told you to file paperwork." I couldn't remember a time when I had this much rage. It swallowed me up and I couldn't breathe, with complete lack of control. I had no idea what I was capable of and I was too far gone to care.

Max was stone still beside me, watching me go absolutely crazy after we had to listen to Sara's rant. And if I'd done half the things she said I'd done, she would have been totally justified. But I hadn't. And instead of Max leaving like I asked him to do, he was standing sentry, ready to bring the noise if I needed him.

"I haven't done anything. I merely informed her that we *would* file after the birth of the child. If you want to make sure your rights as the father are protected then it needs to be done, and it was important she had time to retain adequate legal counsel."

I pulled the phone away from my ear confused as to whether this moron had heard a single word I'd said. Like anything? Because either my version of English was completely off or this guy had his head so far up his ass, he was going to be wearing his colon as a necklace.

"Are you hearing anything I am saying to you?" My whole body shook as the words shot out of my mouth. "I'm that kid's dad because I am going to be there when he or she is born, not because you put my name on a fucking piece of paper. *You* have screwed everything up, and so help me, if I lose either one of them, I will hunt you down—"

"Joey." Max cut in, the shake of head giving me the it's-not-a-good-idea he didn't need to say.

I took a breath. "Shit will not be good for you." My censored version nowhere near what I was feeling.

"This isn't the first time I've worked with musicians, so I get how highly strung you creative types get." His response seemed completely unaffected. "Because of that, I am willing to overlook the threats. And it is against my advice, but if you don't want the motion filed, we won't. Okay?"

Did I stumble into the land of fucking Oz? Because for the life of me I can't understand what fairytale this guy was trying to sell me. As for the musicians he's worked with, I didn't give a fuck. This wasn't about me being a prima donna needing my ego stroked. This was about my life, and how some guy I barely even knew had lit a fire inside my house. There I was, powerless watching the thing burn.

"You say that like it's going to fix anything. She thinks this was *my* idea, that I'm just waiting to dump her like last week's news."

I'd die before I'd hurt Kenzie, take a gunshot right to the chest if it meant I could save her from feeling pain. Yet in some fucked up twist of fate, she'd been hurt anyway.

"Well, I can't control what she thinks, Joey. That's not my job." The bastard had the nerve to sound indignant.

"No, it's not your fucking job. None of this was your fucking job," I screamed into the mouthpiece and killed the call, the phone that had been previously sitting in my hand getting thrown across the room. The soft thud when it landed on the bed not nearly as satisfying as the smashing of glass I'd expected.

My body lost control as I dropped to my knees and screamed. The frustration burned through my veins as my brain completely disconnected.

She thought I was leaving her, like it could have even been an option.

"Joey, focus, brother. You need to hold it together." Max sunk to his knees beside me. "We will work this out."

"Dude, you need to give me time to cool off. I can't be around anyone right now." I sunk forward and stared at the floor, my thighs absorbing the weight of my body as I let go.

"I don't think that's smart. You want to throw shit—trash the room—I won't stop you. But I think it's best you do it with an audience." Max shot me a look of concern, like he half expected me to take a razor to my wrists.

"I'm not going to trash the room, or myself, if that's what you're thinking." I looked him dead in the eye so he knew I was on the level. "But I need to make some calls." Or figure out a way to fix this.

"I'm going to talk to Rusty and Angie and get them up to speed. We also need to fire that son of a bitch." Max shifted on his feet, not sold on leaving. "We're with you on this, whatever you need."

"Thanks. Not sure what anyone can do right now, but I

appreciate you being so tight about this." *And allowing me to have my fucking breakdown without making feel like a complete pussy.*

"Please, being tight is the least I can do. You do what you can." He nodded to the phone. "And we'll make sure the asshole gets his walking papers." He turned and walked out the door.

It was so fucking quiet that I could hear my own heartbeat hammering in my chest. It was keeping tempo with the quick in and out sucks of air my lungs were doing. I needed out of here and I needed it now.

I slowly rose to my feet; the muscles in my legs accepting my weight as I came to full height. My phone, which could have been a casualty, remained intact lying on the mattress of the hotel room bed. As much as I wanted to call Kenzie, there was someone else I needed to call first.

I waited for the call to connect, the voice answering pretty soon after.

"Hello."

"Hey, it's Joey." I rested my head on my fists as I lowered my ass onto the mattress.

"Joey, long time no hear. I'm guessing this isn't a social call, is it?"

"No." I swallowed hard, not having any other ideas. "I need a massive favor and I swear to you, I will owe you."

"You're assuming you have anything I want."

"I'm handing you a blank check, you can cash it anytime you want. I've never given anyone that." I didn't care what it cost me, whatever the price was—it would be worth it. But I needed this.

"Keep your blank check." There was a pause. "If it's that important, I'll do it for free."

"It doesn't get more important than this." I closed my eyes and waited.

There was a pause, but only for a sec. "What do you need?"

•••

Max sent me a message to say Angie and Jase were on the phone to the James and Alex and the other powers that be at Metamorphous, our label. Rich had been fired, but if they had their way, he'd never work with anyone in the music industry again. They were just as pissed as we were, and were leaving no stone unturned as we waded through the misery dipped in sin that I was left to deal with.

The band knew me enough to give me my space, which I appreciated, more because I was seriously on the clock than because I wanted to be alone. It was going to be touch-and-go with the high potential to blow up in my face, but I had to try. And I was already running out of time.

"Dude, let us in." Max rapped on my hotel door, my time limit for solitude apparently expired as I opened the door. Max, flanked by Angie and Rusty stood on the other side, their faces wearing some of my strain.

"I'm glad you're all here. We need to talk." I stepped aside and let them in, my plan pretty obvious once they saw my packed suitcase on the bed.

"You're leaving." Angie looked to the case and then back to me. It hadn't been a question and she didn't seem surprised.

"I'm sorry." I took a seat beside it on the bed as they took up residence on the hotel provided sofa. "I need to go to Kenzie. If there was any other way I could do this without leaving, I'd do it. But the only way I can fix this is by going back to New York. You guys aren't just a band to me; you're my family and this is fucking killing me right now."

I didn't want to have to make the choice. To have to put it on the line like that, but that was my child and the woman I loved. I couldn't pretend that I was going to be able to play tonight even if I did stay here. I needed to go all in and if I lost, it was going to be big but I was all out of choices.

"Joe, we know." Rusty nodded, his face reading like he had been expecting me to pull the pin. "We'll cancel the show, simple. No one can make us play."

"You can't cancel the show." Telling seven thousand people who had paid their hard-earned money they weren't going to see the band wasn't an option. I'd disappointed enough people, besides we were out of time. "We're supposed to be on stage in four hours."

"Okay, maybe we program the bass parts into the preset." Angie started brainstorming, her eyes clocking our bass player as she tried to execute the trouble-shooting of the century. "And Max can take the kit tonight. It won't be fantastic, but we can make do."

Max was an amazing bass player. But the all-round talented dude was also solid on guitar as well as being able to keep steady time on the kit. Nothing fancy, but he could drive the beat and keep the main tempo happening. But going out on the stage with a backing track wasn't what Black Addiction did.

"We aren't a band who plays a pre recorded set, even if it's just one channel for one show. We'd be cheating and you all know it." Looking at their faces confirmed they knew I was right. We were a lot of things; frauds weren't one of them. It was a hundred percent on that stage or not at all.

"So what are you suggesting?" Rusty let out a half assed laugh. "We set up a kit and let you play it via Skype?"

"No, you won't need me tonight."

"What the hell are you talking about?" Max looked me over like I had clearly lost my mind. "I'm thinking if we take the stage without a set of beats behind us, someone is going to notice."

I was just about to fill them on my plan when the there was a knock at the door. If shit hadn't been so time sensitive and completely fucked up, I might have smiled knowing what was on the other side. Instead I pulled it open and let it all unfold without the dialogue.

"Troy?" Angie jumped to her feet as Rusty and Max did the same swivel what-the-fuck between me and the door. Their feet also hitting the floor as they greeted our new guest.

"Don't all say hello all at once." The big guy walked into the room and threw his overnight bag onto the floor. My anxiety levels knocked down a few notches by the smile he had on his face.

"Wait a second. Troy is going to play drums tonight?" Angie proved what a quick study she was by connecting the dots.

The Power Station heavy hitter was one of the most proficient drummers I knew. It also helped that he'd been a friend of Angie's since forever and had a history with the band, Black Addiction being their opening act for their last stadium tour. Oh, and he and his band buddies also owned the label we were signed to.

"Well, I really had a hard-on for the triangle, but Joey tells me you need a drummer. So I guess I can sit behind the kit for a night." Troy cocked a grin.

"No offence, dude," Rusty moved closer, his hand rubbing the back of his neck. "But do you know our stuff?"

"Ha." Troy barked out a laugh. "Considering I heard it most nights for months while we were on tour together,

I'd say I'll be able to pull through. I've got all the MP3s downloaded as well, I'll have them squared away within the hour," he said with an absolute confidence that no one could question.

If anyone could pull it off, it was the dude standing in front of me, and there was no one else I trusted more to do the job.

"Troy, thank you." Angie threw her arms around the big guy and gave him a hug. Our lead singer rarely got handsy, but Troy was like the brother she'd never had and he'd more than proven his friendship to all of us.

"Joey already thanked me." He gave me a nod, the unspoken understanding flowing between us. "And honestly, I think it will be a good time. I can't remember the last time we played together."

"I think I was sixteen. This is going to be fun." Angie smiled for the first time since she'd walked in my room.

The keys to my ride for the night were in the hands of someone I knew would take care of it. Who knew what was going to happen when I got to New York, but at least I hadn't fucked up this family too. I don't think I could have forgiven myself if I had.

"Go, we've got this." Max grabbed my suitcase off the bed and handed it to me. "Go to her." His hand grabbed my arm in a show of support.

"Okay, I need to get to the airport." I checked my pocket to make sure I had my phone and wallet, hopefully able to catch a direct flight. I hadn't had time to check schedules, and honestly I didn't give a shit which route I had to take as long as I got there tonight.

"My driver's downstairs ready to take you." Another trademark Troy grin. "And, I chartered a jet. It's just sitting on the tarmac with nowhere to be until I'm done."

"You chartered a jet?" Rusty, Max and I echoed in stereo, Angie obviously not so surprised.

"Have you tried to get out of JFK in an hour?" Troy laughed, proving how ridiculous the alternative would have been.

"Thanks, I owe you." I threw out my hand, the gratitude I was giving him nowhere near what he deserved.

"You owe me nothing." He clapped my palm with his own. "Go do what you need to do. I'll see if these guys can keep up."

"Guys—" My mouth dried up as I looked at each one of my band—my family—unable to thank them for their support.

"We know." Angie gave me a squeeze and looked to the door I would soon be walking out of. "Go."

A strange sense of calm came over me as I accepted our fate. The knots in my stomach slowly relaxed as I became more resolved in my decision. Joey and I needed to talk and the more time that went by the harder it was going to be. The sooner, the better.

If he had freaked out and wanted to go back to the way things were in the beginning, then I wasn't going to beg. And as much as it would hurt, I'd rather know now than have him fake it until the baby was born. That would have hurt so much more. Either way, we were adults and we would get through this.

Right.

Big girl panties on.

I picked up my phone— the same device I'd been avoiding for days that now had so many missed calls, messages and texts that I was surprised it hadn't disintegrated under the pressure—and scrolled through to his number.

I hesitated.

Maybe I should listen to his messages first? Or read the texts?

No, I needed to stop stalling and just call.

Crap, what time was it? He had a show tonight. He might be getting ready. My brain threw out a few more roadblocks as my finger hovered over his number.

Gah.

Stop.

Press the number and call for God's sake.

The call connected directly to voicemail as I held the phone to my ear.

"Hey this Joey, you know the drill. Wait for the beep." *BEEP.*

God, he sounded good. His voice like water to my thirsty ears as I cleared my throat.

"Hi, it's me." I cringed wondering if I should specify who the *me* was before continuing. I decided to leave it and press on. "I know this is about two days too late, but I just needed some time to get things straight in my head." A long breath I'd been unconsciously holding spilled out from my lips. "I'm not sure what happened or why it happened, but I need you to understand that I'll be okay. It's okay that you changed your mind, and as much as I hated hearing it from that lawyer, I'm glad I know." I kept going before I lost my nerve. "I will never keep you from our child—no matter what happens between us—but if you need paperwork, I'll agree. I know when we started this we promised we'd stay friends and as long as we can do that, then we'll get through this. It's been crazy, right?" A soft laugh escaped my throat. "I know we've gone through a whole lot in the last few months but I wouldn't change it. I never told you, Joey. I am glad you're the baby's father. Even if it has to be like this. I'm not mad, but I'm not going to let this get ugly either. I'll talk to you soon, bye."

I breathed out a sigh of relief. At least it hadn't timed out, that's something. It would have been completely awkward if I'd only been able to leave half my message. And I didn't cry *or* tell him how much I loved him. All positive things. Whether or not waiting to call him had been the best decision, it sure made the things I wanted to say easier.

I eased back into my armchair as I wondered what he would think when he heard the message. If he would call me back right away or let it sit. I couldn't be mad if he decided to give it a few days before he called. It was a lot to take in but I already felt lighter having the one-sided conversation. It had been easier being able to get it out without interruptions.

Oh, shit. I sat up suddenly as I felt a slight panic wash over me. I should have told him that I felt the baby move. It's something he should know, something I'm sure he would want to know. It was also something I probably should have told him *when* it happened, cheating him out of sharing the moment. Still, I wasn't going to beat myself up about it. I'd had a valid reason for keeping it to myself and now was better than a week or two later. Or three months from now when he gets back.

I hit the redial button again, internally cringing at having to leave another message. Shit. What if he answered this time? Considering I left that awesome all-together and levelheaded message, it would be hella awkward if I turned into a stuttering mess. My heart pounded a little harder as I waited, his voicemail once again kicking into gear. I waited through his prerecorded message and the all-important beep.

"Hi, it's me again." Lame. I scrunched my eyes tight as I focused on my task. Get in, get out—don't stumble and try not to sound like a jackass. "I forgot to mention in the last message. I-I felt the baby for the first time. A couple of days ago. It was sort of weird at first, like butterflies were trying to get out, but I felt it again today. It was . . . it was really cool. Anyway, I thought you should know. Bye."

What was that? I shook my head as I slowly exhaled, my hand lowering the phone away from my ear. My second effort had not been nearly as polished as the first, so I probably should quit while I was ahead. And I'd done what I'd set out to do. Hopefully find us some middle ground where no one else would interfere—just us, doing what we had intended to do from the beginning.

As I settled back into the chair, my thoughts wandered

back to Joey. That smile of his that always spelled trouble, his dark sultry eyes and his amazing hair. I thought about how strong his arms were and how nice it had been to be wrapped in them.

I missed him.

I missed everything about him.

It was with mixed sadness when I slowly rose to my feet and walked to my bedroom, the ghost of memories just as vivid in there. I could remember and not be sad I told myself as I slowly undressed, slipping into one of his old T-shirts I had decided should be my sleep shirt. It was comfortable and smelled of him, the fabric against my skin like the hugs that I was missing.

I was just about to lay down, my head desperate to get reacquainted with my pillow when I'd heard a knock at the door. The groan had been automatic, knowing it was probably Sara or Brandon, even though I had told them I needed space. Whoever it was, they wouldn't be staying.

My bare feet padded to the door, my shoulders squared as I opened it.

And then my heart skipped a beat.

"Joey, what are you doing here?" My eyes not believing he was in front of me, blinked and refocused. "Don't you have a show?" The only thing I could think of to say.

He didn't answer, crashing through the doorway and pressing his mouth to mine. My lips opened for him as his tongue teased them apart, our kiss deepening as he cradled my head with his hands. I'd known this kiss; it was one of desperation as he pulled me closer, his mouth dominating mine.

My body responded, the arms that had previously hung lifelessly by my sides got in on the action and wrapped themselves around him. Fingers wandered aimlessly, trying to touch as much of him as I could, as my foot kicked the door closed.

Slowly he pulled his mouth away, moving it just far enough so he could speak. "I listened to your message." His eyes locked on mine. "You are so wrong; I'm not done with this, with you."

"But—" His fingers moved to my mouth and I stopped talking.

"No, for days I lost my mind." He pressed his lips against my forehead. "Literally, lost any sanity I had, not knowing what happened." His lips moved down my face, small kisses following in their wake before he moved back to look at me. "What that asshole did, wasn't me. But I should never have given him those paternity results." I watched as he swallowed, his fingers locking into mine. "That was my fuck up, I'll own it. He took my words and twisted them into something they weren't. I would never need paperwork to know you would do right by me, even if we weren't together. I'm sorry. I'm sorry that I didn't pay enough attention and that I let someone come between us."

My eyes welled as the stress of the last few days melted between us. The wave of emotion crashing over me as his words sunk in.

He hadn't wanted to leave me.

He wanted to be here, with me.

"God, I didn't want to let you go." I gave up trying to stop the tears, no point really—sooner or later they were coming. "But I thought it's what you wanted."

"No, I never wanted to leave." He kissed my lips gently. "I don't ever want to leave." His fingers traced my jaw as he pulled his mouth away, my lips immediately mourning their loss.

"I did this once for the wrong reasons." He sunk to his knees in front of me and I felt like my heart stopped beating. "You asked me if I loved you, and that was the only reason I should propose." He looked up at me from his place on the floor, his gaze unfaltering. "I love you. I've loved you for a while, but was either too stupid or too scared to tell you. But it's how I feel, Kenzie. I love you. I'm in love with you, and I'm down on my knees asking you to marry me. Marry me, because I can't live another day without you. You, me—that's the kind of stuff that defies the odds and I want a forever with you. Trust me, and I promise you I will not fuck it up."

It was like an explosion happened inside of my chest, with every cell in my body waking up all at the same time. The words ringing in my ears as I replayed them in my head and I couldn't breathe.

He loved me.

He wanted to be with me.

He wanted to marry me.

It was that one-in-a-million lightning strike, the possibility you didn't even dare to hope for, and here he was—on his knees—for me.

"You need to say something, babe." He kept his fingers interwoven with mine as he rose to his feet. "I need to know if you'll marry me."

"I love you too," I blurted out, the words I'd been dying to say finally coming out of my mouth.

"Marry me," he asked again, hugging me close to his chest, the steady rhythm of his heart beating proudly beneath his shirt.

"Yes." I nodded, my lips finding his. The kisses we'd shared not long enough as I craved more of him.

"I still don't have a ring," he mumbled against my mouth.

"It doesn't matter." I laughed, not caring if he ever bought the jewelry or not. I had what I wanted, and that meant more than any diamond he might buy.

"Also, just because I've come to my senses doesn't mean in the future I won't make mistakes." His hands moved restlessly over my body like he hadn't touched me in years. "Know that I love you, I didn't mean it, and please ask me before you write me off, okay?"

The guilt crept up on me like a big ugly blanket. As hard as it was to admit, I had played a part in this mess. Listening to everyone else instead of listening to my heart.

"I'm sorry, I should have asked you." I shook my head, not believing how close I'd come to losing all of this because I was too scared to confront him. "I just got so confused, and Brandon was here when the lawyer called, so you can imagine how that went."

"Yeah, let's just say we should keep away from your brother for a while." There was not even a hint of humor in his voice. He and Brandon weren't going to be hanging out, drinking beer anytime soon.

"He means well." I half-heartily tried to defend him. His intentions were good even if the execution blew hardcore.

"Babe, I respect the hell out of him, and I'm sure he loves you." He brought our interlocked hands to his lips and kissed my fingers. "But he tried to fuck with my family, so he's now on my shit list. I'll calm down before the wedding, I'm sure."

Wow, a wedding. And for the first time ever I wanted to be married.

To him.

Forever.

I was probably going to cry again. Damn it.

"So did you listen to both my messages?" I moved our conversation into a happier direction, hopefully one that would stop me from becoming a blubbering mess. He hadn't mentioned the *other* more awkward message, the one where I'd told him about our little person making their presence felt.

"No, when I heard the first, I couldn't listen to the second." He didn't need to tell me why, his eyes still held the pain. "I figured if it was important enough you could tell me to my face. Or maybe you wouldn't need to say it."

He had wrongly assumed the other message would have been worse and possibly hoped we could bury it now we were together. He had no idea that he actually *wanted* to listen to that message.

"No, it still needs to be said." I smiled, hoping it would alleviate some of his worry. "Listen to your messages."

"Can't you just tell me?" He fished out his cell from his pocket, no doubt wondering why the hell I wouldn't just say it, but humoring me all the same.

He punched the numbers into his phone and brought it to his ear, his face unreadable as he listened. Annnnd then his expression changed; his eyes on me the entire time as he gripped the phone so tightly, I was sure it was going to snap.

"He moved? And I missed it?" He pulled the phone away from his ear, not even trying to hide his disappointment.

"Or she." We still had no idea of whether it was a boy or girl. "But you wouldn't have felt it, I barely did." I wrapped my arms around him, laid my head against his chest. "You'll be here for the next time."

"You bet your ass I will be."

He dropped to his knees and pressed his lips to my belly. "Listen here, buddy, this is your daddy. I just told your mommy how much I love her, but you need to know that I love you too, and we're done fucking—I mean *messing*—around. We're going to be a family now, so you do whatever it is you need to do in there and I'll take care of everything else out here. Also, if you hear your mom or me swear, those are grown up words and not for you." He kissed my stomach and then got back onto his feet.

"I love you." I smiled, unable to stop saying those three words. It was like a sickness and I was happy to be infected.

"God, I love hearing that." He grinned, obviously just as far gone as I was.

"Me too." I snuggled closer.

"Now, I'm going to need to make love to my future wife." He wrapped his arms around me and lifted, my feet losing contact with the ground. Our new destination set as he moved us into my bedroom.

"Wait, aren't you supposed to be on a stage somewhere?" My back hit the mattress as he lowered me down, my mouth asking questions while the rest of me screamed to *shut the fuck up*.

"It's cool, I got a fill in." He joined me on the bed, kicking off his shoes. His eyes telling me he was done with the conversation.

"Who did you get on such short notice?" My stupid mouth once again let down the team. Seriously, why couldn't I shut up?

"Stop talking, I need to get you naked already." He

laughed against my throat, his hands wandering against the hem on my sleep shirt.

"So, tell me who and I'll strip." I wriggled around underneath him, my fingers moving to the fly of his jeans.

"Troy Harris, from Power Station." He pulled off his T-shirt and tossed it to the floor as I got to work on his pants.

"Whoa, he just had nothing better to do than a stand-in gig?" I unzipped his jeans and palmed him, the thickness of his cock erasing any need I had to discuss anything further. In fact, what was I even talking about?

"What can I say, he needed the challenge. We're done talking about him and the band." His fingers ripped off my sleep shirt, getting impatient as his eyes steamrolled over my mostly-naked body. "God, you're beautiful."

"Touch me." My back rose off the mattress desperate to feel his hands on my skin.

He didn't answer; a low growl rose from his throat as he kicked off his jeans and moved his mouth to my breast, his lips wrapping around my tight peak.

Yes.

I had meant to say it out loud but my mouth refused to operate, instead a strangled moan came out as I writhed underneath him.

"I've missed this so much." His mouth moved to my other breast, his hands moving over every inch like he was trying to remember me by touch.

"More," I managed to moan, the sensation of his

tongue against my nipple driving me insane. My hands reached for the bulge in his boxers as I palmed his cock, his erection jerked at my touch.

It wasn't close to enough as my hands dove beneath the material, my fingernails grazing his skin as he continued to worship me with his mouth.

"Fuck," he hissed, using one of his hands to push his boxer shorts below his hips, giving me better access. "You're driving me crazy with those hands."

With the added encouragement and an ache between my legs I couldn't describe, my fist wrapped around him and tightened. The slow journey up and down his length deliberate as his fingers moved to the edge of my panties.

I wanted them off in the worst way, hoping he could read my telepathic message to rip them as I continued jerking him off.

And what do you know? He was a mind reader, the tear of the fabric just audible over our heavy breathing. The cool air against my naked skin made me gasp as he moved his fingers against my core.

Oh.

My.

God.

I wasn't sure if it had been that long since he'd touched me there or if some weird biology had happened to my body, but it had never felt like this. His fingers got busy, moving against me before he plunged them inside. His thumb paid close attention to my clit as the sensations sent me into overdrive. My body bucked against his hand while I tried to keep my hands on him, the movement up and down his cock slowing down as every nerve in my body tingled.

"Joey." I had no idea what I was even asking for, just needing to say his name as his mouth moved back to my breast and sucked.

I didn't stand a chance.

An internal detonation exploded inside of me with enough force to make me scream, my body a shaking, twitching mess.

"Yeah, that's my girl." He gave me a satisfied grin, his fingers still moving inside of me.

My eyes blinked, vaguely aware that my hand was still clamped around his dick but had stopped moving. The shivers of the orgasm still rolling through me as he moved his mouth to my throat and sucked gently.

Maddening.

It was the only word I could use to describe it as my body responded to his touch despite coming only minutes before. Tingles prickled my skin as I felt another wave building.

"In me. I want you in me." My broken sentence making enough sense that he nodded in response. The head of his hard length pushed against my entrance as my hips tilted toward him.

"Slow down, baby," he warned, trying to steady me as he slid in slowly, the tip of his cock barely entering me an inch.

"No, I can't wait." My hands grabbed at his ass as I pulled him against me, the sudden motion making him lose balance as he fell toward me. His heavy body covered me as he entered in one hard, sharp unintentional thrust.

"Kenzie, I'm going to hurt you." He scrambled to his elbows and lifted himself off me just enough so I could breathe.

"More," I begged, unashamed at how much I needed him. "I'm going to come."

Taking the words for the green light they were intended, he thrust inside me again—hard. My fingers clawed at his back as I rocked my hips against him, unable to stop.

Everything was amplified, like I tripped on some sexual acid, as my body bucked against him out of control.

"Kenzie, you're going to make me—"

He didn't finish the sentence, my body shattering into a million pieces for the second time, just as violently as the first. He chased my orgasm with one of his own as he filled me with his hot load while his body jerked. His breath ragged and out of control matched mine as he kissed me fiercely on the mouth.

"Don't take this the wrong way." He slowly rolled to his side, my body feeling the loss as he pulled out of me. "But what the hell was that?"

"Everything is super sensitive." I rolled onto my side to

face him. "I read about it, but didn't know it was going to be like that."

Understatement of the century.

The information I'd read said you *might* feel enhanced sensation—not stimulation overload. If that's what it would feel like every time, then I was in serious trouble. I already had a healthy appetite for sex; with my body's new groove, I was going to turn into a glutton.

"It's quite possible I'm going to turn into a sex fiend. Fair warning."

"Babe, as long as you give me a couple of hours to play and occasionally eat, I'll happily take care of all those urges." His teeth gently bit against my shoulder.

"Good." My fingers traced the toned muscles of his chest. "Because I want to do that again."

Joey

I could have laid in that bed with her forever. Literally.

Or at the very least stayed in her apartment. My need to be anywhere she wasn't, non-existent as I watched her sleep peacefully by my side. I couldn't imagine not having this, and knowing what it now felt like, there wasn't a chance I would give it up.

Unfortunately, reality would be an asshole whether we wanted to deal with it or not. The tour I was on still had three months left, and there was no way I would fuck the band over by dropping out now.

So there we were. All the happy-happy-joy-joy short lived as I tried to imagine getting on a plane and leaving her again. Yeah, I'd rather rip my fingernails out one by one.

"Hey." Her eyes cracked open, giving me a perfect view of those beautiful baby blues. "Did I break you?" She treated me to the biggest smile that would have knocked me on my ass if I wasn't already sitting down.

"It's going to take a lot more than that to break me, sweetheart." I brushed her tangled waves off her face. "But I'm going to have to fly back today."

"Oh." The smile faded, the prospect just as exciting for her I guess, as she shuffled up the bed. "When do you have to leave?"

Too fucking soon, that's when. The hours had ticked away through the morning, neither of us lifting our heads until almost noon. I needed to get my shit together, get to the airport, book a flight and be back in Philly in time to hit the stage tonight. Not to mention I hadn't even spoken to the band to find out how last night's gig went.

"In the next hour or two." My eyes locked on hers, already hating the miles I was going to have to put between us. "I'm sorry."

"Joey, you can't be sorry for having to leave. This tour was planned before we even got together. This is an amazing opportunity." She flipped the script, being the voice of reason I should have probably been.

"It doesn't make it easier." I leaned back against the headboard, wishing there was some way I could buy us a few more hours. A day would be even better.

"What if I came with you?"

My head whipped around so fast I wasn't sure I wasn't going to have whiplash, my ears not sure they'd actually heard her correctly. "You would come? With me on tour?"

I didn't care how pussy whipped I actually sounded, even a slight possibility of it happening—rocking my fucking world.

"I woke up early this morning to pee, and it got me thinking." Kenzie, pulled her hair off of her face as she sat up a little straighter in bed. "You put that money in an account for me to use while you were gone. And you said I could use it for whatever I wanted to, right?"

The account that she had been so adamant she wouldn't spend had been getting as much action as my dick had been on tour, i.e. none at all. It was still loaded up with enough zeros that she could have had a fucking field day at Tiffany's, my entire advance from the new album parked in Citibank's finest.

"Well, yeah, but I've checked the balance and you haven't spent a dime." Which is what she'd warned me about when I had given her access in the first place, her hard-ass routine not likely to thaw anytime soon.

"What if I used it to fly back to New York on Fridays?" She threw out her suggestion. "Do my two nights with the *Beauty Queens*, and then take a red eye to wherever you were. We'd have most of the week together. It's three months, so that's like roughly twelve flights? I've seen the amount of money you put in that account, Joey; I could fly to Hawaii twelve times with what's in there."

The asshole in me wanted to fucking sweep her into my arms and tell her yes. That she was coming back with me and would be playing tag with NYC and whatever city

I'd be in. Because let's face it, leaving her here was becoming less of an option the more time I spent in bed with her. But to be shuttled back and forth like a cheap yo-yo for my benefit was a dick move and I knew it. She was pregnant; all that flying couldn't be good.

"Kenzie, I don't know, babe. All those miles, the back and forth?" I played devil's advocate even though my heart was telling me to shut the fuck up and let the woman do what we both wanted.

"Well, what choice do we have?" Kenzie waved me off like her mind had already been made up. "We clearly suck at being apart from each other." She gestured between us, the events of the last few days something I'd rather be forgetting rather than having it signposted for me. "And I have all these urges that are going to need to be taken care of." She smiled seductively. "I mean, I can only masturbate so much before it becomes a liability, and I'm no use to the *Queens* without the use of my hand."

"Jesus." I laughed, wondering how the fuck I got so lucky. "Well, far be it for me to get in the way of what you want. And I'll happily take care of whatever needs doing." The last bit said with intent. Like it would even be a hardship. I don't know what fantasyland she was living in, but that shit would be my fucking pleasure.

"Don't get too excited, buddy." She arched her brow, face full of I'm-not-buying-it. "Your new job description is playing in your band and *then* having sex with me. I bet the novelty wears off really fast."

"Awww, babe." I wrapped my arms around her and pulled her close to my chest, my throbbing hard-on ready and willing to prove the point. "You're so cute when you're wrong."

"Pfft, when have *I* ever been wrong?" She playfully pushed against my chest, trying very unsuccessfully to hide the smirk.

"Do you want a list?" I barked out a laugh, loving seeing her like this—happy. "Not sure we have that kind of time."

"Whatever, *you* have made being wrong an art form." She tipped her chin in the opposite direction in an attempt at cold-shouldering me. She didn't stand a chance as my hands cradled her face and turned it back toward me.

"Why don't we agree we've both had our moments, and we're going to be smarter from here on out." Lord knows I was taking that fucking commitment to heart, my stupid dumbass shit well and truly in the past.

"I can agree to that." She gave me a smile that just about slayed me.

There was no point holding back any longer, my mouth fused to hers, sealing the agreement. My lips as hungry for her as the rest of my body, a small whimper coming out of her mouth as my tongue slid in.

It was a compromise, kissing her like that and promising my dick it would get its chance later, because as much as I wanted to lay her back and make her scream my name, the clock was still ticking. We needed to get from Brooklyn to JFK and get a flight to Philly. Also somewhere in between all of that, we needed to throw some of her stuff into a case and tell her band she was hitting the road. And even though I was Jedi-mind-tricking the fuck out of the analogue display that was sitting on her nightstand, the minutes hadn't rolled back. Which translated into hurry the hell up.

Reluctantly peeling my mouth from hers, I left her to pack while I went to shower alone. Lord knows I couldn't be trusted. If it were up to me, I'd have her up against the tile before the spray had even hit the floor. So we played it smart, with her getting her wash-n-dry after I was out and on the phone to the airline.

It was actually a pretty awesome team effort, getting our shit sorted, the cab ordered and hopefully coming soon to get us on the road.

Kenzie called Sara and gave her the low-down, extra time needing to be spent explaining that what happened with the lawyer had been a huge misunderstanding. Sara took a little convincing—not surprising given how tight they were—but eventually came around. Kenz let her know that we were not only together, but that I'd come to my senses and taken a knee. Cue the tears on both sides of the phone.

And as much as I didn't want to rush my girl, we needed to move this along, hauling our packed bags out of the apartment to the waiting cab. I even triple-check the stove and the locks so she wouldn't have a panic attack on the plane, her tendency to forget shit lately giving her a temporary case of OCD.

The drive to the airport was standard. Lots of stop-start, hurry-up-and-wait but we made it to the gate with time to spare. She used the few extra minutes to call her parents and fill them in, which was interesting considering her brother had already given his version of events. Her folks and her pain-in-the-ass brother also hadn't been part of the make-up, so were dumbfounded as to why she was marrying a guy who had apparently broken her heart. Cue more drama than a fucking UFC title shot on fight night.

I assumed that was the reason why she waited until we were at the gate and past the TSA security checkpoint before she called them. Smart actually, meant she fulfilled her daughterly obligations—telling them about her change in relationship status and her temporary revolving address—but didn't have to deal with them showing up on her doorstep. Not like they didn't know that once Kenzie's mind had been made up, there was little to change it. Besides, there was no doubt their attitude toward me would thaw once they realized I was here for the long haul, and I loved her with all my heart and soul and I wasn't going anywhere.

The boarding call meant I had to sideline my own explaining, the band still in the dark as to what was happening with us. And other than a quick text while the final doors of the plane were closing, they hadn't even known I was on my way back.

Trust me, if anyone would understand it would be those three people. We'd grown up together, shared our dreams and tried to build something great. I'd spent more time with Max, Rusty and Angie than I had my own family, and I loved them no less.

A lump formed in my throat when we'd finally hit the runway, the short flight coming to an end and delivering us to our destination. My tally of fucking awesome was ridiculous and I had taken well above my share. The band, the success, Kenzie, the baby—it almost didn't seem fair. That one guy—a not so-bright kid from the Bronx—had managed to win the million-dollar lottery a few times over just didn't seem logical. But I'd be damned if I was handing any of it back.

"Hey, you okay?" Kenzie looked at me as she unhooked her seatbelt, my eyes blinking fast as I grabbed her hand.

"Yeah," I coughed clearing my throat. "Everything is perfect."

She didn't look like she believed it, but did me a huge favor in not pushing it. Breaking down on a Delta flight wasn't my idea of a good time, so I managed to pull my shit together as we got off the plane and onto the jet bridge. Getting out of the airport and back to the hotel my top priority.

Kenzie's hand stayed locked in mine as we exited the arrival gate and walked to baggage claim. A few people had recognized me—something that was happening more times than not these days—so I'd stopped for a photo or two. My hand around Kenzie didn't deviate; keeping her tight by my side, which of course attracted inevitable attention to her. And if I'd had any doubts that she would be able to handle life on the road with me, they were put to fucking bed as I watched her smile and chat with the fans. She was flawless— absolute perfection— and she was mine.

"What the fuck?" My lids peeled back wide as we rounded the corner of the baggage carousel, my eyes needing to do a double take. Max, Angie and Rusty standing in front of us, the complete lack of surprise on their faces as they saw me with my arm around Kenzie.

"Thought you might need a ride." Max grinned, his chin tipping hello to my girl. "Had a hunch you might be returning with extra luggage."

"Incidentally, you might want to bring your A-game tonight. Troy raised the bar last night and lucky he's already got a gig or your sorry ass would be replaced." Rusty popped me in the arm before turning to Kenzie with a laugh. "FYI, I have no objections to you playing rhythm if you want, Kenz. The added value will just make me sound more awesome."

"In your dreams, Rust. I play lead or not at all." Kenzie grinned back. "Oh, and my future husband will blow the doors off tonight." My girl giving me a twofa by going to bat for me, and revealing we'd decided to tie the knot.

"Congratulations." Angie joined in, her grin genuinely happy. "Seems like every time we go on tour our entourage grows. I think we're going to start needing to take out extra insurance."

"Speaking of which, Alison, Jase and Zack are all waiting to have dinner. If we're done with the Hallmark moment at the airport, maybe we could get something to eat." Rusty reminded us that part of our entourage—his and Angie's significant others—were still back at the hotel.

"Yeah, we should do that." I hugged Kenzie tighter, loving the weight of her body against me. My silent resolve intensifying that I'd never let her go.

"I've got everything I need."

Epilogue
Joey

It had been hours.

Not just felt like hours, like literally hours as we paced the floor of the hospital room. The baby had still yet to make his or her grand entrance as Kenzie bent over the bed while another contraction took hold.

"God, I hate you," she screamed, her hand crushing my fingers so tight I wasn't sure she wasn't going to snap a bone. "I can't believe you did this to me. I want a divorce."

Nice, she was feeling charitable this time around, leaving out threats to my dick and balls as she tried to breathe through the pain. She'd already threatened me with my walking papers no less than five times, so I wasn't even flinching at this point. Just hoping like hell this kid would be born soon so this cycle of agony would end for her.

"Breathe through it, baby. I love you." My hands rubbed circles on her back even though she'd warned me not to touch her. Her body sagged as the tension slowly eased out, hopefully a little closer to the end.

Kenzie's water had broken early this morning, and like all first-time parents we'd taken our pre-packed bag to the hospital excited to meet our son or daughter. *Someone*—cough, Kenzie—had decided we should wait until the birth to find out, so we were still clueless as to whether we were going to be vomiting pink or blue onesies. Not that it mattered—I would be happy with either—but I digress.

While we were admitted quickly, smiles beaming and ready for action, we soon found out that we weren't even close to getting this baby born. A bunch of irregular contractions and a few hours later and the good doctor decided to start an IV.

What the chick in the white coat had failed to mention was that she was injecting Satan juice into my wife. While the bag-of-whatever had brought on regular contractions —its intended purpose—it also turned the beautiful woman that I loved into a crazed psychopath. No shit, that crap needed a warning label and a side of Valium for whomever else was in the room. And a priest; because if that *wasn't* demonic possession happening in front of my eyes, then I had no fucking idea.

Of course after the wave of pain eased off, it was like a shot of reality hit and she was instantly sorry for anything she said. Her tear-filled apology making me feel like an asshole even though I hadn't done anything. Until the next one, and then she'd tell me exactly why I *was* an asshole and which piece of my body she wanted to dismember.

The divorce threats came about four hours in. She'd looked me dead in the eyes as the pain intensified and told me she was done. She also never wanted to see my penis again, and if I even thought about sex she would remove my testicles one by one with a blunt knife.

It became a trend over the next few hours. Each time the needle would spike on the monitor attached to her stomach, I would brace myself for whatever wrath she had prepared. Her insults intensifying as did the contractions, the pain relief they'd given her not even making a dent.

"Hey, doc." I nodded to Kenzie's Ob-something as she walked back in to check the progress. "You want to crank up the volume on the pain meds? My girl is struggling."

It wasn't about the insults, or even the anger—fuck, I would take all of that with a smile if it meant I had a healthy baby and wife at the end. It was watching the unimaginable pain on Kenzie's face that was doing me in. Her eyes pleading for relief while I sat there, unable to help. It was my own private hell.

"I know." She smiled sympathetically having heard some of Kenzie's greatest hits. "I think it might be time for an epidural."

"I can't do this anymore," Kenzie moaned as her head fell forward on the bed. "It hurts so much."

"It's okay, baby. We're going to give you something that helps. You're doing such a great job." My heart fucking bleeding that I couldn't do more for her right now. We were never doing this again. I would happily only have one child and be fucking thankful if they both made it out of this in one piece.

"How can you say that? I have been nothing but horrible. I told you I wanted a divorce four times." The tears streamed down her face as she turned to look at me, the baby giving her a minute or two reprieve.

"Actually it was five, but considering you haven't mentioned chopping my balls off the last few times, I'd say we're all good." My effort to try and make her laugh backfiring as it just escalated the waterworks.

Which led to another contraction. This one so strong she couldn't even yell at me anymore, she just cried and screamed, her face contorted into something that no longer resembled a human.

Awesome.

We are never doing this again.

Ever.

We'll adopt. Or get a dog. And I was going to go straight down the hall and ask someone for a vasectomy. Hell, just give me the knife and I would do the damn thing myself.

"Baby, look at me." I wrapped my arms around her, hoping like hell I wasn't making it worse. "You are fucking amazing, I would have tapped out by now—no question. Please let the doc give you something to help. I love you so much, baby. I hate to see you like this."

She nodded, too tired to give me actual words but I didn't care, just fucking ecstatic she'd given up the superwoman routine.

We quickly went through the risks and signed the waver, Kenzie so exhausted at this point she could no longer stand. Her body curled on its side on the bed as we waited for them to put in the epidural.

She had two more contractions before she was able to be still enough for the line and then—a fucking miracle.

Fat baby angels descended from heaven as the cloud of evil lifted from my wife. Like a television evangelist had placed his hand on her head and cast the demon out, she opened her eyes and wept tears of joy. I might have wept too but I was too busy giving the dude who hooked her up a huge bear hug, my emotional gratitude met with an awkward smile.

Kenzie's body slowly relaxed, the meds doing their job as she closed her eyes. The breath I hadn't realized I'd been holding slowly expelled from my lungs as I sat beside her and watched her sleep.

I caught a few Z's myself, my hand around hers as I floated in and out. It was going to be a long night. Or day. I had no actual idea of what time it was. Nor did I care. As long as I was here with her, the world could end outside and it wouldn't have mattered.

"It's time." I heard the doc's voice and I peeled open an

eye, Kenzie already sitting up with her knees spread apart.

Shit. What had I missed?

"Nothing yet." The nurse answered, my internal dialogue being less internal than I thought.

"Okay, Kenzie." The doc moved to the business end of the bed, her gloved hands disappearing under the sheet. "Next time you feel a contraction, I need you to push."

Kenzie nodded as I flew out of the chair, my feet hitting the floor like a soldier called to attention. "I'm right here, baby." I grabbed her hand ready to do whatever I could to make this easier.

"Just don't leave," Kenzie begged as she tightened the death grip around my fingers.

"Never." I looked her in the eyes, the easiest promise I'd ever have to make.

Before the baby was born, we had done what most future parents did. We read the books, we watched the videos, and we even went to the prenatal classes to get "ready" for when it was show time. But all that shit we read and watched could never prepare us for what happened next.

They don't tell you that watching the life you created take its first breath makes you feel like a greater man than anything you've ever done. They don't tell you that the love and respect for your wife is going to multiply by a million and you're going to feel like a douchebag because you hadn't known it sooner. And they don't tell you that your heart is going to expand so much that your chest aches when you hold your daughter for the first time.

She was perfect.

Just like her mother.

Our little girl had let out a yell that would put Ozzy Osbourne to shame and hadn't stopped until they'd laid her on Kenzie's chest. Her eyes scrunched tight as her hand curled around my finger.

"You did it, baby. I'm so proud of you." I fucking cried like a pussy as I kissed my wife's forehead and repeated the same action on my beautiful little girl. "She's going to be just like you."

"We did it." Kenzie wiped her eyes with one hand as she cradled our daughter with the other. "I couldn't have done this without you. I'm sorry for all those things I said."

"I knew that wasn't you, and I would have taken a hundred times worse just to have this moment right now." I brushed her hair away from her face. "So, I was thinking about a name."

"I'm not sure I have the mental energy, baby." Kenzie laughed, our previous name debates always being fruitless.

"Layla," I whispered. "She's got me on my knees and turned my whole world around." The words of the Eric Clapton song ironically appropriate. I was even willing to overlook he wasn't American. It was still a great name.

"I like that. A lot actually." Kenzie smiled before looking down at our little girl. "Layla. She is totally going to be a rock star."

"Of course." I grinned. "With us as parents, how could she not?"

To keep up to date with all T Gephart's

news,

*appearances
and releases,*

please subscribe to her mailing list at

http://eepurl.com/bws5Av

Acknowledgements

Thank you to my family who has been there every step of the way. Gep, Jenna, Liam and Woodley, you are my pit crew and cheerleaders. Love you all so much.

Thanks to my amazing extended family and friends. Whether there are blood ties or not, we stand together, always.

Special thanks to my beta team who are quick and insightful. MK, Maz and Danielle, you guys are the bomb diggity.

Thank you to the authors who tolerate my madness and welcome my friendship. Your love, support and respect are more than I could have ever hoped for. Lili Saint Germain, JB Hartnett, Monica James, Skyla Madi, CJ Duggan, Lilliana Andersen, Rachael Brookes, JD Nixon, Natasha Preston, Kirsty Mosely, Jane Harvey-Berrick, Ker Dukey, LA Casey, Jill Patten, Tillie Cole, Andie Long, Abbi Glines, Chantal Fernando, Helena Hunting, Christina Hobbs and Lauren Billings, Penelope Louleas, Jay Crownover, Kim Karr, SC Stephens, Joanna Wylde and Kylie Scott—and to anyone I've left out.

Hang Le—you are a master, perfection every time. Thank you so very much.

Thank you to the bloggers and blogs who have and continue to support me. Your shout outs, shares, likes, comments and reviews are invaluable. I adore you.

Thanks to the T Gephart Entourage for the love and the laughs.

Alexander Skarsgård—Just because.

Thanks to my Fictionally Yours, Melbourne team with special mention to Penny Rudge. #MemesAnd Obscenities, I laugh so hard every time.

Thanks to my editor, Nichole Strauss, from Perfectly Publishable. You get me and all of my fucks, Troy Harris forever.

Thank you to my proofreaders for picking up pesky mistakes.

Thanks to Max Henry from Max Effect for her stellar formatting, epic work.

And lastly, a HUGE thanks to my readers. Whether you've been there from the start or we've just met, thanks so much for enjoying my words. I hope you meet as many of you as I can across my travels, you rock my world.

About the Author

T Gephart is an indie author from Melbourne, Australia.

T's approach to life has been somewhat unconventional. Rather than going to University, she jumped on a plane to Los Angeles, USA in search of adventure. While this first trip left her somewhat underwhelmed and largely depleted of funds it fueled her appetite for travel and life experience.

With a rather eclectic resume, which reads more like the fiction she writes than an actual employment history, T struggled to find her niche in the world.

While on a subsequent trip the United States in 1999, T met and married her husband. Their whirlwind courtship and interesting impromptu convenience store wedding set the tone for their life together, which is anything but ordinary. They have lived in Louisiana, Guam and Australia and have traveled extensively throughout the US. T has two beautiful young children and one four legged child, Woodley, the wonder dog.

An avid reader, T became increasingly frustrated by the lack of strong female characters in the books she was reading. She wanted to read about a woman she could identify with, someone strong, independent and confident and who didn't lack femininity. Out of this need, she decided to pen her first book, A Twist of Fate. T set herself the challenge to write something that was interesting, compelling and yet easy enough to read that was still enjoyable. Pulling from her own past "colorful" experiences and the amazing personalities she has surrounded herself with, she had no shortage of inspiration. With a strong slant on erotic fiction, her core characters are empowered women who don't have to sacrifice their femininity. She enjoyed the process so much that when it was over she couldn't let it go.

T loves to travel, laugh and surround herself with colorful characters. This inevitably spills into her writing and makes for an interesting journey - she is well and truly enjoying the ride!

Based on her life experiences, T has plenty of material for her books and has a wealth of ideas to keep you all enthralled.

Website:

http://tgephart.com

Facebook:

www.facebook.com/tgephartauthor

Goodreads:

www.goodreads.com/author/show/7243737.T_Gephart

Twitter:

https://twitter.com/tinagephart

Books by I Gephart

The Lexi Series

Lexi
A Twist of Fate
Twisted Views: Fate's Companion
A Leap of Faith
A Time for Hope

The Power Station Series

High Strung
Crash Ride
Back Stage

The Black Addiction Series

Slide
Sticks
Stand